The Journey of Shine Rivers

by

R.K. Bennett

PublishAmerica
Baltimore

© 2009 by R.K. Bennett.
All rights reserved. No part of this book may be reproduced, stored in a retrieval system or transmitted in any form or by any means without the prior written permission of the publishers, except by a reviewer who may quote brief passages in a review to be printed in a newspaper, magazine or journal.

First printing

All characters in this book are fictitious, and any resemblance to real persons, living or dead, is coincidental.

PublishAmerica has allowed this work to remain exactly as the author intended, verbatim, without editorial input.

ISBN: 1-60836-517-4 (softcover)
ISBN: 978-1-4489-2938-2 (hardcover)
PUBLISHED BY PUBLISHAMERICA, LLLP
www.publishamerica.com
Baltimore

Printed in the United States of America

Dedication

To my wife, Pam, without whose love and support this book would not have been written

Chapter 1
Day One—Monday, June 4, 1962
12:07 AM

Finally, mercifully, he died.

The two black men stood silently, watching and waiting until they were sure the young black man was dead. They then quickly but methodically finished their preparations.

"Let's go," the smaller of the two said.

The other, a very large, powerful man, effortlessly hefted the dead body over his shoulder as if it were no more than an overcoat and followed the smaller man, the only person on earth he feared, three blocks to the Square.

After positioning every detail to his satisfaction, the smaller man poured charcoal lighter fluid over the body, lit it, and walked away casually, in no hurry to flee the scene. The other man followed, scared they would be seen but not wanting to show that fear by hurrying.

The faint glow caught the eye of Charleston Police Officer Carl Ellis as he drove past the Square on routine patrol. He stopped his squad car on the dark, nearly deserted street to get a better look. It appeared that something was burning at the base of the statue of Francis Marion, the Revolutionary War hero for whom the Square, located in the center of Charleston, was named.

Not wanting to lug his fire extinguisher all the way to the center of the Square, he slowly drove his car over the curb onto the wide concrete walkway that led to the statue, just as the dispatcher was beginning the hourly check.

"One A M," his radio squawked. "All units report in order."

The hourly report served several purposes. It ensured that each policeman was okay and in his vehicle; it gave the policemen in the field a feel for who was on the road and where they were (in case immediate help was needed); and it let the dispatcher know the location of his units.

"Unit 10. At the marina," Unit 10 reported.

Ellis, in Car #35, would have to report soon. As his car neared the statue, he could make out what it was that was on fire. "Sweet Jesus!" he muttered aloud.

Ellis hurried out of his car, retrieved his fire extinguisher from the trunk, and doused the flames that were consuming the body which was propped in a sitting position leaning against the concrete base of the statue. He quickly returned to the car and picked up his microphone.

"Unit 35," he said.

"Go ahead 35."

"I've got a DB in the center of Marion Square. It was on fire. I put it out."

"Roger—a dead body. Any other details, 35?"

"Negative. I can't tell from here whether the victim is colored or white or male or female."

"Ten four, 35. Secure the scene and stand by. I'll alert the M E and Lt. Cassidy."

"Ten four. 35 clear," Ellis said. He sat in the squad car to wait for the Medical Examiner and the detective. Curious as he was, he knew that Lt. Cassidy would be very angry if he contaminated the crime scene in any way. He lit a cigarette and sat and waited.

Chapter 2
Day 1—Monday
8:00 AM

"Charleston! OUR time has come!" the tall, black minister began. "Next January First, we will celebrate the one hundredth birthday of the Emancipation Proclamation. We have waited patiently for one hundred years to take our rightful places as full-fledged citizens of this country. Our patience is now at an end. We will wait NO LONGER! Charleston! OUR time has come!"

Pausing for the audience to quiet down, which they did instantly, Reverend Jeremiah Abraham Brown looked down from the lofty pulpit at the sanctuary and saw that his prayers had been answered. The African Methodist Episcopal Church, located on Calhoun Street at the edge of one of Charleston's many black neighborhoods, was full. Every pew in this largest black church building in Charleston County was packed, and those who couldn't find a place to sit were standing in the aisles.

"Our brothers and sisters in Alabama and Mississippi have risen up against the injustice of the white man against the Negro. It is now our turn to say…NO LONGER! No longer will we be treated as second class citizens in our own country. Charleston! Our time has COME!"

A few, scattered "Amens" were heard from the congregation, mostly from the older women, as they sat swishing their cardboard church fans, imprinted with the legend "Compliments of Geddes Funeral Home," in a losing contest against the gradually rising heat in the overly packed church—heat trapped by the windows which had been closed for privacy.

"No longer will we follow the rules of the white man—the rules that say we cannot sit down at the Woolworth counter for a bowl of soup or a cup of coffee. Charleston! Our time has come!"

"No longer will we observe the rules that don't even allow us to go to the bathroom in a public facility. Say it with me, brothers and sisters. Charleston! Our...time...has...come!"

The congregation now had the rhythm, and they joined in with one loud voice.

"No longer will we obey the rules that make us sit in the back of the bus when we pay the same fare as the whites sitting up front."

"Charleston! Our...time...has...come!"

"No longer will we accept the rules that relegate our children to separate schools with lower budgets, poorer buildings, and untrained teachers."

"Charleston! Our...time...has...come!"

"No longer will we tolerate any rules, laws, customs, or practices that deny us full equality and full opportunity in this city that started a war to keep us as slaves."

"Charleston! Our...time...has...come!"

He had brought the assembled crowd to a fever pitch. However, the primary reason for his opening speech was not for the congregation, but rather for two purposes. The reporters would print it word for word in tomorrow's papers, and he would repeat the speech, word for word, on the steps of Charleston's City Hall in less than two hours. He wanted the marchers to participate in the speech at City Hall, as they just had in the church. Now, they knew their lines, and it was time to calm them down and begin the serious business ahead.

He walked slowly down the winding steps of the pulpit and stood facing the congregation, his back to the altar, waiting for the emotion he had built to abate.

"Good morning," he said in a calm voice.

"Good morning," they answered, just as they did every Sunday morning, when it was time for the preacher to make the announcements about youth outings, women's circle events, and various other meetings to be held during the week.

"As they agreed, it's now time for the reporters to leave. While we're waiting, why don't some of you near the windows open them up. It's getting warm in here, and I promise it's going to get warmer."

The congregation laughed, as three reporters from AP, UPI, and the New

York Times, who had been sitting in the front row, rose and hurried out through a side door near the pulpit, anxious to write and file their stories as quickly as possible. They were followed by a CBS Radio Network correspondent and his sound technician, lugging their microphone and tape recorder.

When the door was closed, he looked around the audience. "Will all the white people here please stand up," he said.

A murmur ran through the crowd, as eight young men and women, actually four pairs, stood.

"Thank you. If any of you who just stood up are from Charleston, please raise your hands."

No hand was raised.

"Okay. Nobody from Charleston. If any are from South Carolina, raise your hand."

Again, no hand came up.

"Do any of you live in the South?"

No response.

"We appreciate your help and support, but I am going to ask you to leave the congregation and remain in the church office for thirty minutes or more after we begin the march and then quietly leave. And I don't mean you should merely leave the church. You should get out of South Carolina today."

A sound of surprise emanated from the crowd.

"Please try to understand," he went on. "You have shown us the depth of your feeling about the condition of the Negro in the South by being here today, and for that we will be eternally thankful. But if you join us in this fight, you may do more harm to our cause than good. Furthermore, I don't believe you understand the danger you would face—more danger than any of us Negroes face. If I let you stay with us, at least one of you will probably be killed before this Sunday comes." Several members of the congregation gasped. "So, please, now, go to the church office. Brother Watson, here, will show you the way."

The young white men and women, all college students, slowly gathered their belongings and followed Brother Watson out of the sanctuary, tears in the eyes of the four young women. Reverend Brown waited until Brother Watson returned and nodded.

Brother Watson took his place with fourteen other black men, all in their best Sunday suits, standing side by side in front of the choir area facing the congregation. Each of these men, wearing a large wooden cross on his chest suspended from his neck by a small piece of rope, was a preacher with his own church somewhere in Charleston County. In front of these ministers were four evenly placed, empty chairs. Reverend Brown, "Jab" Brown to his friends, stood in front of the empty chairs facing the congregation.

"Okay, folks," he continued. "Let's get started. We have several things to discuss before we go out there." He pointed towards the church entrance behind the congregation which led out to Calhoun Street.

"First, let me explain the business with the white kids I just asked to leave." He spoke in conversational tones rather than his normal preaching delivery. This was serious business, not church. It was important that they understood what they were getting into.

"They had to leave for two reasons. First, they are outsiders. They are not from here. I know, I know," he said, raising his hands in protest, "neither are you, Reverend Brown, some of you are thinking. I'll get to that in a minute. They are outsiders. This is not their fight. Second, they are white, and this is not the fight of the white man. Our message must be simple, clear, and to the point. The Negro people of Charleston will no longer tolerate the injustices of the past. If we allow other issues to become involved, the white man will seize those issues and use them to cloud and obscure our simple message, and that will hurt our cause, not help it."

He began to slowly pace up and down in front of the congregation. "As for me, I am not an outsider. I was born in a two room apartment less than four blocks from this church and lived here until I was fourteen. When my father got out of the Navy at the end of World War Two, he took me, my mother, and my two brothers to Detroit, where he had been offered a job at a General Motors assembly plant by an officer whose life my father saved. It was in Detroit that I found two things that would change my life and allow me to be here today—a real school that could teach me something and basketball. The first year, I nearly flunked right out of school. That's how far behind the others I was. Gradually, I caught up and finished my senior year with all A's. The basketball came easier. I reckon that God gave me that gift, as well as my height, so I could go on to do his work. From the time I was seventeen, that was seventeen years ago, what I wanted most of all was to be here doing what I am doing today. The basketball and my grades got me to college. After college, I went to the seminary and was ordained a Minister in the African Methodist Episcopal Church eight years ago."

"I can tell you," he continued, "that Detroit is no better than Charleston. Oh, yes, it's different. I got an education and an opportunity there that I would never have had if I had stayed here. Yes, it's different, but ultimately it's not better. Down south, the whites don't care how close we get, as long as we don't get too big. Up north, they don't care how big we get, as long as we don't get too close. The Negro is discriminated against all over this country, this land of opportunity. Up north, the discrimination is more subtle, rooted in daily practice. Down south, the discrimination against us is more open, the result not only of daily practice but also of laws which exclude us from certain places and services. These Jim Crow segregation laws make it easier to fight against discrimination down here. That's why the struggle—the movement—has begun in the South. The struggle for equality up north will come later. Some might put forth the argument that the southerners are more honest in their discrimination against us. But we are not here to put forth or support arguments on behalf of the white man; we are here to put forth and support arguments on behalf of the Negroes of this city who will no longer tolerate or accept that discrimination. When the movement finally began, I went to Dr. King and requested, demanded, pleaded to lead the marches in Charleston. Praise God, Dr. King said, 'Yes.' Last week, I moved my family here and with the kind concurrence of Pastor Lyle," he turned to his left and acknowledged the Pastor of the Calhoun Street AME Church, standing with the other ministers behind Jab Brown, "I have been appointed Associate Pastor of this Church. Brothers and sisters, I am not an outsider. I have come home."

He walked over to a table near the pulpit and took a sip from a glass of water, as much to signal a change of subject as to moisten his dry mouth. He put down the glass and walked behind the empty chairs.

"See these chairs here? We invited four religious leaders of Charleston's white community to be here with us today to acknowledge that God is on the side of justice and against injustice. We did not ask them to march with us—just to be here this morning to join us in prayer. As you can see..."

He touched the back of each chair in turn as he spoke each name.

"Monsignor O'Brien of the Blessed Sacrament Catholic Church...Bishop Carroll of the Episcopal Diocese...Pastor Boyd of the Ashley River Baptist Church...and Rabbi Cohen of the Charleston Hebrew Temple...all had other more pressing engagements this morning."

Again, the congregation laughed.

He walked back in front of the empty chairs. "I want to thank each one of you from the bottom of my heart for being here today. This marks a beginning. Most of you are not doing this for yourselves, but for your children and grandchildren. The struggle we are about to undertake will be long, hard, and dangerous. Some of you will personally suffer for your participation. A few may experience physical harm. One or more may even die. Brothers and sisters, this is serious business, but it is also important business."

He began pacing again. "In a few minutes, we will begin today's march. We will walk single file from here to King Street, down King Street to Broad and then to the corner of Broad and Meeting. As most of you know, at the four corners of that intersection are the City Hall, the County Court House, the Federal Building, and St. Michael's Episcopal Church. Each day, except Sundays, we will march from here to that intersection and back. I notice that many of you sisters are wearing very lovely dresses and your best high heel shoes. I suggest that you do wear those dresses—they look very nice—but you might want to consider wearing shoes that are more practical for the job we are about to do. Each day we will stop and preach and sing and pray in front of one of these four buildings. Today, our first day, we will march to City Hall."

He reached into his coat pocket and removed a slip of paper. He wanted to be sure that these next instructions were complete.

"Here are the rules you must follow. Walk in single file. Do not talk, sing or make any sound until we reach City Hall. Have a smile on your face. Look straight ahead at the back of the person in front of you. We will not stop for red lights. Keep on walking, and keep very close to the person in front of you. If a policeman or anyone else tells you to stop to let traffic through or for any other reason, do...not...stop. Keep on walking. If a policeman tells you that you are under arrest, do...not...stop. Keep on walking. If a policeman or anybody else puts his hands on you and holds you, sit down. If they want to arrest you, make them carry you. If someone starts to beat you, roll yourself up in a ball, your knees to your chest, and cover your face with your arms, like this."

He got down on the floor, put his knees to chest, and buried his face in his arms. Many of the congregation stood to get a better look. After a few moments, he rose to his feet and resumed pacing.

"Above all, if they jeer you, do not respond. If they throw things at you, keep on walking and smiling, looking straight ahead. If they hit you, protect your body, but do…not…hit…back. If at any time you have any questions, are not sure what you should do, or feel you need help, go to one of the ministers standing behind me. You can recognize them by the crosses around their necks."

"Brothers and sisters, can you do these things?"

"Yes, brother," they answered with one voice.

"Are you ready, then?"

"Yes, brother," they responded enthusiastically.

"Pastor Lyle, will you lead us in prayer?"

As Pastor Lyle prayed for strength, Jab Brown's heart was pounding, not from fear but from excitement in the knowledge that this day had at long last come. He, a kid from the slums of Charleston's Ansonborough district, one of the worst slums in the city, would lead the fight out of the slums, both physical and cultural, into the mainstream of American life and the dream it offered to everyone—everyone, that is, except its black people.

The prayer ended, the doors were opened, and they stepped out, Jab Brown at the front. It was a beautiful day, typical Charleston weather for this time of year. Although scattered showers were in the forecast, you wouldn't know it by looking at the morning sky—a deep blue with a few white, high clouds. It was warm, but not yet humid. It would get warmer before the day was over, warmer in many ways for many people.

Jab Brown's excitement grew, as a surge of adrenaline flowed through his body. He had prayed, hoped, prepared and worked for this day for so long that he was somewhat surprised at the feeling. As he stepped off at the head of the line forming behind him to begin the first civil rights march in Charleston, his mood grew to elation. He was almost heady. The last ten years of his life had been dedicated to and aimed directly at this moment, and he had achieved it. If they killed him tomorrow, he would be sorry for his wife and children, but they could never take this moment from him. He, Jab Brown, a kid from the Charleston projects, was leading the civil rights movement in Charleston. His dream was fulfilled.

"Central, this is Traffic 5." Bobby Moore pulled his Police Harley Davidson motorcycle to the curb, so he could hear his radio.

The dispatcher put down his doughnut, washed the last bite down with some coffee, and answered. "Go ahead 5."

"I think we got a problem."

"What're you talkin' about, 5? What problem?"

"There's a whole bunch of Negroes walking down the sidewalk."

"Why is that a problem, 5?" The dispatcher said sarcastically.

"Well, they're walking single file, very close together, and they're blocking traffic when they cross the street. They're not stopping for red lights."

"How many of them are there?"

"I cain't tell."

"Wadda you mean, you cain't tell? Is it ten, twenty, a hundred?"

"I mean that the head of the line just turned south from the northwest corner of King and Calhoun and they're still coming out of the AME Church across from the Holiday Inn."

Shit, the dispatcher thought, being somewhat brighter than the motorcycle cop. It sounded like a civil rights march, something that Charleston had not yet experienced.

"Stay there, 5."

"What do you want me to do? Traffic's startin' to back up."

"Do nothing. I'll get back to you."

Moore sat back on his Harley, loosening the chinstrap on his helmet. He was relieved to hear that he was not to do anything. The opportunities to screw up in a situation like this were too many to count.

"Central to 5. The Sergeant is on his way."

"This is 5. Roger." That was even better. The more he thought about it, the more he was convinced that whatever they did now would later be judged as wrong. Now, the blame would be on the Sergeant.

The Sergeant, who had been rounding the bend at the marina heading towards Spring Street, made it back to Moore, siren wailing and lights flashing, in 2 minutes. As he sped through the marchers, they opened a path for him and closed it behind him, as if he were a hand passing through water. He stopped his motorcycle beside Moore's, took a look at the situation, told Moore to go to the Holiday Inn parking lot and wait for instructions, and took off for headquarters. He didn't want to broadcast over the radio what he was seeing.

Chapter 3
Day 1—Monday
10:00 AM

"Where's Shine?" Jimmy Long asked no one in particular, as he emerged from the office area into the shop, having concluded the regular Monday morning meeting to plan the fleet work for the week and review the backlog of the other customers.

"He's on vacation this week, Mr. Jimmy," one of the black mechanics called out.

"Oh, yeah," Long remembered. Engrossed over the past few weeks with finding a new, larger location for his business, he had forgotten that Shine Rivers, his best black mechanic, had asked for this week off. He had thought at the time that the request was unusual, since Rivers, a preacher on the weekends at a small, black Pentecostal church way out on Wadmalaw Island, usually took Christmas week off because of the festivities at the church.

"Stand by for lots of fish when he gets back," Long said, again to no one in particular. Among his other talents, Shine Rivers was one of the best flounder fishermen in the county.

Long had been on several flounder fishing trips with Shine. They made a funny looking pair. Shine Rivers was a big man, 6'3" or more—big but all muscle, while Jimmy Long was short and stocky, probably no taller than 5'6". When Jimmy spoke with Shine, he would stand back an extra foot or two, so he wouldn't have to crane his neck straight up.

Shine was also one of the better automobile mechanics in Charleston. After working his way up to foreman in the service department of Charleston's Oldsmobile dealership, Jimmy Long had left and opened his own garage, Low

Country Automotive. The first mechanic he hired was Shine, who had worked for him at Oldsmobile. Jimmy Long was probably the best auto mechanic in Charleston. Shine was a close second. Both men could drive a car around the block and from the feel and the sounds tell you exactly what was wrong with it. Of course, since he was a black man, Shine couldn't be a master mechanic.

In the office, Long had a cashier, a bookkeeper, and a parts buyer. In the shop were two white master mechanics, one responsible for the six bays on the right side of the shop and the other for the six bays on the left. There were twelve black mechanics, one for each bay. Shine's bay, number one, was the first bay to the right as you left the office. This morning, it was empty and quiet. Each of the eleven other bays was occupied with either a truck or a car on the lift in the process of being repaired. A master mechanic would deal with the customer, diagnose the problem (unless he needed help from Jimmy or Shine), and supervise the repairs, which were performed by the black mechanics.

Low Country Automotive had been successful from the first day. Long had secured two fleet contracts before opening the business, which insured that he could at least pay the rent and meet the payroll. His reputation for honestly repairing cars correctly on the first try for a fair price and with quality parts spread rapidly, and he soon began to find long lines in front of the shop each morning. He had added mechanics and the two master mechanics over time and now, having no room to grow in this location, found he was having to turn some customers away. After a diligent search, he thought he had at last found a suitable location on the other side of town, near East Bay Street, where he could grow to twenty four bays, if he wanted to. The appointment to inspect the building was this morning.

"I'll be back in about an hour," he told one of the master mechanics.

He got in his car and headed for the appointment. As he turned onto Liberty Street and headed towards King Street, he was surprised to see a line of cars stopped in front of him, waiting for the light, some of them blowing their horns, an unusual occurrence in Charleston. It was also unusual for traffic to be backed up on Liberty. In fact, Long couldn't remember when he hadn't driven to the light, turned right onto King (even if the light was red, which was legal), and proceeded on, which is why he often used this route.

The light turned green, and the traffic still did not move. Long, impatient as usual, jumped out of his car and began walking towards King Street to see what was going on. Halfway there, he stopped, not believing what he was seeing.

A steady stream of black people, walking very close to each other in single file, was moving south on the sidewalk, headed down King Street. When the line kept coming, Long knew immediately what it was—a civil rights march. With what was going on in Mississippi and Birmingham, he had known that it was only a matter of time before the marches would start in Charleston. He would find a way around them, keep his appointment, and then he had a few calls to make.

As he was about to return to his car, something caught his eye, and he turned back towards King Street. There, coming into view, a large wooden cross suspended around his neck, was Shine Rivers. You couldn't miss him. Long had never seen him in a suit before, but he had worked with this man for over 15 years. There was no mistaking who it was.

Long stood there, exploding inside. This was a direct affront to him and to everything he had done for Shine over the years. He secretly paid Shine more than the other black mechanics. He had personally paid the bills for the births of the eight of his nine children who had been born since Shine began working for him. And he gave one hundred and fifty dollars each year to Shine's church.

Now, this. It was a direct slap in his face. Shine and everyone else knew how Jimmy Long felt about the blacks. Suddenly, he was convinced that Shine was, for some reason, doing this just to embarrass him. Just like the blacks, he thought. Ungrateful bastards.

The appointment was forgotten. Long would make those calls now. The regular monthly Ku Klux Klan meeting, scheduled for that night, would now have a different agenda.

He pulled his car out of line, cut through the parking lot across from the Arcade Theater, and began the drive back to the shop. Within two blocks he cooled down enough to realize that he should first make sure that what he assumed was happening was in fact happening. He turned left and paralleled King Street to Broad.

Sure enough, there was the front of the line, moving down Broad Street towards City Hall. He again circled south, headed east on Tradd Street, and parked his car in the parking lot behind St. Michael's Episcopal Church. He stood on the corner opposite City Hall and watched as the head of the line, led by a black man he didn't recognize who was also wearing a wooden cross, reached the front steps of City Hall and stopped. He would wait and watch so he could report at the Klan leadership meeting exactly what happened. He moved to a better vantage point.

Chapter 4
Day 1—Monday
10:35 AM

The law offices of Middleton, Heyward & Rutledge on Broad Street were very busy with messengers running to and from offices, associates researching facts and points of law, partners meeting with clients and dictating into their machines, and secretaries typing their dictation.

That is, all of the offices were busy except one. Gedney Middleton, Managing Partner of the firm, was sitting in his chair, feet up on his desk, thinking. He always scheduled two periods each day for thinking, one in mid morning and the other in mid afternoon. Somebody around here had to think and plan.

Today, however, he was not thinking or planning about the law firm, whose billings were already headed for a fifth consecutive year of record highs. He was thinking about Charleston, his city.

His passion for Charleston developed only after he had left the city to attend college. After finishing near the top of his class at a private boarding school in upstate South Carolina, he had entered Columbia University in New York City, unsure of whether to pursue a career in law or journalism. Since he had a couple of years to decide before declaring his major, Columbia, which had an excellent reputation in both fields, seemed like the logical choice. His father, Managing Partner of the law firm of Middleton, Heyward & Rutledge, which was an old line Charleston firm founded by Gedney's grandfather and two other men, wanted him to pursue a law career and eventually take over the firm, when the senior Gedney retired to the position "Of Counsel," which meant a lot of money for relatively little work. It was agreed, however, that

Gedney would decide for himself, and Gedney felt that there was more to life than what he saw his father doing every day.

In New York, two things happened which would point Gedney to the path he would take. When he first arrived at Columbia, he experienced culture shock, living in the multi-racial, multi-ethnic New York City environment. Charleston, at least the Charleston he had grown up in, was overwhelmingly white, primarily English and Scots Irish, and Protestant. Charleston had more Episcopal Churches than either Catholic or Baptist, and he knew of only one Jewish Synagogue. Manhattan was overwhelmingly mixed, and a person couldn't avoid confronting the cultural consequences of that mix every day. During his freshman year, he found that he couldn't adjust to this cultural stew. At least he hadn't yet.

Then, halfway through his sophomore year, he was mugged on the subway on the way to his apartment in Greenwich Village after studying late at the school library. The muggers were two black men, who not only took his money but also beat him up fairly badly for good measure and for no good reason, since he had already surrendered his cash before they beat him.

The mugging brought his underlying distaste for the multi-cultural environment of New York City to the surface. Gedney now saw Charleston as a haven against the madness of the outside world, a haven that must at all costs be preserved.

After completing his second year at Columbia, he transferred to the University of South Carolina with a major in pre-law. This abrupt change in his educational path was greeted with mixed blessings by his father. Although Gedney had decided to pursue law and join the firm, the University of South Carolina, while a good school, was not Columbia University.

He sailed through both the undergraduate and law schools and returned to Charleston with a very specific plan and agenda. Preserving Charleston's culture was so important that he could not rely on others to do it. He would have to do it himself, and that meant he had to have the power to do it.

With single-minded determination, he implemented his plan. Along the way, he married the "right" girl, Jane Rutledge, the granddaughter of another founder of the firm and a member of another of the old, Charleston families. Whatever Jane's father and Gedney's father agreed should happen in Charleston did happen. They had that much power. Luckily, he had also fallen very much in love with Jane. He had never asked himself whether or not he would have married her anyway. It would have been a stupid question. After about three years, their daughter, Margaret, named after Jane's mother, had come along. And he had fulfilled his military obligation by serving in the South Carolina National Guard with a waiver which exempted him from having to attend any drills.

His plan had two elements. He had to gain enough power within the firm to give him the stature in the community and the free time necessary to achieve the second, more important part of the plan. That meant he had to become Managing Partner, a position held by his father.

He was named Managing Partner by unanimous vote of the partners when he was forty years old, and he did it by becoming both the best attorney in the firm and the number one rainmaker, which meant that he consistently brought more new business into the firm than any other partner. His father, although still fully capable and active, voluntarily and happily stepped aside at the age of 65 and went into semi-retirement to make way for his son to take his place as head of the firm and the youngest Managing Partner in the firm's history.

The second part of the plan was the more important. Most of the adult males in the old Charleston families were members of the Ashley Cooper Society, an organization whose roots dated back before the Revolutionary War. The original purpose of the society was to take care of the widows and children of any member who died and whose family needed help, a common problem in the Colonial South where the leaders and most powerful and influential members of the community were land rich, but cash poor.

Although the widows and orphans fund was maintained to the present, the Society had over time evolved into a forum where the top members of Charleston's society could socialize with "their own kind" and plot the future of the City. If you weren't a member, you were nobody. Membership was by invitation only and was limited by practice almost exclusively to men who were born into (or, in some cases, married into) one of the old Charleston families. Wealth, or the lack of it, had no bearing on becoming a member. One year after being named Managing Partner of the firm, Gedney Middleton was elected President of the Ashley Cooper Society, a post he had now held unopposed for four years. He now had the position and power to control Charleston's agenda.

Charleston was founded in 1670 in a mosquito-infested swamp across the Ashley River from the present site of the old city. Heat, humidity, disease, and laziness almost doomed this colony, just like many others which were established in the New World and ultimately abandoned.

Rather than abandon Charles Town, though, the leaders moved the settlement across the river to the peninsula between the Ashley and Cooper Rivers overlooking the harbor (where, according to Charleston's tourism brochures, the Ashley River and the Cooper River meet to form the Atlantic Ocean). The colony gained a foothold and soon began to flourish as a cultural and economic force in the early South. The plantations on the islands surrounding Charleston grew cotton and rice. The city boasted the only deep-water harbor between Jacksonville and New York, placing it in the mainstream of interstate and international commerce.

During the period prior to the Civil War, Charleston, along with several other Southern cities, such as Savannah, Mobile, and Natchez, developed societal structures that remain today as the myth about life in the antebellum South.

There were three distinct societies in antebellum Charleston, living together economically, but very apart socially. First, there was the aristocracy, the plantation owners and others with wealth. The members of the aristocracy were the landed gentry, the developers and guardians of Southern culture and traditions. Second were the rest of the whites—the merchants, blacksmiths, slave traders and overseers who weren't, and never could become, aristocracy. Many of these Middle Class Whites had come to the New World as indentured servants and had eventually opened shops, when their period of servitude ended. Finally, of course, there were the blacks, the slaves who were shanghaied from Africa to work the plantations, the first arriving in 1671.

The Civil War changed everything and plunged the South into a period of economic and social depression which lasted until the end of the Second World War. It was no accident of history that the first shots of the Civil War were fired in Charleston. While most of the aristocracy in the South hated Lincoln and his goal of ruining the South by abolishing slavery and, with it, the plantation system, many in Charleston feared a deeper threat. They knew that the plantation system, based on manual labor, however cheap, was becoming uneconomical. What they really feared was the destruction of a culture and way of life they had nurtured for over two hundred and fifty years, a genteel, polite, cultured society that would be crushed and replaced with a New York-like lifestyle that many had experienced and detested. They weren't worried about the political consequences of freeing the slaves, since there was no talk or threat of giving them the vote, at least not yet. It was simply that the North and the South were as different as different could be.

The North valued capital; the South valued land.
The North was industrial; the South was agricultural.
The North was in a hurry; the South took its time.

No, the two regions, who looked at life so differently, could never understand each other. And it was becoming apparent that the North, either fearing or hating that which it could not understand, was determined to force its culture and values on the South. The Southern Aristocracy simply could not allow that to happen. So, the logical decision was to break off and form a separate country. They tried and failed.

After this failed attempt to control and determine their own destiny, the people of the South were punished by the victorious North—punished politically and economically, until the Great Depression of the 1930's forced the North to turn its attention away from punishing the South and focus on its own problems. The Southerners never noticed the Great Depression. They had been living in one since the end of the Civil War.

The military buildup of World War Two restored economic growth to America, with some of the economic renewal trickling down below the Mason Dixon line. Charleston, with its deep-water port and Naval Shipyard, participated in the economic upturn.

The convergence of several programs and technological advancements during the 1950's jump-started the South onto an economic binge. The construction of the Interstate Highway System, allowing trucks to replace the railroad as the primary mover of goods from manufacturers to consumers, opened the South with its low cost, non-union work force to manufacturers, and there was a wholesale movement of the textile industry from New England to North and South Carolina with some spillover into Southern Virginia and Eastern Georgia.

Technological advances and cost reductions in air conditioning systems made climate control economically feasible for small businesses, homes, and automobiles, offering relief from the hot muggy July and August air of the Deep South.

The installation by AT&T of microwave transmission systems, developed during World War Two for military use, into the nationwide telephone network produced long distance telephone service that was reliable and economical. A company no longer had to be located near New York, Boston, Chicago or Philadelphia in order to conduct business.

Finally, just when commercial jet aircraft were becoming available, the visionary city fathers of Atlanta joined with a small, regional airline named Delta Airlines to build a large airport at great expense south of Atlanta, opening that city as a viable regional headquarters for large American corporations. As a result of all of these factors, the South began a growth spurt that would gain in momentum and continue for more than fifty years.

Unfortunately, however, for much of the South, the damage had already been done. The Civil War, followed by a century of economic devastation, had reduced the once proud, regal cities with their stately, antebellum homes and churches to neglected slums populated by poor blacks, the whites having fled to the suburbs.

Charleston was one of the few exceptions. Somehow, the old Charleston families, aided by General Sherman's refusal to destroy such a beautiful, historic city, had remained in the city and maintained the homes, churches, buildings and the unique Charleston culture that both nurtured the physical city and was, in turn, nurtured by it.

Charleston's post war economic development also differed from the other Southern cities which participated in the renaissance (not all did). The military installations which thrived during World War Two continued their growth during the ensuing cold war, aided by the fact that Charleston's U.S. Congressman—L. Mendell Rivers—was Chairman of the House Armed Services Committee. Because of the presence of the Naval Base, the Naval Shipyard, and the Air Force Base, any one of which would have been a tremendous economic boost to any city the size of Charleston, the Federal Government became the single largest employer by far in Charleston County.

The downside of such a large Government presence was that Charleston's economy did not diversify. No manufacturing base was built, primarily because employers found they could not compete with the government's pay scales. However, the steady growth in tourism combined with the government payroll brought a sufficient flow of outside money into the city each year to fuel a steady economic growth. The large military presence and the growing tourism also brought something else to Charleston—the night people, those people who owned and worked in the numerous bars in and around the city that catered primarily to sailors, airmen, and tourists.

The now five separate cultures who lived together in a strange combination of detente and symbiosis—the old Charleston families, the middle class whites, the military and Navy Yard personnel, the night people and the large black population—while coming together at the margins of their daily lives, generally led separate and distinct social and cultural lives. This fragile structure required constant vigilance and management, lest it begin to crumble, and the maintenance and management of that structure was the primary function of the Ashley Cooper Society.

The women had their group, the Daughters of the South, which was a women's auxiliary to the Ashley Cooper Society and which concerned itself with the appearance of Charleston and its culture. They orchestrated the debutante season each year, when the daughters of the old Charleston families were "introduced to society" with parties, balls, and tea dances, a throwback to times when daughters were kept close to home until their coming out at the debutante ball around the age of sixteen.

The Daughters of the South also dominated the Charleston Historical Society, which had the legal power and authority through codicils in deeds to control and dictate the outward appearance of most of the old homes and commercial buildings in Charleston's historic districts, both south of Broad Street and elsewhere in the city.

While the women concerned themselves with the appearance of Charleston, the men kept guard over the reality. If Charleston was to maintain its unique culture in these times of change, those who best understood Charleston must set and control the agenda. And those who had the power set the agenda. Keeping that power was, in Gedney's view, the single most important task and responsibility of the Ashley Cooper Society. And, as he was about to learn, the greatest threat yet to Charleston's cultural structure was gathering at that very moment, right outside his building. A knock on the door brought his feet to the floor.

"Yes," Gedney called out. His secretary came in.

"Mr. Layer called to cancel your eleven o'clock meeting," she said. "He doesn't want to walk over here with the demonstration going on."

"What demonstration?" he asked.

"You mean nobody told you? I am so sorry. Go look," she said, motioning to the window.

He walked over and looked out of the window which faced Broad Street. He saw a large growing crowd of black people gathering in front of City Hall and spilling out onto the street. The scene brought a chill down his spine. Even though he had expected it would happen sooner or later, he found that he was surprised by actually seeing it.

"I need you to call the Poets list," he began, as his private line rang. His secretary answered the phone.

"It's Ken Wall," she said, holding her hand over the handset for privacy.

"Good. I'll take it. Get me Beano Martin. Then, I'll tell you what to tell the others." He took the receiver as she left, closing the office door behind her.

"Hello, Ken," he said to the Chief of Charleston's Police Force.

"You know what's going on?" Wall asked, forgetting any opening amenities.

"Yeah. They're right outside my window."

"What should we do?" The Police Chief asked.

"For now, nothing," Middleton replied, thinking furiously. "I'm calling a meeting of the Poets Club for either today or tomorrow. I want you and Buddy Leech" (Leech was the Chief of the Charleston County Police) "to be there. I have to find out where Beano is first. I'll call you back in a few minutes."

"Okay. I'll wait for your call."

Middleton's intercom button lit up. "Mr. Martin is on line two. He's here in town," he heard his secretary say.

Beano Martin, a bachelor, balding, cigar-smoking curmudgeon in his sixties, had been Gedney's Political Science professor at the University of South Carolina. When Gedney had written his senior paper on the Political History of South Carolina, Martin had encouraged him to have it published. The book achieved modest success within the State and brought Gedney a small amount of fame within the State's political circles. While attending law school, he taught a course on South Carolina politics in the undergraduate school, again at the urging of Beano Martin.

Gedney had persuaded Martin to take a position as head of the Political Science Department at the College of Charleston, a real coup for the College and an easy persuasion task for Gedney, since Martin loved Charleston almost as much as Gedney did and was ready to get away from Columbia. Martin's position at the College was in reality his hobby. He enjoyed teaching, even though he was a tyrant in the classroom. The bulk of his income, which was fairly substantial, came from consulting with various politicians, groups and corporations, primarily in the South but also a few outside of the South, who had vested interests in the ebb and flow of political power in the South and shared Martin's conservative political philosophy. Beano Martin was the undisputed expert on Southern politics in general and South Carolina politics in particular and a founding member of the Poets Club.

The Poets Club, organized by Gedney, consisted of a small group of men who met every Friday for lunch in a private dining room at the Colonial Steakhouse, one of Charleston's premier steak and seafood restaurants, located on Vendue Range, a short, out-of-the-way street a few blocks north of Broad Street near the Cooper River. The publicly-stated purpose of the club was a social, lighthearted weekly gathering of friends over lunch to celebrate the coming weekend. POETS was an acronym of "Piss On Everything, Tomorrow's Saturday."

In reality, the Poets Club ruled Charleston. Decisions made at these meetings became laws passed by the City or County Councils or policies implemented by Charleston's largest and most powerful businesses. The Chiefs of the City and County Police weren't members, but were occasionally invited to give input and receive direction on matters too important to risk second or third hand passing of instructions.

"Beano," Gedney said. "How was Washington? When did you get back?"

"Same ole' shit," Beano answered, his cigar clenched in his teeth. "I got back yesterday. I was just about to call you. I guess the pig's in the ditch down here."

"Yeah," Gedney responded. "They're right outside my window. Looks like they're gathering in front of City Hall."

"I hope those cretins that pass for cops haven't started cracking heads."

"Not yet. I just got off the phone with Ken Wall. I told him to do nothing until I got back to him."

"Good," Beano said through his cigar. "We don't need those photographers sending pictures and film up North like we see from Birmingham. That idiot Bull Conner" (Birmingham, Alabama's Chief of Police, whose police officers repeatedly attacked civil rights marchers with clubs, attack dogs, and streams of water from fire hoses) "is the answer to the Kennedy brothers' prayers."

"What photographers?" Gedney asked.

"Look around, son. Just look around. They're there."

"I will. Beano, I want to call a meeting today. Can you come?"

"Poets?"

"Yeah. I haven't called the others yet. I wanted to be sure you can be there."

"Damn straight I'll be there. The whole world is watching Charleston now. We have to present the right picture, or we could lose the whole ball game. I'll be in your office in a few minutes."

"Good." Gedney disconnected and buzzed his secretary. "Call the list. Tell them we are meeting today. They should arrive as usual. Also call Ken Wall and Buddy Leech and tell them to be there."

Gedney Middleton didn't ask people to attend meetings (except, of course, Beano Martin). He told them to attend meetings, and they always came. Gedney's power didn't come from his position as head of the law firm, nor did it arise solely from the fact that he was President of the Ashley Cooper Society. He was powerful because he was the political kingmaker in the lower half of South Carolina. He raised enormous amounts of money, which he both funneled to candidates to finance their election campaigns and spent independently on their behalf. The candidates he supported won; and those he abandoned lost. Best of all, his candidates never had to engage in the tedious and sometimes unpleasant task of fund raising. Gedney provided all of the money they needed to trounce their opponents. In return, they submitted to his bidding.

Gedney walked back over to the window. Sure enough, half a block up Meeting Street, he saw two still photographers and a film cameraman recording the events taking place in front of City Hall, where a tall colored man whom Gedney did not recognize was beginning to give a speech that Gedney couldn't hear.

Gedney jumped, as the crowd suddenly shouted with one voice, "Charleston! Our time has come!" They would repeat those words several times during the speech. Each time Gedney heard it, another chill ran down his spine.

Had he looked straight down from his second story window, Gedney would have seen the black, curly, close-cropped hair of Jimmy Long. As both men watched the demonstration, each felt personally threatened by what was happening, and each was already planning the actions he would take to combat this affront to the established order. Their actions, however, would take very different paths.

Chapter 5
Day 1—Monday
10:45 AM

"Wake up, Frank."

When he didn't respond, she gently shook his shoulder.

"Wake up, Frank. Come on. You have to get up."

Detective Lieutenant Frank Cassidy opened one eye, looked up at his wife, who was still shaking his shoulder, and glanced at the clock.

Yesterday, he and his family had attended Sunday Mass at Blessed Sacrament Catholic Church. After church, they had driven to the beach, so Scott could run and Melissa could search for shells for her collection. That evening, he had grilled hamburgers in the backyard, while Rita had bathed the kids. All in all, a typical, nice Sunday for a typical family in the suburbs.

But they weren't a typical family. Frank was a police detective with a detective's schedule. His father, also a cop, had advised him to try to lead a normal life away from the job, make non-cop friends and get involved in the neighborhood and the church. Otherwise, if he lived with cops twenty four hours a day, he would end up cynical and bitter, spending all of his time with the underside of life.

Frank had taken the advice to heart and worked hard at following it. But it had proved difficult. For a cop, schedules and commitments were made to be broken. Criminals did not seem to be sensitive to his private life.

The telephone call had come a few minutes after one AM. By the time he arrived at Marion Square, an open park in the center of town and the original site of the Citadel, a military college that had moved to a bigger and more modern campus on the banks of the Ashley River and whose old buildings now housed many County Government agencies, the fire had been extinguished. He found the burned body of a young black man who he guessed was in his early to mid twenties, propped in a sitting position at the base of the statue of Francis Marion, the Revolutionary War hero who had been dubbed "The Swamp Fox" and for whom the Square was named.

Each of the victim's ten fingers had been cut off and placed in a semi-circle in front of the body, each finger pointing towards the burned corpse. Also, his penis had been severed at the base and was missing. Cassidy did not know who the victim was or what had killed him, although he suspected that, since there was no blood on the ground near the body, the fingers and penis had been cut off somewhere else, and the body moved to this location. Besides, Marion Square was a very public place to torture someone, assuming that was what had occurred.

It had been after four o'clock in the morning before he finally finished the paper work. He had seen worse, but never in Charleston.

It was now ten forty-five AM. When he worked late, Rita usually let him sleep until he woke on his own. "What's up," he asked, sitting up in bed and taking a sip from the steaming mug of coffee she handed him.

"Daddy! Daddy!" Melissa and Scott, their daughter and son, came running into the bedroom and jumped on the bed. He balanced the coffee the way he had learned when he had been at sea in the Navy and managed not to spill any. He set the coffee cup on the night table and rough housed with the kids.

"The Chief called," Rita explained. "They need you there for some kind of meeting of all the division heads and all detectives."

In the four years that he had been on the force, there had never been such a meeting. He wondered what it was about and asked Rita if he had told her.

"No. He just asked that you come in as soon as you could. He apologized. He knows how late you worked, but he said it's important."

"What time is the meeting?"

"As soon as you get there."

"Oh, great," Frank said, getting out of the bed and leaving the complaining children. He could visualize everyone sitting around waiting for ole' Frank to show up. "Guess I'd better get a move on."

"What about your breakfast?" Rita asked.

"Just make me an egg sandwich. I'll eat it in the car."

He went into the bathroom to take a quick shower, hoping that it would compensate for the missed sleep and wake him up. As he showered, he wondered again about the subject of the meeting, hoping that it wasn't about some cultural law.

Frank looked at the law and his job very simply. In his view, there were two kinds of crimes, social crimes and cultural crimes. He dedicated himself to investigating and solving social crimes, such as murder, assault, rape, robbery, blackmail, extortion, and child abuse, especially child abuse. These crimes had a perpetrator and a victim. On the other hand, he had no interest in crimes he labeled as cultural, acts that were crimes in some jurisdictions and legal in others. Cultural crimes included gambling, prostitution, and liquor law violations, crimes in which there was generally no victim.

Take, for instance, Charleston's approach to the State's liquor laws. It was illegal in South Carolina to sell liquor by the drink, except in clubs that were truly private. However, the authorities in Charleston, in order to attract the conventions and tourists so vital to the City's economy, ignored that law. As a result, there were bars and lounges all over the city. You could get a cocktail in any restaurant or hotel. There were strict, uncodified but enforced rules on how these bars operated—rules enforced by the two detectives on the force dedicated to vice.

There were three types of bars in Charleston County. Type one, the bars in the hotels and restaurants, closed at midnight, and except for two bottles of liquor passed to the Vice Squad Detectives at Christmas, made no other payoffs to the police.

Type two bars closed at two in the morning. Besides liquor, they were also allowed to have B drinkers, who were attractive young ladies who enticed patrons to buy them drinks (which were actually colored water) or fifty dollar bottles of champagne, which cost the bar five dollars, in return for conversation and maybe a hint of sex later, a hint that usually went unfulfilled. Type two bars, which catered primarily to sailors and airmen and were located along a strip on Meeting Street north of Broad Street and on Market Street, could also offer some simple gambling games. Along with the Christmas liquor, type two bars paid the Vice cops $1,000 per month, which was carefully accounted for and went into a fund to help the families of cops who were injured or killed while on duty.

Type three clubs, which paid five thousand dollars per month, stayed open twenty four hours a day, if they wanted to. None did, but the action, which got underway by 10 at night usually continued until four or five in the morning. These clubs offered food, drinks, live bands, strip teasers, full blown casino-type gambling, and, of course, B drinkers, about half of whom were prostitutes.

Frank thought that this was a rational approach and wasn't in any way offended by the fact that the practice violated several State laws. After all, the only difference between Charleston and Las Vegas was that Charleston was in South Carolina and Las Vegas was in Nevada. Besides, the patrons of these bars and clubs clearly wanted them there, and the police made sure that no one was ripped off too badly.

He dried off, dressed, kissed Rita and the kids, grabbed the sandwich and a fresh cup of coffee, and raced for the Ashley River Bridge, siren wailing and a portable light flashing on the dashboard. If they wanted him there as soon as possible, he would get there as soon as possible.

As he neared the river, he could tell from the aroma that it was low tide. The smell of the shore reminded him of his days in the Navy, especially the day he had enlisted—a three-in-one day. It was his eighteenth birthday, he graduated from high school in the morning, and with the reluctant blessings of his father, he had an appointment to be sworn into the Navy in the afternoon. The next day, he was on a train headed for the Great Lakes Naval Training Center near Waukegan, Illinois.

His father, Timothy Cassidy, a Sergeant in the New York City Police Department and one of New York's Finest, had initially been disappointed that Frank did not want to join the Department, as Frank's older brother, Kevin, had done two years earlier. Cassidy men had been New York City Policemen for three—no, now with Kevin, it was four—generations. But Frank had stood his ground. As a child growing up in a cop's family, he had seen the demands that a policeman's job placed on his father—the long hours, being called into work on days off, ruining picnics and other planned family events, and the relatively low pay that made it tough for the large families traditionally found in Irish Catholic households to make ends meet.

He hadn't been adamantly opposed to the idea of becoming a cop. It was just that he wasn't sure yet what he wanted to do; and he wanted to make that decision himself, not have it made for him. When the shouting, rooted in frustration and disappointment, abated, replaced by calm discussions, his father had finally agreed to his son's request, not sure yet what he would tell the guys down at the station house.

Being reasonably athletic and having been forewarned by older friends who had joined the Navy last year, Frank endured basic training relatively easily, only to get his first shock at the end. "Sir! Seaman Apprentice Cassidy reporting as ordered, sir!" he yelled, standing at rigid attention outside the office of the detailer. Having survived basic training, it was now time to learn what job the Navy in its infinite wisdom had decided was best for Seaman Apprentice Frank Cassidy.

"Relax, Cassidy. Have a seat. And don't call me 'sir'. I'm a Chief Petty Officer."

"Yes, s…Chief," Frank gulped, sitting down in the chair in front of the green metal, Navy-issue desk, not sure if he was supposed to sit at attention or not, not even sure if one could sit at attention. The detailer opened Frank's file, which was now on top of the steadily shrinking pile of file folders in the center of his desk.

"You know," he began, "sometimes we have trouble making these determinations, but in your case, your scores point very clearly to a rating that you seem best suited for. You'll be going to Shore Patrol School. Permanent Shore Patrol is good duty."

As the Chief went on to explain the benefits of being a Navy policeman, Frank barely heard him. He was stunned. He was going to be a cop, after all. Maybe it was genetic. He didn't know. At least, his father would probably be happy.

Frank was mildly disappointed. He had pictured himself at sea, maybe aboard a destroyer, slicing through the waves, handling the lines while the ship was refueling or maybe manning the helm, actually steering the large ship.

Well, if that was the decision, he thought, so be it. At least, Shore Patrol School should be a snap. He had been raised since birth to be a cop.

"Here's a ten day pass," he had heard the detailer say, tuning him back in. "Be back here at oh six hundred hours a week from Tuesday, that's the fifteenth, to catch a train for San Diego. Now, get out of here, sailor."

Frank took to Navy police work like a duck to water. He made every promotion the first time he became eligible. His second shock came after three years when he re-upped, having decided to make the Navy his career. After six years of service, he was promoted to E7, Chief Petty Officer, transferred into the Naval Investigative Service, and assigned to the Naval Base at Charleston, where he met and married Rita, a pretty young girl from a good Catholic, though not Irish, family.

In the NIS, he was primarily a detective, investigating crimes which occurred on the base or in town and which involved Navy personnel. After he cracked the case in Beaufort involving a Marine Drill Instructor from Parris Island, he found himself assigned more and more often to homicides and was regularly sent to other naval installations around the U.S. and sometimes overseas to assist in murder investigations.

When he had put in his twenty years, he retired as an E9, a Master Chief Petty Officer, the highest enlisted rank in the Navy, and accepted the standing offer from the Chief of Charleston's Police Department, with whom he had cooperated in many investigations, to join the force as a Detective. He and Rita had moved from North Charleston to Avondale, west of the Ashley, with Melissa, who was then four years old. Scott came along two years later.

His route to Police Headquarters took him north of the marchers' route, so he arrived at the meeting still unaware of its purpose.

As the meeting got underway, Frank was both annoyed and relieved. He placed the segregation laws in the same category as liquor laws and wanted nothing to do with their enforcement, not so much out of any belief that they were wrong as the fact that involvement in them would keep him from duties he considered far more important. However, he was glad that nothing sensational, like a mass murder or a violent crime against a prominent citizen, had occurred.

"So," the Chief was saying, "we want ya'll to be prepared to go high profile. If downtown decides they want this city blanketed with uniforms, we'll blanket it with uniforms. That means you detectives had better break out your blues and see if you can still squeeze into them. Frank, you're excused from having to wear blues."

He was glad to hear that. Cassidy, who had never walked a beat or ridden in a squad car as a civilian cop, didn't even own a uniform. When he joined the force, he had been sworn in dressed in a borrowed set of blues.

The Chief passed around a handful of photographs of a close-up shot of a tall, slender black man giving a speech in front of city hall. The picture had been taken with a telephoto lens.

"Does anybody know who he is?" he asked.

The men in the room studied the picture.

"Might be Jab Brown," an older cop, sitting in the back, mumbled.

"What?" Chief Wall hadn't heard him clearly. "Speak up, Randy. What did you say?"

Randy Holly had been a Charleston cop longer than anyone else on the force. He had walked a beat for years, religiously taking the sergeant's exam each year and just as religiously failing it. He was a damn good cop; he just couldn't retain what he read in the books long enough to repeat it on the test. Finally, they made him a sergeant anyway, after extracting a promise that he wouldn't try for any higher rank.

"I said, he might be Jab Brown," Holly spoke up.

"Who's that?" the Chief asked.

"Kid from Ansonborough. His family moved up north after the war. He played college ball. Basketball. Good. Could've maybe turned pro. Became a preacher instead. Yeah, I saw his picture a couple of times when he played ball. Could be him."

Wall nodded to one of his aides, who left the room to see if he could get a dossier on Jab Brown.

"What about protection?" Frank asked.

"Protection for who?" Wall responded.

"This guy," Frank answered, holding up the picture. "This Brown or whoever he is. We have to assume that he may be an assassination target."

"Maybe I'll shoot the son-of-a-bitch," one of the assembled cops muttered under his breath. Wall ignored the comment.

"No. Until we receive different orders, we're not to do anything out of the ordinary, anything that would indicate any concern on our part in any way about these marches. We'll let them march and go on about our business."

"We gonna let 'em tie up traffic?" growled Traffic Sergeant Bull Jenkins. Bull always growled.

"For now, yes. Bull, your division will babysit them. We think they'll continue to take the same route for as long as they intend to keep this up. If we ignore it and they don't see any reaction or effect, they'll eventually get tired and give it up. You know how the coloreds are. They can't stick to anything for very long. Meanwhile, people will just have to drive a few blocks uptown or downtown to get around the marches. Anything else?"

"I think we should at least draw up a plan for high profile protection, so we're ready if the order comes down," Frank persisted.

"Frank, you wanna bet whether or not we get such an order?" Wall asked. "It's more likely we'll get an order to start arresting them than protecting them. But if it makes you feel better and it doesn't interfere with your other duties, you can work up a plan. That's all for now. Be sure dispatch knows where ya'll are at all times. And I mean at all times. Frank, let's talk about last night's case. That's all for now."

The group grumbled, as the Chief and Frank left the room for the Chief's office. Many of them occasionally visited certain places that they wouldn't want known. They would have to figure out what to do about this order to be constantly reachable.

"Whatcha got?" Chief Wall asked, as they reached the office and poured themselves a cup of coffee from the Chief's personal pot.

"Young, Negro male, early to mid twenties. Body was set on fire. Every finger was cut off at the top knuckle. His penis was also cut off. I'm not sure what killed him. At first, I thought he burned to death. But then why did he just sit there and burn? I think he might have been killed or at least rendered unconscious somewhere else and the body moved to Marion Square and set on fire. The severed fingers were placed in a semi-circle pointing at the victim. We didn't find the penis. We haven't made the victim yet. The tip of each finger is missing, and without finger prints, it may take some time. I don't know if the burning of the body in Marion Square and the pointing fingers were supposed to be a message or not. That was pretty risky. It's such a well-lit public place. If it's a message, I don't know who it's meant for. Doc James said he'd expedite the autopsy. I'm going over there about three."

"Cut off his pecker, huh," Wall said, sipping his coffee. "Maybe it was a dispute over a woman."

"Maybe." Cassidy didn't think so. He suspected the victim was tortured in order to get him to reveal some sort of information.

"Well, keep me informed," Wall said, ending the meeting.

Chapter 6
Day 1—Monday
Noon

The Colonial Steakhouse was located in an old warehouse near the Cooper River. As you walked in the door and up three steps, the cashier's area was straight ahead. A door behind the cashier led into the spacious office of Bob Howe, the owner. The wood paneled dining room, decorated in deep red, was to the right, forming an el around the kitchen. A large glass window between the dining room and the kitchen area allowed patrons to watch their steaks being cooked on a gas-fired grill.

A hallway to the left of the cashier led past the restrooms to the bar. Past the bar were the private dining rooms, two small rooms in the front and one large room in the rear. The POETS Club always met in the rear large private dining room, primarily because it featured a door in the rear which led directly to the parking lot behind the restaurant and allowed the members of the POETS Club to assemble discretely and avoid speculation as to why this group of powerful men was meeting together.

They came singly or in pairs, arriving at pre-set, five-minute intervals beginning at noon. Arthur Manigault, the owner of the News and Courier (Charleston's only morning paper) and the local radio and TV CBS affiliates, was the first to arrive. He usually came alone. Next, John Mason, President of the Old South National Bank, the State's largest bank, and David Smith, President of the Tidewater Savings and Loan, the second largest savings and loan mortgage bank in the State, arrived together. They were followed by Jeremy (call me Jerry) Anderson, Mayor of the City of Charleston, accompanied by Tom Thompson, Chairman of the County Council. J. Alfred

Whittington, Presiding Judge of the County Court, and Jim Tucker, the largest real estate developer in the county, came with Reverend Roger Wilson, Rector of St. Michael's. Beano Martin and Gedney Middleton, who came together, were the last to arrive. When they were invited, Ken Wall and Buddy Leech, the Chiefs of the City and County Police Departments, showed up early and were waiting in the private room when the others entered.

Peaches Parker, the beautiful, blond waitress whose braless breasts were always struggling to burst out of her tight blouse, was permanently assigned to serve the POETS Club at the insistence of several members. She had prepared the room in advance. A large round dining table in the center of the room was set today for eleven. A smaller table in the corner served as a bar with a bucket of iced beer, carafes of red and white wine, and several bottles of liquor, including Black Jack Daniels for Beano. When Gedney Middleton and Beano Martin arrived, Peaches went to Howe's office to alert him.

"Mr. Middleton's here," she said as she walked into the office. Bob Howe rose and accompanied Peaches to the private dining room to greet the POETS members, especially Gedney Middleton, his brother-in-law.

After Howe and Peaches left the room, closing the door behind them, Middleton took his seat and motioned for the others to do the same. Beano filled a glass with ice and brought the bottle of Jack Daniels to the dining table, pouring himself a generous drink along the way.

"Let's get started," Middleton said, as the others took their seats. "We have a lot to cover. I assume that ya'll know about the civil rights march this morning."

The men all nodded in the affirmative.

"Ken, what can you tell us?"

"They assembled at the AME Church on Calhoun Street across from the Holiday Inn," the Chief of the City Police reported. "They marched down King Street to Broad and over to Meeting, blocking traffic the whole way. The guy in front—we assume he's the leader—is Jeremiah Brown, nicknamed Jab. He grew up in Ansonborough and moved to Detroit over fifteen years ago. Guess he's come back home."

"We haven't had any communications with them," the Mayor jumped in, miffed that Middleton hadn't called on him first. The short, rotund man patted his sweating bald head with his cloth napkin. He always sweated when he was upset, even in the cool air conditioning of the restaurant. This morning, he had been in a continuous sweat. "...so we don't know at this point what their demands will be."

"There may not be any demands," Middleton said, impatient that Anderson had spoken without being asked. "This may well be only a skirmish in a war that will be fought in Washington. Beano will get to that in a moment." Turning to the owner of the newspaper and the TV station, he asked, "Arthur, how are you going to treat this?"

Arthur Manigault, who fancied himself a patrician and had affected a manner of speech he thought appropriate to a person of his ancestry and position in the community, paused for effect before responding. He always paused for effect.

"Our position is that these people"—he almost sneered the word 'people'—"are seeking publicity, that publicity of their marches is their main goal. We refuse to be used in such a manner and have therefore decided to ignore their actions. Unfortunately, Gedney, I can't do anything about the northern newspapers or the TV network. I expect Walter Cronkite to mention the march tonight."

"Okay," Middleton said, leaning back and taking a sip of ice water. "Beano, tell them what you told me a little while ago."

The men sat patiently, sipping their drinks, while Beano had one of his persistent coughing fits. He took a large drink of Jack Daniels to clear his throat and began. "Washington is watching Charleston very closely. They expected the reactions that the civil rights marches got in Alabama and Mississippi, but they're waitin' to see what happens here. If we screw this up, President Kennedy'll be all over us like a frog on a cricket."

"In what way?" asked City Council Chairman Thompson. "How will he be all over us?"

"His brother Bobby, the Attorney General, is personally overseeing the drafting of two pieces of legislation, the first of which they are calling the Civil Rights Act."

"Somebody ought to shoot that sonofabitch," mumbled Mason.

"Which one?" asked Tucker. "Jack or Bobby?"

"Both of them," Mason replied. The men chuckled.

"The provisions of the first bill which most directly affect Charleston," Beano went on, ignoring the interruption, "are, first, a requirement that all companies who provide goods and services to the Federal Government must offer equal employment opportunities to all people regardless of race, religion, or country of national origin."

"What does that mean?" asked John Mason, who had sizeable Navy and Air Force accounts in his bank.

"It means that if they don't think you have enough nigras working in your bank, they will ask you to prove that you don't discriminate against them in your hiring practices. If you can't or don't satisfy them, they will not only take away your Government business, they can also fine the bank."

"That's…that's blackmail," Mason exploded. "They cain't do that. It would…"

"Let me finish," Beano snorted. "It's worse than you think. In the bill's latest draft, which I saw last week, this requirement flows through the direct suppliers and contractors to the Government to their suppliers and so on down the line. It will affect virtually every business of any size in this city."

Beano took another slug of whiskey and refilled the glass to the brim. He had another coughing spasm and then continued. "The second provision of the bill of concern to us covers public accommodations, primarily hotels and motels but also restaurants and arguably businesses that offer goods and services to consumers. These businesses will not be able to refuse customers based on their race, et cetera."

"And how does our esteemed President think he's going to circumvent the states' rights provisions of the Constitution?" Judge Whittington asked, his quiet voice mirroring his quiet demeanor.

"The argument," Beano explained, admiring the question from the only other person in the room besides himself and Middleton who Beano believed had a brain, "is that businesses that serve the public, especially hotels, serve the traveling public, hence people from out-of-state. Therefore, refusing to serve them is a violation of interstate commerce."

Judge Whittington sat silent, a worried look on his face.

"If anyone in this room still believes that this is a government of laws, not men," Middleton said, "this should convince him otherwise. Ours has always been a government of men, powerful men, who if they don't like something, merely pass a law to make it the way they want it to be. Abraham Lincoln injured states' rights, FDR pummeled it, and Kennedy will bury it."

"I'm almost afraid to ask," said the Judge. "You mentioned that they are working on two bills."

"This one is the killer," Middleton said, nodding to Beano to continue.

"The second bill is called the Voting Rights Bill. It will give the Federal Government the power to knock down any practices which have the effect of denying nigras of their right to vote. They are particularly targeting poll taxes, literacy tests, property ownership requirements, things like that."

The Mayor got up and went to fix himself a stiff drink.

"You seem to be more worried about the Voting Bill than the other one, Gedney," Dave Smith said. "Why?"

"Both of these bills threaten Charleston's very existence, at least its existence as we know it today," Middleton began. "The primary source of outside money that comes into this city is tourism. It's our lifeblood. We don't have a large manufacturing base or a solid financial industry or a thriving import/export flow. True, we have all of these things, but they tend to be regional, primarily serving the low country. Our economy and with it our city grows from the dollars that tourists spend when they visit. If that revenue drops off by twenty five per cent, we will go from a thriving, growing community to a dying one just like that." He snapped his fingers.

"Then we have to fight this public accommodations thing," an agitated Tommy Thompson demanded. "If the nigras come into our hotels and restaurants and go to our beaches, it'll drive the tourists away."

"I don't totally agree, Tommy," Middleton said calmly. "That may very well be the area where we have to give a little bit."

Everyone at the table except Beano began to argue with Gedney at once.

"Fellows," Middleton said, holding up his hands for quiet, "let me finish. Then, we can discuss these issues 'til the cows come home, if you want. First, though, we'd better order, or we will be here all afternoon."

He rang a small bell. Peaches, waiting outside the door, unbuttoned the top button of her blouse and checked herself in the mirrored wall of the corridor. Colonial Steakhouse waitresses wore red blouses and black skirts. Most of the skirts came down to the knee. Peaches' skirt stopped at mid thigh. With one less button to contend with, her breasts were now halfway out of her blouse. She opened the door and entered the room to take their lunch orders.

Peaches had already had sex with four of the men in the room. Her goal was to lay all of them, all, that is, except that old Beano Martin. As she moved between each of the men to take their order, Buddy Leech casually put his hand on her thigh and moved it up under her skirt. A bra was not the only item of underwear that Peaches didn't wear. He caressed her bare derriere as she calmly took his order for a strip sirloin, medium rare.

When Peaches had left, closing the door behind her, Middleton resumed. "As I said, the Voting Rights bill is the killer. It is vital that we have a white voting majority in Charleston. Beano tells me that our friends in the Senate may be able to delay that bill for a few years if we appear to be phasing segregation out."

He again held up his hands to forestall any protest while he continued.

"Gentlemen, we need time. The nigras are growing as a percent of Charleston's population at an alarming rate."

"Yeah, they breed like rabbits," Jim Tucker said, taking a sip of his beer.

"Actually, that's not true," Middleton said. "Their average family size is not much different than the whites, and that's important. The reason that their percentage of the population is growing is that the nigras are moving into the city from the county while the whites are moving to the suburbs. If we can increase the white population of the city and stop them from moving out—we can't do much about the nigras moving in—we'll be alright. But it will take time, and we need that time."

"How are we going to do that?" Again, it was Tucker, who smelled a real estate involvement.

"In three steps," Middleton responded. "First, we have to handle this civil rights march situation correctly. Arthur, I agree that the local press should play it down. No sense in running off what tourists we have or worrying our citizens too much. Let them march. Sooner or later, they'll get tired. Ken and Buddy, I understand that some of your cops are members of the Klan. Get word to them that the Klan is to lay off. They are not to lay a hand on any nigra for any reason for the time being."

"Okay, Gedney," Ken Wall answered. "I'll tell the day shift today and the night shift tomorrow morning. I don't think anything will happen tonight. They aren't that well organized." Buddy Leech nodded his agreement.

"Second, soon, maybe next week, we loosen up a little on the nigras. Let them have a cup a coffee at Woolworth's. Allow them into one of the movie theaters as a phase-in to opening all of them. Let them use the rest rooms. They must feel like they are making headway. We'll play how fast we go and how much we open up by ear. Hopefully, these actions will buy us the time we need for the third step, the most important one."

He stood up, retrieved some papers from his briefcase in the corner, and walked to an empty table at the side of the room. "Come on over here," he said to the men. He spread out a map of the city. "The third step has two parts. The first involves Ansonborough—here." Gedney pointed to the Ansonborough district. "We began the process to regain this area when we built the Convention Center. Already, Holiday Inn has built one of their first high rise Inns here near the Convention Center. Now, though, we have to advance our schedule. Ansonborough used to be one of the finest areas north of Broad Street. When the whites left, the entire area became a slum."

"Jerry," Gedney said to the Mayor, "I need a list of all of the owners, the slum lords, who own all the homes and buildings in the area I have outlined. Your inspectors will then start continuous inspections—health, fire, zoning violations. We know that practically every dwelling houses multiple nigra families. We need to make the slum lords' lives miserable and costly."

"John and David," he said to the bankers, "let's find out who holds their mortgages. Make them get up-to-date and don't tolerate late payments, even one day. Jim," he turned to the real estate mogul, "I want you to buy up the entire area."

"Whoa there, Gedney," Tucker said. "I can't take on a project like that. And what do I do with these places? How does this help…"

"Easy, Jim," Gedney interrupted. "Let me explain. First, the banks will lend you the money on favorable terms. We will stand good for it, so there's no risk. Second, when you renovate the homes and put them on the market, John & David will offer attractive mortgages. Believe me, the whites from the suburbs will buy them. When you have sold all the units, we will target another area for reclamation."

Gedney walked back to the round table. The other men followed, taking their seats. A knock on the door announced that the food had arrived.

When the servers had left, the assembled power brokers dug into their lunches, while Gedney continued. "The second part is to annex white portions of the county, probably west of the Ashley, into the city. I doubt if we can bring in the areas east of the Cooper, so we should concentrate first on west of the Ashley."

Gedney began to eat while several men asked questions about the plan. When they were finished, each man had his assignment. They agreed to meet again the next day for lunch to assess the situation and report progress.

Bob Howe finished the paper work and leaned back in his chair. He could see through the window of his office that the POETS luncheon was finished as the men began to leave in the reverse order in which they had arrived. Howe felt a stirring in his groin. Peaches would be in as soon as she finished busing the private dining room.

As he waited, he thought about how important Peaches had become to him. It had all started last fall, when he had to pay to repair the damage from the hurricane, damage not covered by insurance. When his financial position became shaky, he became impotent with his wife, probably because of his continual worry over finances. His daughter was scheduled to have her Debutante season in a few months, a very expensive undertaking, and he didn't even have the tuition money for his son's second semester at Harvard. Somehow, he had to cover both situations, or his position in the community would suffer, not to mention his wife's anger and humiliation.

It was an afternoon in December. He was sitting in his office at the end of the lunch period, sipping a drink (he was drinking too much during the day), when Peaches had come in to talk about one of the new girls. Seeing how tired he looked, she offered to give him a back rub. He gratefully accepted. It might help, he thought.

Howe moved over to the couch, removed his shirt, and lay face down. Peaches straddled his legs and began to massage his back, beginning at the neck and gradually moving down. When she reached his waist, she asked him to loosen his pants, which he did with some difficulty. She rose, pulled his pants and undershorts off, and again straddled his legs. She continued massaging his waist and then moved down, massaging his buttocks. Howe became aroused, which was both surprising and uncomfortable, since he was quite large. "Turn over," Peaches said softly, rising up on her knees, so he could twist around.

After that day, they had sex at least three times per week—on the desk, in the chair, on the floor, standing up. One day, when they were relaxing and having a drink after a particularly long and active session, Howe had mentioned his financial problems. That night, Peaches mentioned the problem to Danny Costellano, the owner of the High Hat Club, where Peaches worked as a "B" drinker and sometimes prostitute each night after the Colonial Steakhouse closed. The next day, Costellano called Howe and suggested a meeting. At the meeting, Costellano offered to lend Howe fifty thousand dollars at twenty percent annual interest. When Howe protested the size of the interest,

Costellano stated that his normal rate was twenty percent per month, but that he was doing this for Peaches. Anyway, that was the offer. Howe could take it or leave it. Howe took it.

The tuition was paid, and the Debutante season had been a success. Howe had even managed to resume sex with his wife. Also, business had been good, and Howe was on schedule to raise the sixty thousand he would owe Costellano at year's end. If the summer tourist season held, he would make it. But these civil rights marches were beginning to worry him. If the tourists stopped coming to Charleston, he might fall short, and his instincts told him that would not be a smart thing to do. He was beginning to worry again.

Chapter 7
Day 1—Monday
1:45 PM

"Damn," Rich Newton said out loud. Standing on the long porch which ran the full length along the front of the rambling, white farmhouse, he guessed that this was one of those small, fast-moving rain squalls so common in Charleston in the summer. One minute, the sun would be shining. The next minute, it would be pouring. He remembered many years ago riding his bike as fast as he could up the long driveway to the house in an attempt to outrun one of these squalls. He could see and hear the line of heavy rain behind him, edging closer with each turn of the pedals. He had almost made it.

He sat down on one of the rocking chairs on the porch to wait for the rain to pass. When his father had died unexpectedly, Rich had had to leave college, where he had been in pre-Divinity, and come back to Charleston. In order to support his mother, Rich had been working the evening shift as Assistant Restaurant & Bar Manager at the downtown Holiday Inn, which allowed him to take almost a full load at the College of Charleston. Now that he was on summer break from college, he could begin rotating his shift at the hotel with Charley Innis, the Restaurant and Bar Manager, working mornings one week and evenings the next, which might allow him to resume some semblance of a social life. This week he was on evenings. The rain stopped as suddenly as it had started. He refreshed his coffee, got in his car and drove to work.

Several years earlier, the Ashley Cooper Society began implementing a plan designed to halt the "white flight" to the suburbs and, perhaps, even lure back some of those who had already left the city. The first area targeted was Ansonborough, a residential neighborhood east of Meeting Street and just south of Calhoun Street, which had once been one of the better neighborhoods north of Broad Street with its tree-lined streets and some of the finer homes and town houses in the City. After World War Two, Ansonborough had rapidly deteriorated into a slum of multiple black families crowded into single-family homes and townhouses, interspersed with vacant, rotting, vandalized buildings.

The City floated bonds to finance the construction of a large, new Civic Auditorium and Convention Center on the western edge of Ansonborough just three blocks east of Meeting Street. A vital part of the reclamation plan was the construction by Holiday Inn of one of their first high-rise, hotel-style downtown Inns at the corner of Calhoun and Meeting Streets, two blocks from the Convention Center and also near the central part of the City.

This hotel, now two years old and a showcase for Holiday Inn, was six stories high with twenty four rooms per floor on floors 2 through 6. The ground floor sported a spacious lobby on the eastern end with entrance doors on the front and elevators to the rooms above at the rear. The Innkeeper's office was behind the front check-in desk in the northeast corner of the building. A central corridor, which ran between the bar and lounge facing the front of the building and the private dining and meeting rooms at the rear, connected the lobby with the restaurant, located on the western end of the building, adjacent to Meeting Street. There was a basement parking garage which ran the full length of the building and which was accessible from the building by either the central stairwell or the elevators. This new hotel was directly across the street from the AME Church, the Civil Rights marchers' headquarters.

Rich pulled his 1957 Ford Fairlane 500 into the underground parking lot and rode the elevator to the lobby. He had passed the very end of the line of marchers as they entered the church across the street, having finished the day's march, but he took no notice of a few black people going into a church. As he passed the front desk and headed for the restaurant, the front desk clerk called out to him.

"Rich," she said. He stopped and turned around.

"Hi, Kathy," he answered.

"Hi, yourself. Mr. Mackey asked that you come into his office when you came in."

"Okay. Thanks." Rich reversed direction and walked to the Innkeeper's office behind the front desk.

Russ Mackey had been transferred to Charleston from Denver, Colorado four months earlier after serving as Innkeeper for many years at Denver's oldest Holiday Inn, an aging facility which the Company had decided to sell rather than renovate. The previous Innkeeper in Charleston, hired locally when the hotel had opened, could never quite get the hang of running a hotel the way Kemmons Wilson, Holiday Inn's founder and Chairman, demanded, especially a flagship property like this new downtown high rise Inn. When the decision was made to close the Denver motel, Holiday Inn's top management saw a way to kill two birds with one stone, both keeping one of their better hotel managers in the family and solving their problem in Charleston.

After fighting a losing battle to keep a badly aging motel in Denver up to Holiday Inn's high standards, Mackey, when he learned that he would become the Innkeeper at one of the Company's newest properties, had prepared to relax and fine tune the hotel into one of the nation's best. Now, having hardly had the chance to learn his way around this city with its one-way streets that seemed to go wherever the cow had wandered, his proud new hotel was in the front lines of the Integration Movement, a dispute which was foreign to him and in which he didn't want to become involved, not having a lot of sympathy with the white Southern position. Neither did Charley Innis, who had been Mackey's Restaurant and Bar Manager in Denver and who, to Mackey's relief, had agreed to accept the offer to join him in Charleston, providing the hotel with a seasoned management team accustomed to working together.

"Hi, Rich," Mackey said as Rich entered the office. "Please close the door and have a seat."

Rich, noticing Innis standing by the window, complied. For a split second, he wondered if he was about to be fired, although he couldn't imagine why.

"Rich, you may not know, since you just came in, but there was a civil rights march here today," Mackey began.

"Here?" Rich asked. "Here in the hotel?"

"No, thank God," Mackey responded, managing a small laugh. "I mean here in Charleston. The march started and ended at that church across the street." He pointed at the AME Church, which could be seen through the office window.

Rich said nothing, waiting to learn why a civil rights march from the church across the street warranted a private meeting in the Innkeeper's office.

"Based on what has happened in Georgia and Alabama, I have been told to expect them to march every day for the foreseeable future. We also expect them to send someone, probably a well-dressed, older couple, over here to try to register for a room or, more likely, to try to eat in our restaurant."

So, that's it, Rich thought. "What are we going to do?" Rich asked.

"I spoke to Memphis an hour ago. They said we should follow the local custom, which translates into do not serve colored people in the hotel." Mackey held his hand up as he continued. "Please don't say anything until I finish. The suggestion, which is probably the best way to handle it, is that if they come in and ask to be seated, we ask them if they have a reservation. When they say, 'no', we'll tell them that we're sorry, but we're all booked up with reservations."

"Won't they then just call for a reservation?" Rich asked, forgetting Mackey's admonition to say nothing.

"We won't take reservations from calls we get from outside the hotel, only from calls placed from hotel rooms. If someone calls from the outside, we'll tell them that reservations aren't necessary. They should just come in." Mackey took a deep breath and went on. "Charley and I talked it over, and we agree that because we are outsiders and not Southerners, it would look better if you are the one who greets them and declines to seat them."

Mackey hurried on, again raising his hand as a signal to Rich not to say anything until he was through. "I am not telling you to do it or ordering you to do it or anything like that. If you don't want to, just say so, and it won't in any way affect your job or our opinion of you or…"

"Mr. Mackey," Rich interrupted, "I don't mind. If the Company says don't serve them, I'll turn them away. If the Company says to serve them, I'll seat them. It doesn't matter to me either way."

Mackey, relieved, sat back, realizing that he had been sitting on the edge of his chair. He had not been entirely honest with Rich on two counts. First, it had been Memphis who had wanted a Southerner, preferably someone local, to meet any of the protesters who came in. Mackey feared that if Rich knew it was Memphis who wanted him to do be the front person to deal with this problem, it might put undo pressure on him to agree to it. Secondly, he would not tell Rich that both he and Charley Innis were having internal struggles, based on personal convictions, with Memphis's directive and had agreed between themselves that if Rich refused to handle the situation, they would resign before doing it themselves. Mackey was relieved for many reasons.

"Okay, then," Mackey said, "for the time being, we'll change your hours.

Since we don't expect them to come in at breakfast because the marches usually begin in the morning, you should come to work in time for lunch—some time before twelve—and stay until three. Then, you can take off until six and leave for the day around ten. Charley and I will handle opening and closing each day."

Rich agreed to the new hours and headed for the restaurant to check in the evening shift, which had to be in and ready to work by three, when the day shift got off. After they were checked in, he would then open the bar.

While Mackey was relieved with the result of the meeting, Rich was bothered. What bothered him was the fact that he wasn't bothered by the task he had been asked to perform. Somewhat to his surprise, he had discovered during his time away at college that he wasn't a racist, having become friendly with several blacks, a few Chinese, and two Jews. Yet, having grown up in Charleston, he knew that this threat to past customs and the status quo would be fiercely resisted by most, if not all, of the white people, and he reasoned that maybe the resistance was right, if it could slow down the changes, thereby preserving the good aspects of Southern culture while replacing the bad.

On a deeper level, though, he wondered if maybe he should care more. If he planned to become a minister, shouldn't he care about all of God's people, regardless of their race? And if he should, why hadn't the ministers of Charleston's churches made an issue of it before? He would be interested to see if Reverend Tolbert said anything on Sunday. Maybe he should talk with Tolbert about it, although he suspected that he would get the same answer as last time—he must work it out for himself. He checked in the four white evening waitresses and then went into the kitchen to check in Marvin Watkins, the evening cook, and his all black kitchen crew.

Chapter 8
Day 1—Monday
2:00 PM

The marchers had all returned to the AME Church. After a quick speech by Jab Brown, congratulating them on their first day and advising them to get some rest, the tired but elated marchers, standing tall, began their trips home.

Jab Brown and the other fourteen ministers who comprised the Strategy Council for the movement in Charleston retired to a classroom behind the sanctuary for a brief meeting to recap the day's events and plan tomorrow's. Reverend Brown closed the door, as the men found seats.

"Today went well," he said, and the assembled group applauded. "I hope ya'll are clapping for yourselves and for those brothers and sisters out there, because the credit goes to ya'll. Not one incident to mar the effect of today's march."

He started to pace. It helped him concentrate. "Remember, though, that today, we caught them by surprise—off their guard. Tomorrow may be different. They're probably having their own meeting right now. Today, we announced our broad theme. Starting tomorrow, we will begin to express the end of our patience in specific areas. What should tomorrow's topic be?"

"Education," one minister offered.

"Jobs for our men, so they can better themselves and their families' lives," another spoke out.

Reverend Lyle remained silent, pondering.

"There are many, many issues here," Brown went on. "I agree that education is as good a place to start as any. It will also point out that this movement is really about future generations. One more thing," he continued.

"It is very important that what we discuss in these planning meetings remains in this room. You are to tell nobody, and I mean nobody. It is essential that we keep as much of the element of surprise as we can. Can ya'll do that?" To a man, they nodded their assent.

"Good. That's all for this afternoon. Brother Jordan and his wife have volunteered to go across the street tonight to the Holiday Inn to try to have dinner. We'll target the Holiday Inn for several reasons. First, it's a national, publicly owned chain. The adverse publicity from refusing us will be difficult for them to withstand. Second, we have several national labor unions that are ready to send telegrams to Holiday Inn headquarters after they refuse us entry into their restaurant stating that none of their members will stay in Holiday Inns until the policy is changed. Third, it's very convenient." The ministers laughed. "Brother Jordan, ya'll please be here at seven thirty. I'll brief you then. I'll also arrange for a reporter to accompany you. I'll see the rest of ya'll bright and early here tomorrow morning at eight."

Jab Brown adjourned the meeting and went outside in front of the church for a press conference. This routine would be repeated each day. An opening speech to the marchers which would be repeated at the destination of that day's march, the march itself, a planning meeting, and then a press conference. The microphones were in place and reporters were waiting outside, as Reverend Brown joined them.

After leaving the planning meeting, Shine Rivers made several shuttle trips in his 1956 Pontiac, helping to ferry those marchers who lived too far to walk home to their neighborhoods. By three thirty, he was finished and began his trip home to Wadmalaw Island near Seabrook Beach, a trip which normally took forty five minutes to an hour during rush hour but which today would take only thirty minutes.

Shine was not tired. He was elated, high on the knowledge that at last they were doing something. He could have begun another march all over again right then. He turned off the highway onto the gravel road leading to his church, noting that the sign on the highway, which read "Wadmalaw Island Evangelical Church" and gave the hours for Sunday services, could use a new paint job. He would make a note when he got home to ask for volunteers this Sunday, knowing that Amos Cantrell, a professional sign painter by trade, would insist on doing the job and defy anyone else to touch that sign.

He was proud of their small, gleaming white church. It could only seat about one hundred and fifty worshipers comfortably in the pews they had rescued from a church downtown, when it had been renovated with new pews. The men of the church had repaired, sanded and painted the pews, and after they were installed, they looked brand new. The Hymnals and Bibles had also been donated by a white Episcopal Church in the City. Sometimes, they used the Hymnals, but usually they sang old Negro spirituals that the island people knew by heart, accompanied by the ancient upright piano that was constantly in need of tuning. In the rear of the church were several small rooms that served as a nursery, Sunday school, and the smallest room as his office with its most valuable and important feature—a telephone.

Shine steered the car onto the dirt road that veered off to the right past the church and continued into the woods to his modest house which wandered off in several directions, the result of adding rooms one-by-one as his family had grown, one-by-one. When the house came into view, he honked the horn and headed for the garage, pulling in next to the pick-up truck. At the sound of the horn, kids came running from everywhere. As he turned off the ignition, he said his usual prayer, thanking God for his family, his church, and, above all, for Rebecca, his wife. After all these years, he was still amazed that she had married him.

They had met eighteen years earlier at a county-wide, week long revival held at a farm on Johns Island, having been introduced by his aunt who had gotten her dentures from Rebecca's father, a dentist in Charleston. They were an unlikely pair. She was pretty, petite, light skinned and educated, having just completed her sophomore year at Howard University in Washington, DC. Shine was tall, big, dark skinned, menacing looking, and had dropped out of school after the eighth grade, believing at that young age (with help from some of the island men) that an educated Negro in the South was a frustrated Negro.

While searching around for a trade to learn, he began shining shoes in front of Hunley's Drug Store on King Street, riding into Charleston every day with an uncle who worked as a car cleaner at the Oldsmobile dealership. The nickname "Shine" stuck, which suited him fine, since his real name, Solomon, got him into at least one fight every week. On rainy days, he went with his uncle to the dealership and performed odd jobs for the mechanics, watching them while they worked and occasionally asking questions, but always careful not to get in the way or become a nuisance.

By the time he was sixteen, he began showing up at the dealership every day, and the mechanics were keeping him constantly busy with jobs, which freed them up to finish their work more quickly. Seeing that he had become valuable to the operation of the garage, the foreman put Shine on the payroll, creating the title of Mechanic's Helper. When that foreman left for more money at the Cadillac dealership down the street, Jimmy Long, the most senior Master Mechanic, was selected to become the new foreman. His first act was to promote Shine to Mechanic.

Somehow, Rebecca saw something beneath Shine's rough exterior, and they began seeing each other, sometimes walking through the woods on Wadmalaw Island and other times swimming at Skeeter Beach, which was actually a sandbar on a creek and was the only "beach" available to black people.

But wherever they went and whatever they were doing, they always talked. Shine's limited vocabulary made it difficult for him to express himself, sometimes resulting in anger, frustration, and embarrassment on his part, but Rebecca seemed always to understand what he was trying to say.

As the end of the summer approached, Rebecca knew that she would soon have to make a decision. She could return to Howard and continue her education to become a teacher, or she could stay and marry Shine. She knew that, if she went back to school, in his eyes she would be abandoning him, and she would probably lose him.

One day in August, her decision was made for her. During one of their walks in the woods, they came upon a small church nestled behind a stand of pine trees at the end of a dirt road. Out of nowhere, apparently having come to trust her enough, Shine began talking about his impossible dream to become a preacher and have his own church.

"Why, Shine Rivers," she said, trying to mask her surprise. "You never tole me about that before."

"Doan talk 'bout it much to nobody," he said, looking down at his foot moving the dirt around in little piles. "No cause to. It'll never happen no how."

"Why do you feel that way?" she asked.

"Preachers is smart," he answered, still looking down. Rebecca could tell that this was painful and difficult for him. "I'm not. They can talk good. I cain't. I can hardly read, even."

"Shine," she said softly and tenderly, "you're not stupid or dumb. I know from our talking together that underneath that hair"—she gently touched the top of his head, able to only because he was looking down—"is a very good brain. You just need to learn more words, so that you can express what you think and what you feel. I can help you learn those words."

"I doan know," he said. "Been a long time since I was in school."

"Look," she said. "I've been goin' to college for two years to become a teacher. Reckon I've learned a few things. And besides, you already know how to read some, you want to learn and you're smart. You'll be surprised how quickly it comes."

"But we doan got much time fore you go back," he protested.

"Maybe I won't go," she responded quietly.

"Whadda you mean? You gonna stay?"

"Maybe," she said coyly. "Depends."

"On what?"

"On whether a certain person asks me a certain question."

"Who? Ast what question?"

"Oh, Shine," she said, exasperated. "Do you want it over your head for the rest of our lives that I had to ask you?"

"You mean...," he stammered, "do you mean you want me to ast you to marry me?"

"I accept," she said, not taking any chances.

"Rebecca," he said very slowly and quietly, "is you sayin' that a pretty, smart, educated woman like you wants to marry up with somebody like me?"

"Not someone LIKE you. YOU! Yes, I will marry you."

Shine started jumping up and down, whooping. He jumped so high that he hit his head on a tree limb. Rebecca laughed, and her laughter caused Shine to start laughing. Soon, they were both laughing so hard they had tears running down their cheeks.

When the laughter subsided, Shine took her by the hand, looked her straight in the eye, and said, "Rebecca, is you sure?"

"I'm sure," she said, looking up at his face. "I love you, Shine Rivers, and I want to be the mother of your children."

Shine knelt, motioning Rebecca to kneel beside him, and said a prayer, a prayer he would repeat every day for the rest of his life, thanking God for Rebecca.

The next day, she checked out eighth grade level reading books from the public library. Two hours later, she returned them and checked out sixth grade books. Shine was not embarrassed or angry. If Rebecca believed that she could teach him to read at an adult level, that was good enough for him. They just had to find the right starting place.

They were married in October.

Shine's reading progressed at the rate of one grade level every two months. After one year, he was reading college level texts. For their second anniversary, Rebecca, very pregnant with their first child, gave him a new Bible and a concordance to help him with Biblical words and passages.

Rebecca discovered that she was not just a teacher; she was also a student. Shine possessed a stronger faith in God than she had ever encountered before. His faith was truly that of a child, totally without reservation, and yet he was not a naive or simpleminded person. In fact, as his vocabulary caught up with his innate thoughts, Rebecca found that he was much deeper than even she had suspected. And yet he had this simple faith. Whatever happened was ordained by God. If we didn't understand it, that was our problem, not God's.

Eight years ago, he had been named an Associate Pastor of the church, and in only three years, when the Pastor was killed in a farming accident, Shine Rivers became an ordained pastor of the Wadmalaw Island Evangelical Church. It was an unpaid position in the poor church. But that didn't matter. He was a minister with his own church, his dream now a reality.

As the children came and grew, Rebecca was determined that they would grow up speaking correctly. Therefore, Gullah was banned from the house. This was, at first, hard on Shine, because he had been speaking the unique Lowcountry black mixture of modern English, old English and African since he learned to talk. But he gradually improved, as his knowledge and comprehension grew. Five years ago, he had stopped wearing his mojo, a voodoo mixture of herbs worn in a bag suspended from the neck to ward off evil spirits, having grown in his Christian belief to the point that God and God alone could protect one from evil. However, the small voodoo totem remained in the front yard near the driveway. His congregation had not progressed as far in their faith as he had in his. Nevertheless, the only remnant of voodoo that remained in his household was the folk medicine taught to Rebecca by the island women.

Shine got out of the car, mobbed by the younger children, and walked with them into the house. He would spend time with each child before bedtime, after which he and Rebecca would talk, read the Bible, and work on his Sunday sermon. Tonight, he would have a lot to tell her.

Chapter 9
Day 1—Monday
2:45 PM

"Time to go see the M E, Frank," Sergeant Holly said. Frank Cassidy put away the file and followed the uniformed officer out to the parking lot to Frank's unmarked car. Holly drove them to meet with the Medical Examiner about the burned body discovered the previous night, making a brief stop at Krispy Kreme for a dozen doughnuts.

Charleston's Detective Squad was unusual in two respects. First, there was no leader—no Captain or Chief of Detectives. The individual detectives, all Lieutenants in rank, reported directly to the Chief of Police. Secondly, except for the two cops who were dedicated to Vice, the detectives were not paired off as partners. They worked individually. Any time they felt that they wanted or needed a partner on a specific case, they were free to take a uniformed policeman with them. Frank always used Randy Holly.

The Medical Examiner's office was also unusual. The Police and citizens of Charleston were fortunate that Coroner Carlton James had selected lifestyle over fame and fortune. Carlton James (every time he filled out a form requesting last name first, the person reviewing the completed form would inevitably tell him that he had it backwards, and he would patiently explain that his first name was Carlton and his last, James) was one of the more renown forensic pathologists in the country and had authored texts used in most medical schools on the analysis of the contents of a murder victim's stomach and their use in establishing the time of death.

When the University of South Carolina Medical School, located in Charleston, approached Carlton James to head their Forensic Pathology

Department, he agreed, provided that the school allotted space to the County at no charge for a morgue. The school complied, and constructed one of the most modern morgues in the country, complete with an overhead amphitheater, so Dr. James could instruct students while performing actual autopsies.

"Hello, Doc," Cassidy said, as he walked through the double swinging doors into the autopsy room. Sergeant Holly went down the hall to pass doughnuts out to the staffers, after swiping a jelly one for himself. "Whatcha got on our John Doe?"

"For starters," Carl James began, filling his ever present pipe and opening the file on the table in front of him, "he's no longer a John Doe. I've got a name and an address. Don't know if the address is current, though."

"How in hell did you do that?" Cassidy asked, filling a cup with coffee and taking a seat, sitting backwards in a wooden chair and resting his arms on the chair's back.

"Dental work." He lit the pipe with a special pipe lighter that could double as a small flamethrower. "There's a nutty colored dentist in this town who signs his work. Swear to God. I gave him a call. He knew the guy right away. Work was done about…" he turned a page in the file, "about 8 months ago. Expensive, too. Your victim had money. At least he did then. His name is…was Sammy Boutry. Lived at 1514 Huger Street." (He pronounced Huger as you would say the letters "U G"). "Twenty four years old. I've got the rest of the vitals in the report."

Cassidy made a note of the name and address. He wouldn't have to take additional notes during this conversation. Carl James was as thorough as he was skilled.

"What else do you have?"

"Well, to begin with, I'm not sure why they burned the body. The mutilation and murder took place somewhere else, and the body was brought to Marion Square. From what I could see, they poured some kerosene on the body, lit it, and left. There was no evidence that they used any kind of fuse to give them time to get away before the fire became visible. Pretty risky. Also, they didn't use enough kerosene to destroy evidence. Either they didn't know what they were doing, or the fire was started for another purpose."

"I have a theory," Cassidy interjected, "which I'll get to later. Go on."

"Okay," Dr. James said, referring to the file again, so as not to omit any details. "The index and middle fingers of the victim's right hand were severed before he died, probably with a sharp knife. His penis was also cut off before he died."

"Yeah," Cassidy said. "We never found the penis. Guess it was left at the murder location or discarded."

"No," James said, "I found it."

"Where?"

"Down his throat. That's what killed him. He choked to death on his own penis. I've seen a lot, but I've never seen that before. Pretty brutal. Frank, you've got to find these guys."

"We will. You keep saying, 'they'. You're sure that there was more than one perp?"

"Had to be. Who's going to sit still while someone cuts off two of his fingers and his penis? The other eight fingers were severed after the victim had died. The perps tried to make it look like a voodoo ritualistic murder, but they did a lousy job."

"How do you mean?"

"It wasn't so much what they did as what they didn't do. For instance, there should have been blood from a freshly killed chicken sprinkled in a circle around the body. You see any blood?"

"No."

"Whole thing's kinda weird. Anyway, his last meal was fried chicken and some greens, which he washed down with a beer. You tell me when he ate, and I'll tell you within half an hour either way when he was killed."

"What kind of beer?" Frank meant it as a joke.

"Pabst Blue Ribbon," James replied matter-of-factly. "What's this theory you have?" James asked, closing the file folder and apparently finished for now with the briefing.

"Well, what you told me reinforces it. I think that…" he looked at his notes, "this Sammy Boutry was tortured to make him talk, to reveal some information, was probably killed to cover up the identities of the perps, and the body arranged in that way and burned to send a message to someone or a group of someones. That's about as far as I've gotten."

"Sounds plausible," the Coroner said. "Fits what I have."

"Okay, that's what we'll go with for now. I owe you a fifth of Scotch for identifying the victim. Still drink Teacher's?"

"Yep," James said, relighting his pipe. He hadn't had to buy his own booze for at least three years.

Cassidy located Randy Holly shooting the breeze with an ambulance driver, and the two of them drove to the Huger Street address. There, they learned from another tenant in the same building that the Boutry family had moved about three months earlier to Ansonborough. They got the senior Mr. Boutry's first name, called a special number at South Carolina Electric and Gas, learned the Boutry's new address, and drove to Ansonborough.

Cassidy showed his badge to the young woman who answered the door. She could see Sergeant Holly's uniform. Along with the added protection a uniformed officer provided, detectives took them along when they went into the black neighborhoods to help identify themselves as policemen. White men in suits in black neighborhoods were assumed by the residents to be either police or bill collectors. They were more likely to answer the door for a policeman than for a bill collector.

"Sammy Boutry?" Cassidy said.

"Which one?" the young woman, probably his sister, asked.

"About twenty four years old," Cassidy answered.

"He ain't here. What's he done?"

"Does he live here?" Cassidy pressed.

"Yeah. Didn't come home last night, though. Whatcha looking for him for?"

"Is your mother or father home?"

"Just a minute." The girl left them standing at the front door and went into the back of the house. An older woman came to the door, taking off her apron and straightening her hair. Her daughter returned and stood behind her. "Yes?" she asked.

"Mrs. Boutry?"

"Yessuh?"

"I'm Lieutenant Cassidy, Charleston Police. This is Sergeant Holly. Is Sammy Boutry your son?"

"Yessuh. Is he alright?"

"May we come in?"

"Yessuh. Of course."

She opened the screen door, and the two men walked into the living room.

"Did you used to live at 1514 Huger Street?"

"Yessuh. We used to live ova to Huger Street. What's this all about?"

"Did your son have some dental work done by Dr. Wiggins within the last year?"

"Yessuh. What's happened?"

"Mrs. Boutry, we have a body down at the morgue. We believe that it's your son, Sammy."

"Oh, no!" The woman put her hand to her head and, for a moment, appeared about to faint. "Oh, lordy!"

"What happened to him?" the daughter asked.

"He was murdered. I'll spare you the details, but it was pretty brutal. We'll need some information about him."

"Do you know who did it?" the daughter was asking the questions. Her mother had sat down hard in the nearest chair and was continuing to say, "Oh, lordy! Oh, no!"

"No, we don't, at least not yet. We only just identified him. It happened sometime last night. We need the information, so we can find the person or persons who did this."

"How'd he die?" the daughter persisted.

"I'd rather not go into that just now." Let the mortician tell them how Sammy Boutry had died, if he wanted to. Frank had no intention of telling them himself. "Do you mind answering a few questions?"

"I tole him," the daughter wailed. "I tole him this would happen."

The mother regained her composure and stood up. "Hesh, girl," she said to her daughter. Then, she turned to face Cassidy. "Let us see to our son's burial," she said. "After the funeral, then we'll answer your questions."

Frank felt sure that after the funeral, the daughter would tell him everything she could, even if the mother wouldn't. No sense in pressing it now. If the killers were going to flee, they were already long gone. Frank suspected, however, that they were still in Charleston and would not flee, believing that they had successfully masked Boutry's identity. After giving Mrs. Boutry his card containing his name and telephone number, Frank had Holly drive him back to the station. He now had more paperwork to complete.

Chapter 10
Day 1—Monday
7:30 PM

The farmer who provided the field for the monthly Ku Klux Klan rally was an ardent Klan supporter. He must have been. The section of his James Island farm he had set aside for the rallies had been rendered unsuitable for farming by the cars and trucks parking for the rallies and by the beer cans and liquor bottles discarded during the meetings. For providing a meeting place, he had been included in the ruling council, even though the Klan leaders didn't much care for him.

The huge cross was flaming. The sun had not yet set. When it did, the burning cross would provide the only light for the meeting. Jimmy Long, dressed along with the other council members in Klan robes without hoods, stood in the cowboy boots he always wore under his robe to add a couple of inches to his height and surveyed the crowd that was gathering to hear his speech. He guessed that there were about two hundred people finding places on the ground to spread their blankets and sit, four times the number who usually attended the rallies. Although he thought that the Klan's work was man's work, he was not too disturbed to see quite a few women in the crowd. For the fight ahead, the Klan would need the support of all white people.

While he waited in front of the microphone attached to the battery-powered sound system, he thought about the council meeting that had been held an hour earlier. I should have become a psychologist, he said to himself. I played them perfectly.

The Klan had four committees—Negro, Jew, Catholic, and Homosexual. Each committee head was responsible for planning and implementing the Klan's actions against one of those specific groups.

Jimmy Long headed the Negro Committee. He had opened the council meeting with a description of the march he had witnessed in Charleston that morning. Then, he insisted that they—the Klan—had to make a swift and decisive response to nip this movement in the bud. "Today, they marched," Long said, "probably a little scared, not knowing what to expect. Well, nothing happened to 'em. If we don't do something, then tomorrow they will have more confidence, not as scared. Every day that nothing happens, their confidence will grow even more. We need to hit 'em and hit 'em hard—tonight!"

"My Chief told us all that if we knew any Klan members, we ought to tell them to lay off," said one of the council members, a sergeant in the County Police Department.

"Mine said the same thing," said an officer in the city police force. "He looked straight at me when he said it," he added, uncomfortably.

"Pussies," Long responded. "They're not going to do anything, not tomorrow, or the next day, or the next. They're just going to let this ball start rolling down the hill 'til it gets up so much speed that nothing or nobody can stop it! That's why we have to do something and do it quick—tonight. We're the only ones with the balls to stand up to these Communist bastards."

"So, whadda you want to do, Jimmy?" another man asked.

"I think we should hang Shine Rivers," Jimmy answered, smiling.

"What?!" the county cop exploded. "Are you fucking nuts?! This place would be crawling with Feds!"

The others jumped in, saying to a man that each wanted nothing to do with a lynching. Jimmy had anticipated this reaction. After berating the group and telling them that they were as weak as the Mayor and the other City and County leaders, he then insisted that they at least give Shine a whipping, or did they think that they—the Klan—should also do nothing?

It was agreed that after the rally, ten members of the council, wearing robes and hoods, would go to Shine's house, where Jimmy Long would administer twenty lashes as a warning to the marchers that they should stop all protest activities. The group would include Long, the two cops, a council member who was a photographer for the News & Courier, Charleston's morning newspaper, a pipe fitter from North Charleston who had never met Shine and would, therefore, be the one—and the only one—to speak during the flogging, and five other men—ten in all. The photographer would take photographs of the whipping, develop them that night, and make sure that copies fell into the hands of the newspaper's editor as well as the Chief of the City Police and the Mayor first thing in the morning. The photographer had agreed to the task, not yet having figured out how to deliver the photographs anonymously. The nine men who were to accompany Long to Shine's house drank more than usual during the remainder of the council meeting.

The crowd was seated. It was time to begin. His back to the burning cross, Jimmy Long stepped up to the microphone. "Good evening," he began, the sound system squealing with feedback. He bent down and adjusted the volume. "It's good to see so many of you out here tonight. Guess you heard about the coloreds marching in Charleston today. I saw it myself. There must have been a thousand of 'em." The correspondents reported the number of marchers as five hundred; the police estimated it to be two hundred; the actual number had been three hundred sixty seven. "This movement is not only a threat to the peace and safety of our community, it is an affront to God's order, and I can assure you that the Knights of the Ku Klux Klan will not stand by and let this Communist blasphemy continue!"

A static of applause and a few "Right on's" rippled through the crowd.

"It is clear that the Nigra is inferior," Long continued, "is different from the white man, and that God intended for them to stay separate. This Yankee, liberal, Communist plot to force the South to mingle with and ultimately marry with the coloreds is against nature as ordained by God." He took a sip from the cup of Old Crow whiskey he held in his hand. "What right does the Nigra have to claim a spot equal to the white man? Name me one thing any of 'em have ever done to better himself or mankind. Name me one country in Africa not ruled by whites which has risen above mud huts, witch doctors, and cannibalism! You cain't, 'cause there ain't any. Anything of any worth ever invented in this world, any progress in business or art or anything else ever made in this world, was made by the white man."

Jimmy Long was not merely a white supremacist, he was a white male supremacist. When he said white man, he meant white MAN. In fact, he was a white protestant male supremacist. He ranked mankind in order of importance as white protestant males first, followed in order by white protestant females, Catholics, non-Christian whites (including Jews), Orientals, homosexuals, and finally, blacks.

"It's against nature! Do the sparrows make nests with the robins? Do they mate together? No! Hell, they won't even fly together. If you see any of 'em together, they're fighting. Same with the Nigra and the white man. It's against nature for the races to mix. Those Yankee preachers tell us that the Bible says we are to love our fellow man. They say that if we don't integrate with the Nigra, we are not following what God and Jesus said we should do. Shame on them! Shame on them! They must think we're ignorant—that we don't know that the Bible was written in Greek and that there are many different words in Greek for the word 'love'. Two of 'em I want to talk to you about—and that is agape" (he pronounced it AGG-a-pie) "and filio" (FILL-e-o). "Agape is the love that God has for us or the love a man has for his wife. Filio is brotherly love, the way we feel for our brothers and sisters and close friends. When Jesus said that we should love our neighbor as ourselves, he said we should filio them. He didn't say we should agape them! Hell, I may filio my brother or my friend, but that doesn't mean I want to live next door to them."

The crowd laughed.

"Them Yankee preachers are lying to us and insulting us by thinking we are too stupid and ignorant to know our Bible. Well, we do know our Bible, maybe better than they do, and we know what God intended. He meant for us to live apart. That's why he made them black!"

The crowd applauded enthusiastically.

"We are going to have a rally here every night until we put an end to this abomination—this insult to God's order. Every one of you who supports what we are sayin' should bring at least one new person with you tomorrow night. The white people must stand together and show the coloreds that we will not put up with this nonsense. We also ask you to become members of the Klan. Our leader, the Grand Imperial Wizard, will tell you how you can do that."

During the recruitment speech, Long stepped out of the light to replenish his cup. Tonight, though, he would remain sober, the adrenalin already starting to flow in anticipation of what was to happen later. All his years of practice, both with the whip and with all of the rifles and pistols in the private arsenal he kept in the shed behind his house, would now pay off. He wished his wife were present tonight to hear him. She might then understand. But eight days ago, he had slapped her around and then fallen asleep for the night, only to awaken in the morning and discover that she had taken off, probably to her mother's house in Walterboro, taking their eight-year-old son with her. His initial reaction was good riddance to both of them. If they had no more respect for him than to steal away in the night while he was asleep, then let the cowards go. He had not even attempted to track them down. They would come back soon, he was sure, and beg his forgiveness.

But tonight, he wished she were here. Then, maybe she would understand that there was more to the Klan than, as she put it, a bunch of rednecks getting drunk and beating up queers. If she had been here, maybe she would see that the Klan was important—that it was the only line of defense of the white man against the black man. Long took another slug of whiskey.

Chapter 11
Day 1—Monday
7:48 PM

The Holiday Inn provided an entrance from the parking lot in front of the hotel directly into the restaurant and bar area, allowing patrons from outside the hotel to avoid the hustle and bustle of the lobby as well as the long walk down the corridor leading to the restaurant. Rich Newton had just completed a walk through the dining area, checking to ensure that nothing was amiss, and was standing at the hostess's podium, when he saw an elderly, well-dressed, black couple come through the door, followed by a younger, white man carrying a tape recorder. Here we go, he thought, as they approached the podium.

"May I help you?" Rich said, stepping around the podium to greet the arrivals.

"Yes," the black man said. "We would like to have dinner."

The young man with the tape recorder stood to Rich's right and held a microphone close enough to record the conversation.

"Certainly," Rich responded. "Your name please. I'll check your reservation."

"We don't have a reservation," the black man said.

"Oh, I am sorry," Rich said. "We're all booked up for tonight, so we can only seat those with reservations."

The black couple and the reporter could easily see that the restaurant was only about one third filled. "Thank you," the black man said, smiling. "Perhaps another night."

"Yes," Rich said. "Maybe when we're not so busy."

The black couple, followed by the reporter, turned and left through the front door. The entire exchange had taken less than thirty seconds. As Rich returned to the podium to work on the week's banquet schedule, the uneasiness he had felt that morning following the meeting in Mackey's office returned. What he had just done was bothering him, and he didn't still know why.

Chapter 12
Day 1—Monday
10:30 PM

A female possum, followed by her three babies, emerged from the dark woods into the moonlit clearing. As she prepared to shepherd her children across the gravel road into the woods on the other side, the first pickup truck turned off the highway onto the road. The mother possum stopped in the middle of the road, her eyes glowing in the truck's headlights, daring the truck to proceed. The driver of the truck hit the brakes and was nearly rear-ended by a second pickup following closely behind, causing the three men standing in the bed of the second truck to grab the roof of the cab to avoid falling.

"Shit," Jimmy Long said, spilling some of his Old Crow on the passenger's seat of the first truck. He was riding shotgun, so he could navigate, since he knew the way. "Kill your headlights."

The driver turned the truck's headlights off. Almost immediately, the driver of the second truck followed suit. The gravel road leading through the woods to the church was clearly visible in the bright moon light, allowing them to drive without lights and not wander off the road.

Satisfied that her charges were safely across the road, the mother possum turned and scampered after them.

"Pull up by the church," Long ordered.

The two trucks, each with two men riding in the cab and three standing in the bed, slowly proceeded a couple of hundred yards down the road until they were beside the church and out of view of the highway. The men got out of the trucks and donned white robes and hoods. Long was still wearing his cowboy boots.

The drivers returned to the trucks and drove slowly and as silently as possible past the church to the house in the woods, stopping in front of the house as Long had instructed. The other eight men, three with shotguns and Long with his bullwhip, walked behind the second truck as the trucks moved into position.

One of the hooded men retrieved a posthole digger from the second truck, walked to a spot approximately 20 yards in front of the front porch, and quickly dug a hole. Two other men followed with the six foot high wooden cross, which they held in the hole while a third man poured in premixed concrete. Within three minutes, the cement had hardened enough to hold the cross upright, and the gasoline drenched cross was ignited.

Jimmy Long's adrenalin was pumping, as Wally Givens, the only one of the group who would talk that night, yelled out, "Shine Rivers! Get your black ass out here!"

One of the hooded men fired his shotgun three times in the air, as Shine, stuffing his shirt tail into his pants, appeared through the front door. He held his hand up to shield his eyes from the glare of the four headlights on high beams which were pointed directly at the porch. He couldn't see anyone, but he could see the now blazing cross in his front yard.

"Who's there? What's goin' on?" Shine asked, fighting to wake up and straining to see where the voice had come from.

Rebecca ran onto the porch, saw the burning cross, and gasped. This couldn't be true, she thought. It couldn't be happening. This was nineteen sixty two, not nineteen twenty two. "It's the Klan," she said quietly to Shine, walking up and standing beside her man.

The ten Klansmen stepped forward, now visible, but backlit by the headlights.

"Shine Rivers," Givens began, trying to sound official in spite of the pint of Jim Beam he had consumed, "you marched today in defiance of the white man and God's natural order! For this, you will be punished! Step forward!"

"Stay put, darlin'," Rebecca said, as the children began coming onto the porch to see what the ruckus was all about. Rebecca's first instinct was to take the children back inside the house, but she immediately decided that they should witness this, whatever was about to happen. She also was suddenly sure that God would not let any real harm come to Shine.

"He's not goin' anywhere," Rebecca called out in a loud voice. "Ya'll just go on back home to your families! Leave us be!"

"Lettin' your woman talk for you, boy?" Givens sneered. "Step forward now. If'n you don't, that man over yonder's gonna start shootin' your family!"

One of the Klansmen took a couple of steps forward and aimed his shotgun at the porch. Shine stepped off the porch and walked, barefoot, halfway to the burning cross.

Rebecca gathered her children around her, taking her two year old son from the arms of her fifteen year old daughter, and began talking to her children in a soft, calm voice.

"Don't fret, children. You know how much your father trusts in Jesus?"

"Yes, Mama," several of the children whispered.

"Move over to that tree yonder," Givens ordered, pointing with his robed arm.

"And you know how your father says that Jesus loves us and answers our prayers?" Rebecca said in a voice that was soft, yet loud enough to be overheard by the Klansmen in the yard.

"Yes, Mama."

The five year old started crying.

"Hush, chile," Rebecca said, putting her free arm around the child to comfort her. "We have to be strong, like your father. Now, I want each of you to say a little prayer to Jesus to watch over your father right now."

One of the silent Klansmen, accompanied by another with a shotgun, walked over to Shine. The two men knew that Shine could take on both of them, if he was so inclined. They relied on the shotgun still aimed at the front porch to dissuade him, but up close, they were still apprehensive.

As they came near Shine, the two Klansmen saw that he was trembling as he stood, barefoot, in front of the burning cross. They mistakenly assumed that he was trembling with fear and relaxed a little, when, in fact, Shine's shaking was the outward sign of the internal battle he was waging against the rage that was welling up inside—a battle he was barely winning.

The man with the shotgun had moved too close. It took all of Shine's will power not to grab the shotgun and, using it as a club, drop both men where they stood. It was not any fear for his own life that stopped him. He was afraid for his family. Besides, he assumed that since they already had not done so, they didn't plan to kill him, although he still didn't know what they were going to do. Then, the Klansman without the gun took a rope from beneath his robe, and Shine suddenly wasn't so sure.

Rebecca gasped again, interrupting her prayer, when she saw the rope. She was on the verge of telling her children to run as fast as they could into the woods and begin screaming as loud as she could, when the Klansman looped the rope around Shine's left wrist and began pulling him towards a tree off to the right. Rebecca watched silently, holding the two children tighter.

The Klansman who worked for the newspaper stepped backward, now out of sight, retrieved his camera, and began taking pictures of the scene, initially without a flash.

When they reached the tree, the Klansman walked the rope around the tree and tied the other end to Shine's right wrist. He pulled the rope tight and tied it off, forcing Shine's chest against the tree, his left ear pressing into the bark. In that position, Shine's face was pointed towards the porch, and he could see his wife and children. In fact, the only way he could avoid looking at them would be to close his eyes, since he couldn't move his head. He kept his eyes open. After checking the tightness of the rope, the Klansman continued around the tree until he was behind Shine. Using a sharp hunting knife, he cut Shine's shirt from top to bottom, leaving a thin, bleeding trail on Shine's skin, and tore the shirt away.

Jimmy Long moved a few steps closer to the tree and took the coiled bull whip out from under his robe. He adjusted his hood to insure that his vision would not become obstructed, flipped the whip out to his right to straighten it out, and with a strong, downward movement of his right arm and shoulder, sent the lethal tip of the whip speeding through the air toward Shine.

Tears began to roll down Rebecca's cheeks when she saw the whip. Now that she knew what the Klansmen intended, she realized the pain that Shine would have to endure and prayed that the devil with the whip knew what he was doing.

CRACK!!!!

Long had misjudged the distance. He was too close to the tree. The deadly tip of the whip hit the tree over Shine's right shoulder as the fatter body of the whip lashed across his back. Shine suddenly felt the pain and the shock. Not able to see what was going on behind him, he didn't know he was to be whipped until the first lash landed.

The photographer was now using flash bulbs and would photograph every lash.

Long took one step backwards, flipped the whip behind him, and brought his right arm forward again. This time, the tip caught Shine on his right cheek, opening a three inch gash from his cheek bone down towards his mouth. Shine came within a half of inch of losing the sight in his right eye.

"Please, Jesus, be with your servant Shine in this time of persecution," Rebecca prayed out loud, as she heard all of the children except the two oldest boys crying. "Put your arms around him and help him endure this wicked, evil assault on his body, which he has pledged and dedicated as your temple."

CRACK!!!

Long, who had taken one more step to the rear, now had the range. The tip cut a four inch gash below Shine's right shoulder blade.

Shine believed in his heart that this, just like everything else that happened on earth, was ordained and willed by God as part of his infinite plan. Shine didn't understand why it had to happen or why he had to be subjected to this unbearable pain. But he knew that it wasn't necessary for him to understand. He was God's servant, and God loved him. He had faith that, one day, God would reveal the reason to him. For now, he would take it like a man—like a soldier of God. He vowed that he would not pass out and continued to look at his family, trying not to let the horrible pain show in his eyes, yet seeing the pain in theirs.

"Pray with me, children," Rebecca said. "Pray loud, so Jesus can hear you. Our father..." Rebecca and the children recited the Lord's Prayer in a combined voice that each of the Klansmen could clearly hear above the sounds of the cracking of the whip. The sound of the children praying made Wally Givens uneasy. He turned his back to the porch, lifted his hood, and took a long drink from his pint of whiskey.

After eight lashes, Shine's back was completely covered with blood, which splattered a few feet with every new crack of the whip. After two more lashes, that part of Shine's brain which receives pain messages transmitted by the body's nervous system shut down, and he didn't feel any pain from the remaining ten strokes. Even though the night was warm and Shine was only a few feet from the blazing fire on the cross, the loss of blood was sufficient to make him feel cold, and he began shivering again. However, he never lost consciousness.

After he had inflicted the twentieth lash, Long coiled the whip and walked back between the trucks, no longer visible to the others.

"If ya'll stop this marching and all other Communist crap," Givens said, more to Rebecca than to Shine, assuming incorrectly that, by now, Shine had passed out, "we won't do anything else to you. But if they march again tomorrow, we'll come back. Tell that to that carpet bagging colored preacher who started this whole thing. He better not mess with Charleston."

The Klansmen got in the trucks, leaving Shine tied to the tree. The driver of the first truck started his engine first. Somewhere, deep in Shine's brain, he registered, '57 Chevy pickup. # 5 valve clicks. Needs adjusting.' The trucks sped away, spraying gravel in their wakes.

Still holding her baby, Rebecca, followed by the children, ran over to the tree. "Shine, honey," she said, "you all right?" Up close, his back looked even worse than she had feared. She was afraid to touch him.

"I'll be okay," he whispered. "Doan know if I can walk, though. My legs feel kinda weak. Are ya'll okay?"

"Matthew," she said hurriedly to her sixteen-year-old son, the eldest, "go get your father's sharp knife out of the garage and drive the pickup 'round here."

"Yes, Mama." Matthew ran into the house to get the keys to the truck.

"We're okay, baby," she said softly to Shine. "We'll get you into the house. Don't you worry. We'll get you into the house."

"Are they gone?" Shine asked.

"Luke, get the key to the phone, run over to the church, and call Dr. Knight," she said to her second oldest son. "The number's on the wall in the church. Tell him your father's hurt bad. Tell him Shine won't die, but he should bring his needle and lot's of thread. You got all that?"

"Yes, Mama," the fourteen year old answered and ran after Matthew to get the key to the phone.

Rebecca took the end of her dress and wiped Shine's brow. She could see that he was shivering, but didn't want to touch his back or put anything over it yet. "Yes, Shine, they're gone. Everything's gonna be all right, now."

"Here, Ruth." Rebecca handed the baby to her eldest daughter. "Take care of Samuel. Give him a bottle, and see if you can get him down."

"Naomi, put a big pot of water on the stove to boil, tear up a sheet into strips and put them into the water, and make a poultice like I showed you when Luke cut his arm. You remember how?"

"Yes, Mama." She ran into the house, heading for the kitchen.

"The rest of you kids get the mattress off my bed and pull it into the living room."

"Shine, Matthew's bringin' the truck 'round. We'll back it right up to here, and when we cut you loose, you can just sit down on the tail gate, and we'll drive you over to the porch. Think you can do that?"

"Yeah," Shine whispered. "I can do that. I think you better hurry, though."

Matthew drove up in the truck and, ever so slowly at Rebecca's direction, backed it up until the lowered tailgate almost touched the backs of Shine's legs. Rebecca stood to Shine's right, as Matthew took the knife and cut the rope. Shine gradually loosened his vice-like grip on the tree and with Rebecca's help slowly lowered himself until he was sitting on the tailgate of the pickup truck. Matthew got back behind the wheel, very slowly pulled the truck away from the tree, and backed it up to the porch, Rebecca walking behind the truck and holding Shine's hands, helping him to sit up. Somehow, Rebecca and her son managed to get Shine into the living room and face down onto the mattress.

"I'm cold, Rebecca," Shine said, as she resumed wiping his forehead with her dress.

"I know, honey," she said through her tears. "We're gonna fix that right now."

Matthew helped Naomi bring the pot of water into the living room. As Rebecca carefully and gingerly spread the hot, sterile strips of sheeting across his back, Shine's shivering began to diminish.

After she had completely covered his back with the hot cloths, Rebecca began removing the strips, one-by-one, and washed the exposed area very gently until it was cleansed of blood. She then rinsed the strip in the pot, wrung it out, replaced it on Shine's back, and repeated the process with the next strip, all the while talking to Shine.

"Bible says to forgive your enemies, Shine. You gonna forgive those white scum who did this to you?"

"Maybe I'll forgive 'em tomorrow," he answered in a soft voice. "Too busy hatin' 'em just now, God forgive me."

"Seems to me God oughta be askin' you for forgiveness, lettin' this happen."

"Now, Rebecca," he gently scolded, "God has a reason for this. We just doan know it yet. Doan you go blasphemin'."

Naomi brought the poultice in from the kitchen, as Luke came running in through the front door, out of breath.

"Doctor Knight says he'll be here directly," Luke said. "How's Daddy doin'?"

"He'll be all right," Rebecca said, as she began removing the cotton strips, again one at a time, placing a portion of the poultice over the wounds and replacing the strips over the poultice. She wanted to give the poultice as much time as possible to draw out the poison from the wounds and then remove it before the doctor arrived. She was afraid that Doctor Knight might not approve of her using folk medicine on Shine. Just as she finished removing the poultice and replacing the cotton strips, she heard a car pull up in the front.

Instead of spending his Wednesday afternoons chasing a small white ball around a golf course, Doctor Roland Knight, a white pediatrician, held free clinics in Shine's church for any of the black families on Wadmalaw Island who wanted to bring their children in. He refused payment for the services, but the proud families insisted on bringing him hand woven baskets, vegetables, chickens, and fish. He discovered that unless he accepted these gifts as payment, the people wouldn't come.

The doctor hurried through the front door, shirt tail out and medical bag in hand. "What happened?" he asked, seeing Shine lying face down on the mattress, his back covered with the cotton strips. "Did he burn himself?"

"You children go on to bed now," Rebecca said.

With a chorus of "Yes, Mama's" and "Goodnight, Daddy's," the younger children, some still sniffling, were ushered by the older children down the hall to the back of the house.

"No," Rebecca answered, when the children were gone, "it was the Klan." She slowly removed the cotton strips from Shine's back.

"Good God!" Doctor Knight exclaimed. "The Ku Klux Klan was here? And they did this?"

"Shine," the doctor said, sitting on the floor, so Shine could see him, "are you okay?" It sounded like a stupid question, especially coming from a doctor, but he wanted to engage Shine in a dialogue in order to judge his state of mind and lucidness.

"I'm okay," Shine responded, some of the pain returning, as the shock began to wear off. "Hurts a little."

The doctor squirmed along the floor, so he could examine Shine's back. "What did this?" he asked. "A knife?"

"No," Rebecca said wearily, the emotional drain beginning to take its toll. "A whip. I believe they call it a bull whip."

"Good God!" he repeated. He had never before seen this much damage intentionally inflicted on one human being by another. "Why? Why Shine?"

"Shine walked in the march in Charleston today," Rebecca answered. "Somebody must've recognized him and decided to make an example out of him."

Roland Knight fought back the anger that was welling up inside. This was not the time. Shine needed all of the cool detachment, skill and professionalism he could muster. He examined the wounds more closely. Rebecca must have used some kind of folk medicine on Shine's back, he thought. The wounds were extraordinarily clean, and the healing process had already begun. He opened his bag, hoping he had brought along enough suture.

"Doctor?" It was Shine.

"Yes, Reverend."

"Do you have white thread?"

"Do I have…oh, you mean suture. Yes, I have white suture." He often used white suture when stitching dark skinned black people because it was easier to see when the time came to remove it. Normally, though, he only used white suture on areas of the body which would be covered by clothing.

"Please use it, then," Shine said, "even on my face."

"Why?" The doctor asked, threading the needle with white suture.

"I'll have to march tomorrow. Reverend Brown may want to make a point about what happened here tonight."

"Shine, I don't think you should," Rebecca said, more worried about Shine's weakened condition and the healing of his back than afraid of further retribution by the Klan.

"Have to, Rebecca," he said, wincing as the doctor began to stitch up his back. "Doubly have to, now."

The doctor concentrated on his work. There would be scars, even on Shine's face. The wounds were too deep and too open. He guessed that Shine would probably want scars. His guess was right.

Damn those bastards, he thought, threading more suture on the needle and blotting a small amount of blood from the next cut he intended to stitch. He vowed to talk with his brother, a lawyer at one of the city's most powerful firms. Maybe his brother could do something or knew someone who could.

Chapter 13
Day 1—Monday
Midnight

After the last customer was politely invited to leave because it was time to close, Rich told the bartender to call it a night and closed the bar himself. His turning away the black couple was still gnawing at him, and he couldn't put his finger on exactly why. Was it because he had lied about the need for reservations?

Rich was far from perfect, but when he knowingly and intentionally told a lie, an act which to him was moral cowardice, it always bothered him afterwards. Or was it because, deep down, he was coming to the view that segregation—separating one group or class of people simply because of the color of their skin—was wrong? He didn't know yet whether his uneasiness resulted from one of these beliefs, and if so, which one, or both, or from some other problem. Time would tell. It always did. Sooner or later, he would work it out. Meanwhile, the last thing he wanted to do right now was go home to bed. He was too keyed up. He decided to drop by the High Hat for a drink.

The High Hat Club, located in the northern part of the city, stayed open until dawn and catered primarily to tourists and conventioneers. The club featured live music, dinner (including one of the better steaks in town), gambling, strip teasers, and B drinkers. The few locals who came in were people like Rich who worked late. If they wanted some place to go after midnight, they had to choose between places like the High Hat or the bars that catered to sailors and airmen. Most locals avoided the military bars. Rich pressed the buzzer on the front door of the club. An eye appeared in the peep hole, and the door opened.

"Hi, Preacher," the bouncer said. "Where you been?"

"Hi, Scrap," Rich answered. "I've been at school."

While his answer was only partly true, Rich wanted to avoid a long conversation with the bouncer, assuming that Scrap Iron was, in fact, capable of sustaining a long conversation. Scrap Iron Riles (Rich didn't know his real first name, only Scrap Iron) had the physique of a heavyweight weight lifter. His neck was bigger than his shaved head, which was perched on top of a huge body. He wasn't very tall, but there was no doubt in Rich's mind that if he wanted to, this man could pick him up and throw him across the parking lot.

"Danny's been askin' 'bout you," Scrap Iron grunted, opening the inner door, so Rich could enter the club.

As Rich walked in, he could see that nothing much had changed since last summer, when he had become an irregular regular during the weeks when he worked the night shift. After his father's death, though, when he had come home from college, he hadn't been back, his time taken up with school in the morning and work at night. Now, with school out for the summer, he could sleep late if he stayed out late.

The public part of the High Hat Club was one very big room. Along the back wall to the left were the band stand and a small stage, where the strippers performed. A four piece band was playing a slow dance, and some of the patrons were dancing with B drinkers. Surrounding the dance floor were dining tables with red and white checkered table cloths and small oil lamps for atmosphere. The room was kept fairly dark. The bar ran the length of the room, front to back along the wall to the right. The gambling tables were situated between the dining area and the bar. The action tonight appeared slow, but then again it was early.

As Rich walked to the bar, Drew Cole, the bartender, poured a Dewars and water and placed it in front of an empty stool. "Good evening, Preacher," Cole said, as Rich sat down and took a sip from the drink. Good memory, Rich thought.

Danny Costellano, owner of the High Hat, had given Rich his nickname after learning one night of Rich's plans to become a minister. Everyone in the place had picked up on it and by this point, none of them probably remembered his real name.

Danny liked Rich, which was unusual. Night people usually had little regard for day people, looking upon them as marks to be taken. Their attitude was 'if we don't take them, somebody else will.' On the other hand, one night person would go to great lengths to help another night person in trouble or need. For some reason, they had anointed Rich as an honorary night person.

"Where ya been?" the bartender asked, perpetually cleaning a glass with a towel that itself could use some cleaning.

"Away at school," Rich repeated the half true excuse.

"Good to see ya," Cole said, as Costellano walked up.

"Preacher!" Costellano boomed, causing a few heads at the gambling tables to turn momentarily. "Long time no see!"

"He's been off at college," Cole offered, relieving Rich of the necessity of continuing the lie.

"Well, welcome back," Costellano said, walking away to check the blackjack dealers. "His drinks are on me," he called to Cole over his shoulder.

Ever since Danny had dubbed him 'Preacher', Rich had drunk for free. It was no big deal, since he never had more than two drinks, but it helped Rich's tight budget and was one of the reasons he had become a regular.

"Hi, Preacher. Want a little bit tonight?"

"Hi, Peaches," Rich answered before turning to his left to see her. "How've you been?"

As usual, he blushed. This particular B drinker offered him free sex every time he came in. He wasn't sure if she was serious or she just wanted to make him blush, which happened every time she brought the subject up. He was pretty sure she was serious, though, which was why he had never called her bluff.

Not that she wasn't desirable. Peaches was tall, blond, beautiful, and built. She was also an airhead, Rich had learned, which had nothing to do with his polite refusals to her offer. The fact was that Rich, even though he had been popular in high school, largely because of the rock band he had formed, was shy. As a result, he was still a virgin and therefore declined her offer primarily because he didn't want her to know of his inexperience. What Rich didn't know was that she would have been even more excited about having sex with him had she known it would be his first time.

"Oh, fine," she said, sitting on the stool next to him. She put her elbows on the bar and hunched slightly forward, providing Rich with a totally unencumbered view of her braless breasts. "How 'bout it. Is tonight the night? We can go to my place."

"Thanks, but I don't think so. Not tonight. Thanks all the same."

"You're a real challenge," she said, laughing. "One of these days..." She let the thought drift off.

She stood up suddenly and took his arm.

"Come with me. We've got a new girl. Her name's June. I want you to meet her."

Rich had no choice. He managed to grab his drink before she pulled him off the stool. She led him down to the far end of the bar, where a girl was sitting, sipping a Coke.

"June, this is...we call him Preacher. Preacher, this is June." Having made the introductions, Peaches walked away in search of a mark that might pop for a bottle of champagne.

"Hello," Rich said, awkwardly. He wasn't sure how tall she was, since she was seated on a barstool. He could tell that she was very pretty, not beautiful like Peaches, more cute like a cheerleader with long, dark brown hair that framed a face of flawless skin. But what intrigued him most were her eyes— her wise eyes. She had the eyes of a twenty five year-old woman in the body of an eighteen year-old girl. Rich felt stirrings he hadn't felt in some time. This girl, woman, whatever she was, was very sexy.

"Have a seat, Preacher," she said, motioning to the bar stool to her right. "Why do they call you that?"

"Please call me Rich. That's my name." For some reason, it was important to him that she know his real name. He went on to tell her briefly why he was known in the club as 'Preacher' and then asked her about herself, not wanting to talk about himself just now.

"My name is June Edwards," she began her usual fib, assuming that Rich was a mark. "And I'm from Valdosta, Georgia." That was an out and out lie.

June Edwards had been born into a poor family in Lake City, South Carolina, about fifty miles west of Myrtle Beach. Actually, her family was officially classified as lower middle class. The black people of the South kept the white people off the bottom rung of the economic ladder. But that didn't matter to June. As far as she was concerned, they were poor.

For as long as she could remember, she hated her life and was determined to escape it. The eldest of six children, she watched her mother grow old before her time, working the night shift at the textile mill, raising the kids and working the vegetable garden, so that they would have something to eat during the innumerable times when she and her husband were laid off from their jobs at the mill. She vowed early on that what had happened to her mother would not happen to her.

She even hated her name—Ellie Mae Jones. And her mother insisted on calling her "Ellie Mae." At the age of six, she had secretly begun thinking of herself as June (her birthday was in June and she always liked the sound of that name), not Ellie Mae, but told no one. When she got away, she thought, she would leave everything, including that horrible name, behind. She was fortunate in one regard. She was a beautiful child, and by the time she was fourteen, it became apparent to her as well as to the older boys in the town that she was becoming a beautiful young woman. As she fought the boys off, she began to plot her escape in detail.

To get some privacy, she took walks in the woods every day that she could, where she practiced walking erectly, the way she had watched the models do on TV. She also talked to the birds and the trees, struggling to cure herself of her rural drawl. Her favorite book by far was Pygmalion. She strongly identified with Liza Doolittle, the cockney flower girl who was trained by Dr. Henry Higgins to overcome her cockney accent and speak "correct" English, thereby entering the ranks of the English upper class. She was convinced that if she, too, could learn to speak well, she could also leave her past behind and move into the upper levels of society.

Sometimes during her walks in the woods, she fancied herself a model, walking down the runway modeling beautiful gowns. Other times, she pretended she was an actress and played out roles with invisible leading men. Or else she was a singer, singing in a Broadway show.

Always her audience consisted of the birds and animals in the woods. If they could talk, they would have told her what they saw—a beautiful young woman with wavy, dark brown hair, maybe a little short for her age, her skin tanned to a light bronze, and a developing body that was in perfect proportion to her size and height. They heard her speech gradually improve and saw her walk become straighter and more graceful. In all honesty, they would have advised her that singing was not her strong point—that she should stick to modeling or acting.

While she knew that she was beautiful, she didn't plan to rely solely on her looks. She did well in school and was determined that some day, some way, she would go to college. But that would come later. Meanwhile, her looks would be her passport out of Lake City. Gradually, month-by-month, she began to overcome her bad English, although she kept this secret, too, from her family, lapsing back into the familiar patois when she left the woods and returned home.

Somehow, she managed to keep the boys at bay.

When she turned sixteen, her father began talking more often about how much additional income they would have if she went to work at the mill on the day shift. She figured that the time had come to get out, that it was now or never. If she dropped out of school and went to work at the mill, she would be trapped, just like her mother.

She had managed to save three hundred fifty eight dollars over the years from baby-sitting and other jobs. It hadn't been easy because she was supposed to give her earnings to her mother to help with the family expenses. But she had held back a dollar here and two dollars there, and it had slowly built up.

One fall morning four months after her sixteenth birthday, she donned her best jeans and favorite shirt, put an extra bra and pair of panties in her book bag along with her copy of Pygmalion, retrieved her money from its hiding place, kissed her mother goodbye, and left for school.

Instead of going to school, she headed for the Greyhound bus station and bought a one-way ticket to Columbia. When she arrived at Columbia, she bought a one-way ticket on the next bus to Charleston.

When she didn't come home from school, her mother was initially worried. Then on a hunch, she checked Ellie Mae's 'secret' stash of cash which she had accidentally discovered one day while searching for one of Ellie Mae's blouses, which had been misplaced. When she saw that the money was gone along with her favorite book, she immediately knew that Ellie Mae, too, was gone.

"Good for you, honey," she thought. "Get out before the mill traps you, too. So young. Still a baby. But you're smart. You'll make it." Her eyes welled up with tears, as she cleaned the small house that would now have slightly more room.

When her father discovered that she had taken off, he attempted to locate her. The Greyhound agent at the Lake City station (actually it was the general store that was also the bus station and the Western Union office) remembered that she had purchased a ticket to Columbia. However, no one at the Columbia bus terminal would remember the young girl who bought a ticket to Charleston. Her trail ended in Columbia. Ellie Mae had vanished.

The bus trip to Charleston via Columbia, which cost her eighteen dollars, took four hours. As she rode on the bus, she realized that she had some decisions to make. She was only sixteen, but she thought she could pass for nineteen, so that would be her age. She would need a new last name. Nothing that she liked came to her, so she put that one off for now.

She would be from Valdosta, Georgia. Her best friend back home, Jill Atkins, was from Valdosta and had talked about it so much that June thought she could answer enough questions about the town to pull it off. Besides, since Valdosta was in southern Georgia, she felt sure that the odds of running into someone in Charleston who was from Valdosta were pretty small.

When she arrived in Charleston, she checked in at the YWCA. Since it was early afternoon, she decided to go shopping for some inexpensive clothes and some make-up and toiletries. She was excited. At last, she was on her own. As she walked down King Street, she spied Edwards Five and Ten Cents Store. Edwards. June Edwards. She liked the sound. That would be her name.

She made her purchases and returned to the YWCA, where she asked the woman at the desk for the names of the best restaurants in town. She had worked over the summer at a fish camp in Lake City on Friday and Saturday nights as a waitress. While a fish camp was a far cry from a fancy restaurant, waitressing was the closet thing to a skill that she had.

The next morning, June was waiting at the front steps of the Colonial Steakhouse at ten thirty when Bob Howe, the owner, arrived. June was honest and straightforward about her experience and her need for and desire to work. Since getting and keeping good help was more difficult in the restaurant business than getting and keeping customers, Howe, impressed by her honesty, enthusiasm, and good looks, hired her on the spot. For the first week she would be on probation, which meant that she would be paid one dollar and fifteen cents per hour in cash. After a week, if she worked out, she would go on the regular payroll.

June literally ran back to Edwards to purchase the red blouse, black skirt, and black waitress shoes she would need as a uniform and was back in time to work the lunch shift. For a day or two, she would train, which meant that the first day, she would follow an experienced waitress around, learning her duties and the system. Then, on the second day, June would wait the tables, and the trainer would observe. Howe asked Peaches to train June.

The Colonial Steakhouse, located on Vendue Range near the Cooper River a few blocks north of Broad Street, was one of Charleston's finest steak and seafood restaurants. It was open from twelve noon until three on Monday through Friday and offered a seafood and salad buffet as well as items from the menu. The restaurant then closed, reopening at six until around eleven. On Saturday, the Colonial Steakhouse served dinner only and was closed on Sunday. Hiring and keeping waitresses who would work such a split shift was a continual problem, but no other system seemed to work.

After lunch had ended, Peaches suggested to June that she should become a B drinker at the High Hat, going there when the restaurant closed in the evening, the way Peaches did. June was at first reluctant and a little bit frightened by the idea of enticing strange men to buy her drinks in a nightclub. However, such an arrangement would allow her to prepare for her dream to go to college. She could live off of the pay and tips she got at the Colonial Steakhouse and save the money she earned at the High Hat, building a college fund while she figured out how to first get a high school diploma.

Peaches also suggested that June move in with her. So, during the afternoon break, June collected her things from the YMCA and moved them into Peaches' apartment. It would take only a week for June to discover that sharing an apartment with a prostitute had its drawbacks. Peaches had understood when June moved out to her own, small studio apartment two blocks from the Colonial Steakhouse.

Danny Costellano, the owner of the High Hat, had liked June immediately, although he wasn't sure that she would be successful as a B drinker. How many drinks the girls hustled a night was not an important issue for him. In fact, the B drinks were merely a way of compensating the girls while insuring that they didn't get drunk on the job. He needed attractive young women in the place to draw the male conventioneers in, so he could make his money from them at the gambling tables. While he didn't know her story or where she came from and didn't want to know, Danny arranged for June to get forged ID cards, including a Social Security card, so that she could get on the payroll at the Colonial Steakhouse, rent an apartment, open a bank account, and conduct other personal daily business that required identification. She was now truly June Edwards.

June told Rich none of this, repeating instead her canned story of growing up in Georgia and moving to Charleston last fall. After June told her brief story, the conversation moved to his job at the Holiday Inn and on to the civil rights marches and Rich's turning away the black couple. He had to talk the situation through with someone and was finding this pretty, sexy, and apparently smart girl easy to talk to.

Danny looked up from the blackjack tables and saw Peaches introducing Rich to June. Two good kids, he thought. Neither one belongs in here. They make a cute couple, too. He walked over and said something to Drew Cole. I must be getting soft, Danny said to himself, after speaking with the bartender.

As Danny was patrolling the dining area, he heard the faint sound of a door chime over the piped in background music, the band having taken a break. He walked to the front door, responding to Scrap Iron's signal.

He opened the inner door. Scrap Iron, seated on a bar stool and looking through the peephole, said, "Junior. Comin' 'round back."

As he hurried through the restaurant to his office in the back, Danny checked his watch. Right on time, as usual. Danny walked around behind his desk, opened the top right hand drawer, and retrieved a snub-nosed thirty eight caliber revolver from its place beside the private telephone. Hearing a knock on the rear door that opened to the outside rear of the building, he put the gun in the right hand pocket of his suit coat and opened the door. Junior Hutto, a black man in his mid thirties whose street name was Hammer, the meanest individual Costellano had ever encountered, walked in and placed a paper sack on the desk. "Pretty good week," he said.

"How much?" Danny asked, taking the bundled bills from the paper sack and putting them in a floor safe, which he then locked. The money would be counted tomorrow by the back office people who came to work at noon, when the first numbers tickets began to arrive. The butter and eggs numbers receipts arrived daily, except Sunday when there was no game, along with the betting slips. The net receipts from drug sales were delivered every Monday night personally by Junior Hutto, when he picked up his supply of drugs for the following week.

"One hundred forty five thousand, give or take," Hutto answered, pouring himself a drink from Danny's personal bar and sitting on the couch.

"That IS good," Danny said. Soon, the take from the sale of drugs, which was growing, would exceed the take from the numbers game, which had remained essentially flat for about a year.

"Doan know if it'll hold, though," Hutto said.

"Why?" Danny asked, smelling trouble.

"There's some new shit on the street."

"Whaddayamean, new shit?!!" Danny exploded uncharacteristically. "From where?"

"Some of my guys tole me they was losing customers to new sources at cheaper prices. I sniffed around and traced it to one of my guys who quit two weeks ago. When I found him, he tole me who the man was."

"How did you get him to do that?" Danny asked. "No, don't tell me. Maybe I don't want to know. So, who the hell is trying to move in on me?" Danny was supposed to have a monopoly in Charleston County on all drugs, numbers, and loan sharking. That was the deal, and for what he was paying, it had better still be the deal.

"Sammy said the man's name's Terrell. Charles Terrell. Says he be operatin' outta a new club up the road. A place called the Jaguar, or sompin like dat."

"Alright, I'll take care of it," Danny said. He was irritated. He didn't need this aggravation. "You just make sure your guys hold the line on prices. Hell, compared to New York, we're practically giving the shit away as it is."

That, too, was part of the deal, a part he never understood or agreed with. He had to keep the availability of drugs to the black community cheap and plentiful. Once, he had raised prices and was immediately raided, losing a week's supply of drugs, which he then had to replace out of his share of the take. He never again attempted to raise prices, although he still thought they could make a lot more money with higher prices. "What do you need tonight?"

Junior Hutto handed over a list, which included heroin, cocaine, marijuana, uppers and downers. Danny went into the next room alone, locking the door behind him, retrieved the drugs from another safe, this one hidden behind a false wall, placed the drugs in the same paper sack, and returned to the office. Hutto took his supply for the week and left.

After double-checking that both doors to his office were locked, Danny reached under his desk and flipped a switch, which caused the letter T on the large neon sign on the roof which spelled out High Hat to flicker, as if it were about to fail. He then checked his watch. Twelve forty five. The call would come in fifteen minutes, at one o'clock, or it would come at two. Danny had no idea how the man he called 'Mr. X' found out so quickly about the signal. He doubted that this man, whoever he was, sat outside his club every night except Sunday for two hours. Nevertheless, the signal system had never failed to work. He decided to wait in his office until one o'clock. He poured himself a drink and went to work updating the records of his drug inventory.

Talk about getting lucky, he thought. As a young button man in the Gambino family in Brooklyn, he had been ordered to take out a minor hood from the Genovese family who had moved across the river from New Jersey and was loan sharking at the Brooklyn Navy Yard, which was Gambino territory. Unfortunately, when Danny made the hit, the hood was driving a car, having just picked up the young son of a Genovese capo regime from school. In the resulting car crash, the child was injured. Although the boy recovered fully from the injuries, the child's godfather, to Danny's misfortune, was Vito Genovese himself.

Danny immediately joined the Navy and was eventually assigned to a destroyer based in Charleston, which he soon discovered was an untapped gold mine. Although South Carolina had laws barring the selling of liquor by the drink, Charleston was wide open and, best of all as far as he could tell, unorganized. With the blessing and financial backing of the Family, he remained in Charleston after mustering out of the Navy and opened a bar. He was just beginning to branch out into numbers, when he got the call from New York.

"Are you alone?" the voice asked.

"Yes," Danny replied.

"Do you know who this is?"

Danny knew enough not to say the name. "Yes," he answered. It was Carlo Gambino's consigliore, the Don's right hand man.

"We have made an arrangement. A messenger will deliver your instructions tomorrow. Follow them to the letter."

The instructions were clear. He was to install a telephone in his office which had an unpublished and unlisted number. The man who brought the instructions from New York would then rig up a light to the phone, rig up a switch for the neon sign signal, and return to New York, bringing the number of the telephone with him. Two days after the man left for New York, Danny would receive a call on that telephone at precisely midnight. He was to comply with the instructions he received. In return, Danny would control all drugs, numbers and loan sharking activities in Charleston.

The phone had rung, exactly as scheduled. "Hello," Danny answered.

"Are you alone?" a man's voice asked. Although the words were clear and unmuffled, Danny believed that the voice was altered.

"Yes. I'm alone," Danny answered.

"First, do not write any of this down. You must commit it to memory. Can you do that?"

Danny put away the pencil he was holding. "Yes," he answered.

"The light next to the phone should be on now. Is it?"

Danny had noticed when he opened the drawer to answer the phone that the light installed by the man from New York was lit.

"Yes, it is," Danny confirmed.

"If I need to get in touch with you, I will call this number. If you aren't in your office, the light will indicate that I have called. I will call again precisely on the hour. You are to check this phone every hour from eleven PM to two AM every night except Sunday. I know you are closed on Sunday. If the light is on, be there for my call on the hour. Do you understand?"

"Yes, I understand."

"There is a button below the light. Push it to turn the light off. Do it now."

Danny pressed the button. "The light's now off," Danny said.

"If you need to get in touch with me, turn on the other switch that was installed. I will get the signal and call you, again, on the hour. When you answer this phone, say 'Hello, Mr. X', if you are alone and free to talk. If not, answer any other way. Our business arrangement will be as follows."

Mr. X explained the deal to Danny. Within a month, all of Danny's competitors had been harassed out of business by continued police raids, and ever since, Danny had operated free from competition and free from any police interference.

Archie MacMillan drove a yellow cab in the city at night, Monday through Saturday. Between the hours of eleven PM and two AM, he always made sure that he drove by the High Hat as many times as he could. His instructions were that if he saw the T in the neon sign flashing, he was to call an answering service and leave a message that Archie had called. Every time he made the call, he would find $25 in an envelope in his mailbox within two days. He hung up the pay phone and returned to his cab, mentally spending the $25 he would soon have.

The call came at precisely one o'clock. "Hello, Mr. X," Danny said, answering the ringing phone.

"What's up?" the now familiar voice asked.

"We've got a problem. My guy tells me that someone is supplying drugs and setting up an organization."

"Do you know who?"

"My information is that his name is Charles Terrell and he owns a new club called the Jaguar here in town."

"Okay. We'll look into it." Click.

While Danny was occupied, Rich and June had sat and talked, dancing a few times, but always talking. Once, when they returned from the dance floor, June found that Drew Cole had put ten stir sticks on a napkin in front of her stool. When June asked him about them, Drew told her that they were from Danny. (B drinkers kept the stir sticks from the drinks they hustled and turned them in for their pay before they left for the night. The sticks were worth two dollars and fifty cents each). Danny had said she shouldn't worry about other customers. It was all right for her to stay with Preacher.

Rich was becoming very comfortable with her and could tell from her side of the conversation that she had a head on her shoulders. June, however, was becoming torn with mixed emotions. She really liked this guy, and she had begun their relationship (if that what it was becoming) with a lie. But then, maybe it didn't matter. Here he was about to become a minister, and she was, in his eyes, a barfly. She had told him about her job as a waitress at the Colonial Steakhouse and that she just did this for extra money, but that probably didn't matter.

Then, he surprised her by suggesting that since they both had the afternoon off, why didn't they go to Hampton Park tomorrow (actually later that day). She accepted, and they made plans for him to pick her up at the Colonial Steakhouse shortly after three, drop by her apartment quickly, so she could change, and spend a few hours in the Park.

Rich left and drove home, not able to get June out of his mind. For her part, June could not get motivated to hustle drinks and went home early. Each lay in bed, staring at the ceiling, thinking of the other and the time they had spent together.

Chapter 14
Day 2—Tuesday, June 5, 1962
8:00 AM

Jab Brown was mad—mad at himself for not believing what Dr. King and the others in Alabama and Georgia had warned him to expect and mad at the Klan for what they had done to Shine Rivers, who was standing next to the pulpit displaying his brutalized back to the stunned audience.

"The battle has been joined!" roared Brown. "Yesterday, we walked together in the sunlight before God and all the citizens of this city in a peaceful demonstration of our desire and demand that we be given our rightful place in society as Americans. Last night, the Ku Klux Klan, those cowards, those despicable thieves in the night, ganged up on our brother, Shine Rivers, and forced him to submit to this savage beating of his body by threatening harm to his wife and children if he resisted. Brothers and sisters, I want you to get up, form a single line here in the center aisle and one by one walk forward and get a close look at what the white man has done to our brother."

As the assembled marchers filed by Shine, each pausing to get a good look at his devastated back and the 847 stitches required to close the wounds, Jab Brown went on, "Today, we were scheduled to talk about education, about how our children will forever be trapped in a second class life unless they can get a first class education. The education of our children is our number one priority. But for today, that priority will have to wait, because today we will talk about the cowardly Klan. Shame on you! Thieves in the night. Shame on you!"

The congregation picked up the chant, roaring 'Shame on you' after every statement Brown uttered about last night's beating.

"Hiding in darkness! Shame on you! Hiding under hoods and sheets! Shame on you! Ten men against one! Shame on you. Threatening women and children! Shame on you! Beating this man with a bull whip, just like your slave-owning ancestors! Shame on you!"

"Brothers and sisters," Brown changed the cadence, "will this cowardly act of violence scare us off?"

"NO!" They shouted as one.

"Will we be back tomorrow, and the day after that, and the day after that, until the white man takes his foot off our backs and treats us as equals?"

"YES!"

"Are you ready to march today, brothers & sisters?"

"YES!"

"Brother Rivers, please lead us in prayer."

Many of the marchers wept silently as Shine prayed that God would forgive those misguided souls who had beat him so unmercifully. Jab Brown was not yet forgiving. He was still angry, partly because it had been Shine and not himself who had been attacked. Was his zeal to lead this movement putting others in harm's way? He wasn't sure. But he was sure that they had the white man worried, and he didn't know if or how the situation would escalate when they marched today and showed that the beating would not deter them from their mission. He prayed that if any significant harm had to come to one of them, it should come to him and not one of the other marchers.

Chapter 15
Day 2—Tuesday
10:25 AM

    Frank Cassidy and Randy Holly climbed the rickety stairs of the faded white wooden building to the second floor over the corner sandwich shop in the heart of Ansonborough. The professionally painted name on the door said "William S. Wiggins, DDS."
    As the two policemen entered the waiting room, Holly cringed at the sound of the high speed drill coming from one of the treatment rooms in the back. He had a real fear of dentists from his childhood, when he had the misfortune of being treated by a dentist who was technically good but rough on his patients. As a result, only a toothache would drive him to see a dentist.
    "May I help you?" the receptionist asked. Cassidy would have been surprised to learn that Dr. Wiggins had several white patients, so the receptionist truly didn't know what they wanted, even though Holly was wearing his blue uniform.
    "Charleston police," Cassidy said, producing his badge and ID. "We would like to speak with Dr. Wiggins, please." Frank was always polite until the other person, regardless of their color or apparent station in life, proved that they didn't deserve politeness or respect.
    "May I tell him what this is about?" she asked.
    "It's about one of his patients," Cassidy answered. "I'd rather not get any more specific until we speak with the doctor."
    The receptionist disappeared down the corridor. To Holly's relief the drilling sound stopped and the receptionist reappeared, followed by a short, fat, black man in a white tunic.

"I'm Doctor Wiggins," the dentist said to Cassidy, extending his hand. "How can I help?"

"I'm Lieutenant Cassidy of the Charleston Police," Cassidy said, showing his badge and ID to the dentist. "This is Officer Holly. May we talk in your office?"

"It's not big enough," the dentist said. "Come. We can talk back here."

The two policemen followed the dentist down the hall and into a vacant treatment room. One look at the drill and Holly excused himself, telling Cassidy he would wait for him in the reception room.

"Will this take long?" The dentist asked. "I have about five minutes while some cement hardens. Then, I really need to return to my patient."

"I'll be as brief as I can. I need some information on a patient of yours by the name of Sammy Boutry. Can you confirm that this is your work and that the patient is Boutry?" Cassidy showed the dentist a photograph of the dental work that the Medical Examiner had used to identify the dentist.

"Yes, it looks like my work, and I remember the phone call from the coroner. Just a minute." The dentist left the room and returned almost immediately with a file folder. "Yes," he said, studying the record in the file. "It's Sammy Boutry, alright."

"When was the work performed?" Cassidy asked.

"Let me see here," he mumbled, flipping through some pages. "Looks like last November, yes, a couple of days before Thanksgiving. That was the last appointment. The work was done over…four appointments in October and November."

"Do you remember how he paid you?"

"Sure do," the dentist smiled, not bothering to refer to the file. "Five crisp one hundred dollar bills. Cash on the barrel head, as they say."

"You remember that, even today?"

"Lieutenant, it's not every day that one of my patients pays with hundred dollar bills, especially five of them."

"Do you know where he got that much cash?"

"No, sir. And to be honest, I was somewhat concerned that they might be counterfeit. I was sure glad when the lady at the bank said they were good."

"Is there anything else you can tell me about Sammy Boutry?" Cassidy asked.

"I don't think so," the dentist replied, screwing up his mouth as he thought hard. "What's this about?"

"I don't think you'll be seeing Sammy again. He was murdered Sunday night." Cassidy paused. "You don't seem surprised at hearing he was murdered."

"I guess I'm not," the dentist said. "He didn't live around here. He lived somewhere over near the park, oh, here it is, on Huger Street. But something about him, I don't know, the way he dressed or the way he carried himself, made me think he was involved in something that wasn't exactly on the up-and-up. Cain't be specific. Just a feeling."

"Just one more question," Cassidy said, seeing the dentist glance at his watch. "Do you know why he came all the way over here to come to you when he lived over by the park?"

"No, I don't," the dentist answered.

"Thanks for your time," Cassidy said, shaking hands with the dentist and walking towards the reception area to fetch Holly.

'Nice guy,' the dentist thought to himself, as he washed his hands and returned to his patient. He washed his hands again in front of the patient. Patients liked to see their dentist wash their hands.

Cassidy and Holly returned to headquarters. Cassidy checked with the South Carolina State Tax Department and could find no record that Sammy Boutry held a job for which taxes had been withheld at any time during 1961. Cassidy suspected that Boutry was either a thief or involved in the sale and distribution of drugs (his bet was drugs) and felt confident that Boutry's sister would talk with him after the funeral. Meantime, he hoped that this killing wasn't the beginning of some kind of drug war. Unlike New York, Detroit, and Chicago, Charleston had never had any fights for territory among drug dealers. The only drug related deaths were the occasional overdoses, so this was a first. He hoped there wouldn't be a second or third.

Chapter 16
Day 2—Tuesday
Noon

As Beano Martin and Gedney Middleton entered the Colonial Steakhouse private dining room from the rear entrance, the members of the POETS club knew immediately that Middleton, normally cool and in control, was angry.

"Everyone please take your seats," Gedney said as Beano detoured to the bar setup to fix himself a tall Jack Daniels. Gedney waited for Beano.

"For those of you who don't yet know," Gedney began in a serious tone, "last night the Klan bullwhipped a Nigra minister on Wadmalaw Island and burned a cross in his front yard. I heard about it from one of my attorneys whose brother, a doctor, stitched up the minister. He said it was very brutal. Then during the march, their leader, Brown, had the one who was whipped remove his shirt. It was bad. Does anyone know any more?"

The two police chiefs and the newspaper publisher all began to speak at once. The policemen deferred to the publisher.

"This morning, I found these photographs on my desk," Arthur Manigault said. "Evidently, copies were also delivered to Ken and Buddy." The two policemen nodded, indicating that they had received the pictures. "I had copies made." He passed copies around the table. Each person visibly reacted when he saw them. "God knows who took them or how he got them on my desk."

There were three photographs. One showed a close-up of Shine's back as the whip was delivering the blow. The second picture from farther back showed Jimmy Long in a robe and hood hurtling the whip tip towards Shine's back. The third was almost a panoramic shot of the entire scene, showing many of the Klansmen, the blazing cross, Shine tied to the tree receiving yet another blow, and Shine's wife and children on the front porch, witnessing the brutal punishment by the Klan.

Beano looked carefully at each photograph, downed his drink, and stood up to fetch a refill. "Anyone care to bet which one of these pictures will be on the front page of the New York Times tomorrow?" He asked, as he ambled towards the bar.

"Do you really think that'll happen?" Jim Tucker asked.

"Hell, yes," Beano snorted, fixing another drink and having a brief coughing spasm. "Bobby Kennedy will jump for joy when he sees this, and I'm willing to bet a year's salary that he will see it. Who wants to take that bet?"

The room was silent as the men looked again at the photographs, especially the wide angled picture showing the children watching their father tied to the tree, his bloody back about to endure another lash from the blurred whip tip that was flying towards him.

"Gedney," the newspaper publisher said, "we have to print this."

Beano, bringing the bottle of Jack Daniels with him back to the table, leaned over and whispered something in Gedney's ear. "I agree," Gedney said. "Front page, center. I think that the Mayor and Chief of Police—both of you—should be quoted about how the people of Charleston will not stand for this type of violence and promise early arrests and vigorous prosecutions of those who did this."

"Beano, can you buy us time?" Gedney asked, as Beano took his seat.

"Depends on what we do," Beano grunted. "If we can arrest this scum quickly and show we will not tolerate this kind of activity, yes."

"How quick is quickly?" It was Jerry Anderson, the Mayor, who was visualizing Federal troops rather than tourists walking the streets of Charleston.

"A week, maybe two, if we can demonstrate progress."

The two police chiefs sank lower in their seats, knowing what was sure to come.

"There's something about these photographs, Gedney," Manigault said.

"Go on," Middleton said, softly.

"Like Beano, I'd bet a year's salary that they were taken by a professional—a newspaper professional. The framing's right—almost perfect. Hell, in a different context, this one"—he held up the panoramic view—"would win a Pulitzer prize, hands down."

"Okay," Gedney began, leaning back in his chair. "Our mistake. We underestimated how fast the Klan would react. Shame on us. Now, it's our turn to react." He leaned forward and addressed Arthur Manigault. "Are you saying that these pictures were taken by one of your employees?"

"Yes. Sadly, I believe so."

The two police chiefs, sitting next to each other as usual, had been engaged in a rapid whispered conversation. They sat back as Gedney now addressed them.

"What is your plan?" he said calmly.

Ken Wall, the City Police Chief, nodded to Buddy Leech, County Chief. "Even though this crime occurred in the County," Leech began, "we agree that Frank Cassidy, one of Ken's detectives, is the best man for the job."

They had all heard of Cassidy.

"Why?" Middleton pressed.

"First, he's the best detective in the county" Leech continued.

"Will SLED" (the State Law Enforcement Division) "and the FBI agree with that?" Middleton interrupted.

"Yes," Ken Wall said, taking over the argument. "Moreover, he's as straight as they come. Sometimes, it's been a problem."

Some around the table snickered, getting Wall's drift.

Middleton cut them short. "C'mon, gentlemen," he exploded. "Don't you people understand what we have here? We could lose the whole ball game." He paused and visibly calmed himself. "Go ahead, Ken," he continued. "What's your plan?"

"We'll put Cassidy, one uniform from the City force, and one uniform from the County force on a task force full time on this."

"Okay," Gedney agreed. "I want reports twice daily on progress, and I want an arrest by this time next week. Is that understood?" Both police chiefs nodded.

"Okay," Gedney went on, now apparently more relaxed. "Let's get Peaches in here and order. Then, we'll discuss progress on the Ansonborough project."

Buddy Leech went to summon the waitress while Tucker and the bankers retrieved papers from their briefcases. Ken Wall left the restaurant without eating, so he could get Cassidy started. One week wasn't very much time.

Chapter 17
Day 2—Tuesday
2:15 PM

During the course of any investigation, many theories are formed. Some are pursued, others discarded. Ultimately, all but one prove to be false.

Cassidy preferred to keep his theories to himself until one emerged as the most promising. Then, he would feed the Chief's insatiable thirst for information. He used Randy Holly as his partner primarily because Holly had proved he could keep his mouth shut.

Cassidy's protests about the county cop had fallen on deaf ears. He would have to be careful with this county cop, suspecting that his main job was to keep Buddy Leech informed about their progress. If Leech had good information before Cassidy briefed Wall, it would be Cassidy's ass. Unfortunately, this problem would slow them down, because Cassidy would have to create a few false trails to keep Leech in the dark.

Frank Cassidy left the two uniformed policemen in his unmarked car and entered the AME Church. After briefly speaking with one of the marchers, he walked down the hall behind the sanctuary and knocked softly on the door of the room from which he could hear voices.

"Come in," he heard.

He entered and saw Jab Brown standing in front of the seated men, all with wooden crosses around their necks. "May I help you?" Jab Brown asked.

"Yes, sir," Cassidy responded. "I'm Lt. Cassidy from the Police." He offered his badge and credentials. "I'm here about the whipping."

"Thank you, sir, for addressing me as 'sir'," Brown began, "but with all due respect, we don't need…"

"Brother Brown!" It was Reverend Lyle, the Pastor of the AME Church. "Excuse me for interrupting, but we know of this man. He's fair to us."

"Then, pardon me, sir. You'll want to speak with Brother Rivers, here." He gestured towards Shine. "We will be through in about five minutes. Would you like to stay?"

"No, thank you," Cassidy answered. "I'll wait outside in the sanctuary." He nodded towards Shine, who nodded in return his agreement to meet.

Cassidy was not a small man and was not accustomed to looking up at someone when he spoke with him. He had to look up at Shine. "Reverend Rivers, I'm investigating the beating. I need you to come to headquarters, so we can take your statement."

"Cain't right now, suh. I have to go see the doctor. My son's outside, waitin' to drive me. I cain't drive 'cause I have to sit forward, you know."

"Okay," Cassidy said. "I'll have to photograph your injuries, right now, if you don't mind. It's really important." They stepped outside, and Shine removed his jacket and shirt.

Cassidy physically recoiled when he saw the extent of the lashes. No, this wasn't a beating of a child, but in a way, it almost was. The panoramic photograph showed the Klansman holding the shotgun aimed at Shine's wife and children on the porch. This huge man had been forced to submit to this torture to protect his family. At that moment, because of his love for his family, he had been as helpless as a child and the bastards who had done this to him had known this. Suddenly, this investigation took on new meaning to Cassidy. It now became personal. He would get these sons of bitches. Cassidy took more photographs than were necessary.

"We can wait until tomorrow for your statement," he said, putting the camera away. "How about I pick you up here tomorrow and drive you to headquarters. We can get your statement, and then I'll drive you home. I'll also have to talk to your wife. Is that okay?"

"Yessuh," Shine answered. "That'll be fine. Thanks."

"No problem," Cassidy said. "I'm truly sorry about this."

"Not your doin'. See you tomorrow."

As Shine walked to the parking lot to meet his son, Jab Brown came through the door for his post-march press conference. Cassidy only now noticed the assembling reporters.

As the press conference began, Cassidy surveyed the area. The Holiday

Inn was directly across the street. To the right, across Meeting Street, was an entire block of buildings with flat roofs. A sniper would have several choices for a good shot. He would talk to the Chief. At least they should have men on the roofs to deny them to a shooter.

Chapter 18
Day 2—Tuesday
3:00 PM

Rich pulled up in his Ford as June came down the front steps of the Colonial Steakhouse. He drove her to her apartment and waited while she changed into jeans and a Tee shirt. She put a basket in the back seat, and they drove to Hampton Park.

Hampton Park, north of the Holiday Inn and near the Ashley River, sported a bandstand, a small zoo, and lots of grass and flowers. They found a spot near the bandstand where Rich spread an old beach blanket he kept in the trunk. It was slightly sandy, but it would do.

"Rich," June began, as she took a container of sweetened iced tea and some grapes from the basket, "I've got something to tell you. I lied to you last night."

As she poured him a cup of iced tea, she told him the whole story of Ellie Mae Jones from Lake City. Actually, she told him almost the whole story, omitting the fact that she would celebrate her seventeenth birthday in less than two weeks. She stared off into the distance as she confessed her life story, allowing Rich the opportunity to watch her closely. Captured by her beauty, he fell deeper and deeper in love with her as she poured her heart out. He wanted to hold her, to protect her from her fears of her family and a life of virtual slavery in the textile mills of the small town South, so he did. He moved over next to her and put his arms around her, stroking her hair. She stopped talking, put her head on his shoulder, and wept softly.

"Please don't hate me for lying to you," she said through her tears. "I was afraid you wouldn't like me if you knew I was a geechie from Lake City."

He moved her head, looked into those beautiful, wise eyes, and kissed her, long and tenderly. "What'll I call you?" he asked. "Ellie? Ellie Mae?"

She looked at him and realized he was teasing her. "You do and I'll kill you," she laughed through her tears, beating him lightly on the chest. "Now, my name is June. I don't ever want to be Ellie Mae again."

He fell over onto his back to avoid the blows. She moved on top of him, looked him deeply in the eyes for a moment, and then kissed him, lightly at first, but then with increasing passion. "Rich," she said into his ear, "I have never made love before. I want to make love to you. Can we go back to my apartment?"

"Now?" Rich swallowed. "I mean, yes, okay, sure."

They got up, gathered their things, and walked, hand-in-hand, to the car. As Rich got behind the wheel, June slid over next to him. Rich put the car in gear and put his arm around her as he drove off.

"Please hurry," she whispered.

He hurried.

June's apartment featured a small living room in front, a kitchen and dining area in the middle, and a bedroom and bath in the rear. They never made it to the bedroom.

Chapter 19
Day 2—Tuesday
6:30 PM

"We gotta do somethin'," Jimmy Long insisted. "We cain't jest sit around and let these coloreds get away with this."

That morning, when he saw Jab Brown display Shine Rivers' back to the crowd of black marchers on the steps of City Hall, Jimmy Long's mood had changed from astonishment that they had marched in apparently larger numbers than the day before to anger that this group of Negroes was defying him personally, throwing his whipping of Rivers back in his face. He had gone back to his shop and started drinking. By the time the Klan Council meeting began, he was drunk. "We gotta do something," he repeated to the Council members.

"Yeah, the whipping stopped them dead in their tracks, didn't it, Jimmy," Monty Simmons, the City cop, said sarcastically.

"We shoulda hung him like I wanted to," Long responded.

"Yeah, that whipping was a great idea," Simmons went on. "They've assigned Frank Cassidy to the case."

"So what?" Long retorted.

"So what? He's the best detective in the whole damn state! That's what! If he finds out we did this, our asses are grass. You know what they do to cops in prison?"

"Quit crying," Long shouted. "He won't find out, unless someone in this room tells him, and that ain't gonna happen. Let's keep our eye on the ball, here. Those old women who call themselves the City's leaders aren't going to do anything to stop these marches, and sooner or later, they're going to start lettin' the coloreds into the restaurants, the movies, and the restrooms, just so they won't scare off the precious tourists. This here is what the Klan is all about. We gotta do something."

"What do you think we oughta do now, Jimmy?" the Council leader asked.

"Exactly what we should have done last night, except we should hang that black preacher that's leadin' them."

"Jimmy," the leader said softly, "I think it's time for you to leave."

"Whadda you mean?" Long slurred.

"Jimmy, you're drunk, and you may be crazy. You are no longer a member of this Council or the Klan. Now, leave quietly, or we'll toss you out."

As Long stood up, Simmons reached into his coat pocket for his gun, fully prepared to shoot Long if he attempted to attack the Council leader. Instead, Long turned abruptly and walked out the door, slamming it behind him.

After Long's exit, the Klan made plans to erect and burn a large cross the following night in front of the AME Church. Two men were assigned to construct the cross and have it in a truck at the meeting the following night.

Chapter 20
Day 2—Tuesday
7:03 PM

Rich, day dreaming about his afternoon with June, did not notice when the elderly black couple and the reporter with his tape recorder came through the door. He had to hurry to catch up with them, as they approached the cash register.

After their love making, Rich and June had spent the remainder of their time together that afternoon discussing the marches and Rich's assignment to refuse service to blacks attempting to eat in the restaurant. He was certain that they would come back.

Continually amazed by June's wisdom and clarity of thinking, Rich had decided that he would carry out his duties tonight, but that tomorrow, he would inform both Mackey and Innis that he would no longer refuse service to blacks, because it was not only morally wrong, he now believed that it was also bad for business. He didn't know what to expect, but he was comfortable with his decision. In fact, he felt better about himself than he had in days. Maybe it was because of the decision or maybe it was because of June and the way he felt about her. Not only didn't he know which it was (or maybe it was both), he didn't care. He was happy.

Rich and the black couple went through the same dialogue as the previous night. All parties now had their lines down pat.

Ironically, at the exact moment Rich was telling the black couple that they must have reservations in order to be seated, Walter Cronkite, on the CBS Evening News, was playing the tape recording for his television audience of Rich refusing the same black couple the previous night. He mistakenly identified Rich as the Holiday Inn Restaurant & Bar Manager, but he got the rest of the story right.

Kemmons Wilson, Founder and Chairman of Holiday Inn, was watching Cronkite's newscast in his office in Memphis. After the segment featuring Rich refusing service to the black couple was over, he picked up his phone, looked up a number in the personal phone book he kept beside the phone, and placed a call to Russ Mackey. Yesterday, he had allowed his staff to influence his decision against his better judgment. He would now correct that error.

Chapter 21
Day 2—Tuesday
11:30 PM

Unlike the equipment at the High Hat which was on par with gambling tables found at a Rotary Club Casino night, the second floor of the Jaguar Club was a smaller copy of the main casino at the Tropicana Club in Las Vegas, complete with dealers in bow ties. Charles Terrell, decked out in a black tuxedo, walked among the tables, greeting the gamblers and checking on his dealers. The action was good, he thought, especially for a Tuesday night and especially at one of the two crap tables. He walked over to check the action.

"Eight. The number is eight," the croupier called, scooping up the dice and moving them back to the well-built redhead with the low cut dress. She was a shill for Terrell, always drawing a crowd of men to her table. As she bent over to retrieve the dice, she rewarded those at the table with an enticing view of her ample breasts.

Just as she was about to toss the dice again, three loud buzzes pierced the quiet elevator music playing in the background. Terrell and the girl quickly walked to a door in the rear of the room as the front door opened. By the time the two vice detectives and the four uniformed policemen entered the room, Terrell and the redhead were safely ensconced in his office.

"Ladies and gentlemen, may I have your attention," one of the detectives called out. "This is a raid. Gambling is illegal in the State of South Carolina, as is liquor by the drink. Please give your name to this policeman here, and you will then be free to leave. If the District Attorney decides to press charges against you, you will be notified."

The crowd began talking to the policeman, telling him which powerful or influential people they knew and threatening the cops with loss of their jobs if they were charged or if their names appeared in the papers. One policeman wrote down each of the names, along with the names of the influential people they named. The list would later be torn up and discarded. However, it had its intended effect; these people would not return to the Jaguar Club to gamble.

The remaining cops searched both floors of the club. After all the patrons were processed and had left, the police brought in axes and proceeded to chop up all of the gambling tables. The slot machines also were destroyed. The liquor was confiscated. After an exhaustive search, no drugs were found.

Still in his office, Terrell picked up the phone and called New York. If they left in an hour or two and drove straight through, he could have a new supply of liquor and gambling equipment in time to open up tomorrow night. After making the arrangements, he placed a second call to an attorney, also in New York. Charleston had fired its opening shot. Now, it was time for his response.

Chapter 22
Day 3—Wednesday, June 6, 1962
8:30 AM

Marvin Watkins, the evening cook at the Holiday Inn, awoke in the bedroom of his third floor, three bedroom apartment in the heart of Ansonborough. He had left his job as assistant cook at the Colonial Steakhouse a year earlier and followed the Colonial Steakhouse manager to the Holiday Inn. Although the manager had been replaced by Charley Innis, Marvin had kept his job. He wasn't a trained chef, but he had studied cook books and had turned himself into a passable cook, good enough for the Holiday Inn. His salary plus additional income from odd jobs was enough to afford this apartment for himself, his mother, and his grandmother.

Everything had been going well, and then these marches had to start. If that wasn't bad enough, the marches were using the church across the street from the Holiday Inn as their headquarters. Marvin was concerned that these marches would scare away the tourists, and the hotel, or at least the restaurant, might be closed. He was worried about keeping his job and hadn't slept well the past two nights.

He put on his robe and sauntered into the kitchen. His grandmother poured him a cup of coffee and turned on the stove to cook his breakfast.

"Where's Mama?" he asked, sipping his coffee.

"Gone since yesterday, right after you left for work," his grandmother said, breaking an egg into the frying pan.

"Gone where?"

"Gone after drugs, I 'spect."

"You didn't give her no money, did you?"

"Course not. I knows better."

"How can she get drugs then?"

"Whoring, I 'spect."

"Don't you call her no whore!" Marvin shouted. "She's my mama!"

"She may be yore mama," the woman said, putting his breakfast on the table, "but she's my daughter. How do you think I feel?"

"I'm gonna find her," Marvin said.

"Eat your breakfast, first. Then, if you want, you can go find her."

Marvin wolfed down his eggs, washing them down with the coffee. Throwing on his clothes, he left the apartment, taking the stairs three at a time. He had to find Junior Hutto.

Three years ago, on his way home from the Colonial Steakhouse at about midnight, Marvin had stumbled upon a situation where three young black gang members were about to beat up Junior Hutto's younger brother in retaliation for a beating Junior had administered to one of them. Marvin had picked up a 2 by 4 lying against the side of a building and, taking them by surprise, knocked two of the young toughs unconscious. The third fled. Ever since, Junior Hutto had treated Marvin like a special friend, putting out the word that anyone who messed with Marvin would have him to answer for and agreeing that none of his people would sell drugs to Marvin's mother. Since Hutto had exclusive control of drug distribution in the black community, this meant that Marvin's mother had to dry up, which she had successfully done until yesterday.

"Marvin, my man," Hutto called, as Marvin walked into the coffee shop where Hutto had breakfast every morning. The two body guards, recognizing Marvin, went back to their card game.

"You know where my mama is?" Marvin asked, sitting down across from Hutto.

"No, I don't. You look like shit. What's the matter wid you?"

"Not sleeping good. These marches got me worried they might close the Holiday Inn. My gran'ma thinks mama's got some drugs. I thought you and me had a deal."

"We do, and I've kept it," Hutto said, buttering his toast. "There's some new shit in town. New dealers. We're workin' on it, but she mighta got some smack from them."

"Who's the man?"

"White guy named Terrell. Charles Terrell. Has a club uptown called the Jaguar. He's tryin' to move in on our action."

"What am I gonna do?"

Hutto could see that Marvin was becoming very upset. "Go on home," Hutto said, motioning to one of his body guards. "I'll put the word out. We'll find your mama. I'll let you know."

"Thanks, Junior," Marvin said, standing up. As Marvin left, Hutto said something to one of the bodyguards, who immediately left to put the word out.

Chapter 23
Day 3—Wednesday
10:00 AM

Rich arrived early, so he could have his meeting with Mackey and Innis in time for them to decide how to handle the situation. As he got off the elevator, having parked in the underground garage, Charley Innis walked by on his way to Mackey's office.

"Charley," Rich called out, walking towards him.

"Ah, good timing," Innis said. "Mackey wants to see us. Glad you came in early."

"Okay, because I have to see y'all, too." They walked into the Innkeeper's office.

"This won't take long," Mackey said, as they entered the office. "Hi, Rich. Glad you're here early. Mr. Wilson called me last night. The policy has changed. We are to serve customers both in the restaurant and the hotel without regard to race. I know how Charley feels. Rich, is that okay with you?"

"Yes, sir," Rich responded, relieved.

"Good."

"What was it you wanted, Rich?" Innis asked.

"Oh, nothing now."

Rich and Innis left to get the restaurant and bar ready for lunch. Rich found it difficult to concentrate on the bar inventory. All he could think of was his date with June at three. Today, they would go straight to her apartment. This time, they might make it to the bed.

Chapter 24
Day 3—Wednesday
1:30 PM

Gedney had to cut the POETS meeting short. This attorney from New York had been insistent on meeting at 1:30, so he could catch a plane back to New York today. Gedney had agreed to the meeting on short notice out of professional courtesy, but he was also curious. Martindale Hubbell listed Anthony Minella as a one man practice, not associated with a firm. It also did not list any clients. Yes, he was curious.

His secretary buzzed at precisely 1:30. Good, he thought. Punctual. Gedney walked to his door and opened it, as his secretary escorted Anthony Minella from the lobby. "Good afternoon," Gedney said, extending his hand. "Please come in."

"Thank you," the attorney said, taking a seat.

Gedney sized him up as he walked around his desk. Expensive suit, conservative. Looks like a successful New York attorney. Okay, he thought, let's see what this is all about.

"I'll get straight to the point," Minella began. "I represent Mr. Charles Terrell, who has recently moved here from New York. Mr. Terrell opened a club, a very nice, tasteful club, here in Charleston—a club like several others here in the city. In order to compete and attract customers, Mr. Terrell features dining, dancing, cocktails, and, of course, gambling, just like several other clubs here in the city. Last night, Mr. Terrell's establishment, called, by the way, the Jaguar, was raided by the Charleston City Police. If this occurs again, we intend to file a law suit against the City of Charleston. The suit will claim that the City is engaging in malicious and discriminatory persecution of Mr. Terrell by raiding his club, when they forebear from similar action against other clubs which are openly engaging in the same conduct and business."

"Why are you telling me all of this?" Gedney asked.

"As you know, I have no standing in South Carolina courts. We, that is, Mr. Terrell wishes to engage your firm to work with me in this matter. I will conduct the case. You or one of your partners would serve as co-counsel to provide standing. We intend to seek publicity about our case, both here and in New York. It will provide your firm with some valuable publicity, not to mention the generous retainer Mr. Terrell is prepared to offer."

"Please thank Mr. Terrell for his generous offer, but we prefer not to take on such cases, especially if we do not have control of the case-in-chief. I'm sure you understand." Gedney rose, signaling that the meeting was ended.

"Thank you for your time. Here's my card, if you should reconsider."

"Thanks," Gedney said, taking the card but not offering one of his, "but I doubt if we would reconsider."

After escorting the lawyer to the lobby, Gedney returned to his office, closed the door, and picked up the phone to make a call.

Anthony Minella hailed a cab and headed for the airport, his mission accomplished. He had delivered his message to the City of Charleston.

Chapter 25
Day 3—Wednesday
2:00 PM

As Minella's taxi sped past Calhoun Street on its way to the airport, the Marchers' Strategy Council meeting was getting underway. After news about Shine's beating had spread throughout the black community, over a thousand people had showed up that morning for the march. Although Jab was still saddened by what Shine had endured, the beating had been a blessing, because it put the Charleston march on the front page of every paper north of Virginia and breathed new fire into the movement.

"Okay," Brown began. "We had another good day. How many marchers did we have?"

"Don't know for sure," Brother Anderson said. "I lost count after eleven hundred."

"Wonderful. I believe that's a new record. Okay. What is our subject for tomorrow?"

All of the favorites were proposed. Earlier that day, Jab had spoken about education and the segregated school system in the South. Now he heard jobs, wages, public accommodations, and then he heard a new topic.

"Reverend Brown," Pastor Lyle began, "I would like to propose that you speak about drugs and the numbers, both of which are enslaving our people."

"What do you mean—drugs?" Brown asked. "Is there a drug problem here?"

"Yes, I'm sad to say," Lyle continued, as others present nodded their heads in agreement. "There are no drugs in the white community, but they are plentiful in the Negro community. Many of our people spend their money on drugs to help ease the pain of their poverty rather than saving their money to help them rise above the poverty. And those who don't buy drugs spend their money on the numbers. These two vices suck precious cash out of our communities, leaving very little to be spent with the merchants and other Negro businesses."

"Is it really that bad?" Brown was surprised. He hadn't known about this problem.

"It may be our biggest problem. If we don't break the bonds of this slavery, we will never rise above where we are today."

"Okay, then. That will be our subject for tomorrow. Pastor Lyle, please meet with me this evening and brief me more on this problem. Our couple will visit the Holiday Inn again this evening. And brothers, please remember, not a word to anyone about our topic for tomorrow."

As the meeting broke, Shine went outside to meet Frank Cassidy. He found him in front of the church, again surveying the nearby rooftops. As the two men got into Cassidy's unmarked police car, Jab Brown joined the reporters in front of the church for his daily press conference.

Cassidy drove Shine about five blocks west to Police Headquarters. He noticed that Shine sat forward on the seat, so that his back would not come in contact with the seat back. If Shine was in pain, though, he didn't let on.

At headquarters, Cassidy, Rivers, and a police stenographer sat in one of the interrogation rooms. Cassidy took Shine slowly through the events of Monday, pressing him to remember every detail. When it came time to describe the beating, Shine's voice got so low that the stenographer had to repeatedly ask him to repeat himself.

Cassidy showed Shine the three photographs. When he saw the panoramic shot with his wife and children on the porch, a tear rolled down each of his cheeks. He was reliving that night all over again.

Police experts had examined every inch of the three photographs. Unfortunately, none of the pictures showed any vehicles or anything on any of the Klansmen, such as shoes, jewelry, or clothing beneath the robes which would help identify them.

After the session, Shine was exhausted and drained. As he and Cassidy left the building so that Cassidy could drive him home and interview Rebecca, Monty Simmons came out of the building dressed in civilian clothes.

"How's it going, Monty?" Cassidy asked.

"Fine, Frank. How's by you?"

"Okay. Off duty?"

"Yeah, just finished up. See ya."

Simmons walked to his pick-up truck as Shine and Cassidy headed through the parking lot towards Cassidy's car. As Simmons started the truck, Shine stopped in his tracks, momentarily confused. Then, it clicked in his mind. He reversed his steps and walked up to the driver's side of the pick-up.

When Simmons saw the big black man walking towards him and staring at him, he almost panicked. Suddenly, he was certain that somehow Shine knew he had been there at the beating. Simmons reached down and took his snub nosed pistol from the holster strapped around his right ankle.

Shine stopped beside the open window. He looked at Simmons for what seemed to Simmons like an eternity.

"I forgive you," he said to Simmons. Then, he turned and walked over to join Cassidy. Simmons, who realized he had been holding his breath, exhaled, slammed the truck in gear, and sped out of the parking lot.

"What was that all about?" Cassidy asked, as they got in the car.

"That pick-up truck was there Monday night," Shine said, carefully getting into the car and leaning forward.

"Where? It was where?" Cassidy asked, as he looked over his shoulder and backed out of the parking place.

"At my house. One of the Klan drove that truck."

"What?" Frank stopped the car and looked at Shine. "Are you sure? How do you know?"

"I heard that truck at my house Monday night. Yes, sir. I'm sure. No doubt. It was that truck."

"So, you think that Monty Simmons was one of the Klansmen who beat you," Cassidy said, more as a statement than a question.

"I'm not sayin' that, Mr. Cassidy. I'm just saying that the truck was there, that's all."

"Yeah, well, it's a good bet that if the truck was there, Simmons was there. These guys don't loan their trucks to anybody."

There certainly wasn't enough evidence to arrest Simmons, Cassidy thought, as he drove to Wadmalaw Island. In the atmosphere surrounding this case, Cassidy couldn't yet even mention this development to the Chief. He would have to think about this one.

Chapter 26
Day 3—Wednesday
7:00 PM

Rich was relieved, when he saw them coming in the door. Now, he could do the right thing. "Good evening," he said to the black couple. "May I help you?"

"Yes," the elderly man said, just as he had the two previous nights. "We would like to have dinner, please."

"Certainly," Rich said, picking up two menus. "Right this way."

Rich led the couple into the dining room and seated them at a prominent table. As he left, a waitress (who was from New Jersey and had come to Charleston with her sailor husband) took the couple's order and went into the kitchen. Almost immediately, she returned to the dining room and walked over to Rich.

"Rich," she said, "there's a problem in the kitchen. Marvin won't cook the order."

"What the…!" Rich responded. "I'll take care of it." Rich walked into the kitchen. "What's going on, Marvin?" he asked.

"I ain't goin' to cook no food for those people," he said tersely.

"Why? What's the matter? I thought you would be glad to see us serve Negroes."

"No, Mr. Rich. I ain't glad at all. These people are gonna make them close down this hotel."

"Nobody's going to close this hotel or this restaurant, Marvin. I promise. Now, cook the order. We can talk about this more after we close, if you want to. Okay?"

"Okay, Mr. Rich," Marvin said, going to the refrigerator and taking out the pork chops. "I still doan like it, but I'll do it."

"Thanks, Marvin." Rich went out front to resume his post.

Chapter 27
Day 3—Wednesday
11:45 PM

"Go ahead, Rich," Charley Innis said. "Go on home. I'll close the bar."

"Thanks, Charley."

However, he wasn't going home. He was anxious to tell June about the incident with Marvin. He wondered if she would be as surprised as he was.

June was dancing with a jerk in a Shriner's hat. Rich walked to the bar, as Drew Cole placed a scotch and water in front of an empty bar stool.

"Hi, Preacher," the bartender said, rubbing a glass with what was probably the same dirty towel.

"Hi, Drew," Rich answered, as Peaches walked up.

"Hi, lover," she said. "Boy, has June fallen for you or what. Guess now I'll never know what you're carrying down there." She patted his crotch. "Too bad."

The dance ended, and June sat down beside Rich. "Hi, you," she said. He could see the love in her eyes. This afternoon had been wonderful, as slow and lasting as the first time had been short and quick. "How'd it go?"

"Crazy," Rich said, kissing her on the cheek. "Wait'll you hear what happened."

While Rich was telling June about the incident with Marvin, Danny Costellano went into his office, just as his private phone was ringing. He opened the desk drawer and lifted the receiver.

"Hello, Mr. X," he said into the phone.

"We won't be able to help with the Terrell problem," the now familiar voice said. "You'll have to deal with it yourself."

"I don't understand," Danny complained. "That's part of the deal."

"Nevertheless, we can't help with this particular problem," Mr. X insisted. "Keep this week's deposit to cover your expenses." The line went dead.

As Danny sat at his desk, trying to figure out what he could do about Terrell for approximately $60,000, which represented one week's deposit into Mr. X's bank account, he heard a knock at the back door. He took his pistol out of the drawer, went to the door, and looked through the peephole. It was Junior Hutto. What was he doing here on a Wednesday night?

"We got trouble with that preacher who leads the marches," Hutto said, as he walked into the office.

A few blocks south, the sky was lit with reflections from the large blazing cross in front of the Calhoun Street AME Church.

Chapter 28
Thursday, June 7, 1962
8:30 AM

Now that the Holiday Inn had reversed its practice and served the black couple, the restaurant was full of journalists having breakfast and waiting for the march to start. Many had already checked back into rooms which they had abandoned for other hotels when the Holiday Inn first denied the black couple entry.

When the front doors of the church opened and the marchers began emerging into the humid, morning air, the journalists, having already paid their checks in anticipation of this moment, bolted from the restaurant. The restaurant, which moments before had been full, was now empty. Well, not quite empty. Seated alone by the front window, Jimmy Long watched as the marchers, accompanied by journalists and photographers, walked single file along Calhoun Street to King Street, where they would turn south. Everybody in town now knew the route and the approximate time the march would begin. The marchers looked over at the large, still smoldering cross as they passed it, and then looked straight ahead, a look of renewed determination on their faces.

Jab Brown, when he arrived that morning, had changed his plan. He would talk about the cross burning on the steps of St. Michael's Church, saving his speech about the drug problem until the post-march press conference. The Klan, he thought, was turning out to be his ally, providing him with visible evidence of the attitudes of many whites toward the Negro.

Long sat, sipping his coffee and watching the long, seemingly endless line of black people coming out of the AME Church. The cross burning hadn't made a dent in their numbers. Merely burning a cross was too subtle, he thought. We have to hit them hard, scare them so much that they will stop this nonsense rather than risk further retaliation.

Kick him out of the Klan, will they? Well, they couldn't. Jimmy Long was in the Klan because he thought like a Klansman, not because some group had voted him in. By taking such weak and ineffective action, these people who ran the Klan were showing that it was they who were not true Klansmen. Jimmy Long was the true Klansman, the true protector of the South. He knew what had to be done, and he was the man to do it. He paid his check and went home to get the things he needed.

Chapter 29
Day 4—Thursday
2:15 PM

The rear of the line of marchers disappeared into the church, and the doors closed. It was time. Long, who had returned to the restaurant for lunch, paid his check and hurried to the underground parking garage. He retrieved his rifle and a suitcase from his car and took the elevator to the top floor of the hotel. Earlier, he had followed the same route and had located the stairs leading to the roof.

He walked across the flat tar and gravel roof to the front of the hotel facing Calhoun Street, selected his spot, and opened the suitcase. First, he took off his shoes and put on his cowboy boots. Then, he took his Klan robe from the suitcase and donned it over his clothes. He wouldn't need the hood. The final item in the suitcase was a sniper scope. He attached the scope to the rifle and adjusted it for the range to the microphones, which he noticed today had been set up in front of the burnt cross rather than in the usual spot directly in front of the church doors. Long moved to his left about twenty feet to get a better aspect to the cross and sat down to wait.

Jab Brown came out to meet the reporters and walked over to the cross. Jimmy Long brought the rifle up and peered through the scope. He focused the sight on Brown.

Word had gone out that Brown was going to give a different speech than the one he had delivered a few hours ago at St. Michael's Church, and a larger than usual crowd had gathered on the sidewalk in front of the church. Many of the marchers had also stayed to hear it. Seeing the large crowd gathering, Rich Newton walked out to the front of the hotel to see what was going on.

Sweat was pouring down Long's forehead. The Klansman robe was proving very hot, especially with the day's high humidity, but the idea of taking the robe off never occurred to him. Today, Long was the Klan, and the world must know who he was and how the Klan had finally taken action to stop this Communist threat.

As Brown stepped up to the microphones, Long again looked through the sniper scope sight. Sweat trickled into his eyes. He lowered the rifle, resting it on the raised edge of the roof, and used the bottom of his robe to wipe the perspiration from his eyes and face.

Flecks of dried mortar floated down in front of Rich, who looked up to see where they were coming from. He spotted what appeared to be a pipe protruding from the top of the hotel. He would have to tell the engineer to see what it was, he thought, as he returned his attention to the church and Jab Brown across the street.

Jab spoke a few words to test the microphones. Sure enough, the feedback had to be adjusted. He waited patiently.

Long brought the rifle up, again dislodging more white mortar flecks. He peered through the scope, found Brown's head in the cross hairs, and began to squeeze the trigger.

When more white specks of mortar came down, Rich looked up again. The pipe had moved. Suddenly, Rich realized that it wasn't a pipe. It was a rifle.

"Hey!" Rich shouted to some of the cops standing nearby.

Jab Brown began to turn his head to see what the commotion was. He saw Rich pointing upward toward the roof of the hotel. Two cops also looked up, saw the rifle barrel, and started running toward the entrance to the hotel.

More sweat flowed into Long's eyes as he squeezed the trigger. His ears heard the shouting from below his position near the front of the hotel. The shouting didn't register in his brain. He closed his eyes against the burning of the sweat as the rifle fired.

CRACK…crack.

The report of the rifle echoed from the buildings around Marion Square to Long's left. Jab Brown fell, knocking over the microphones, dead before he hit the ground, a bullet lodged deep in his brain.

"Up there!" Rich was shouting, pointing to the roof of the hotel. "I saw a rifle up there." More cops ran into the hotel, some taking the elevator and others the stairs. Bull Jenkins walked over to his motorcycle and called headquarters. He knew the Chief would want Frank Cassidy in on this one.

On the roof, Jimmy Long sat and waited for the police to arrive. He would be a hero. He had showed them who he was. He had the balls to do what had to be done. The white people of the South wouldn't let anything bad happen to him. They would understand.

The first two cops to arrive on the roof ran over toward the robed figure sitting by the edge. The first stopped about ten feet from Long and drew his gun. He immediately recognized Long. "Aw, shit, Jimmy," he said. "What did you have to go and do that for?"

The second cop approached Long. "Okay, Jimmy," he said, pistol drawn and aimed at Long. "Stand up and step away from the rifle." Long complied. He didn't want these nervous cops to shoot him and deprive him of the glory that was sure to come.

The photographers had a field day when the cops brought Jimmy down to the parking lot in front of the hotel, still in his Klan robe with his hands handcuffed behind him. As they put him in the back seat of a squad car, Cassidy and Randy Holly drove up in Holly's black and white. The cops asked Cassidy what he wanted done with Long.

"Take him in and book him. Then, put him in a holding cell. Nobody questions him 'til I get there."

As the squad car drove off, Cassidy heard a commotion in front of the restaurant entrance. He walked over. "What's the problem?"

"Hi, Lieutenant," one of the cops said. "We've sealed off the hotel," which meant that nobody could either enter or leave the hotel, "until you arrived. This boy says he works in there and wants to enter."

Marvin Watkins was late. He appeared nervous and out-of-breath.

"Get the names and addresses of everyone who witnessed the shooting and then open the hotel," Cassidy ordered. "Anybody here from management?"

"I am," Rich said, stepping up. The uniformed cop whispered to Cassidy that Rich had shouted an alarm at the moment of the shooting.

"Do you know him?" Cassidy motioned towards Watkins.

"Yes, sir. That's Marvin, Marvin Watkins. He's the evening cook. He's late."

"Okay, let him in," Cassidy said to the cop. Then, he turned to Rich. "Mr…"

"Newton, Rich Newton."

"Mr. Newton, I'm Lieutenant Cassidy," Frank said, writing Rich's name in his book. "I'll want to talk with you later. Will you be here?"

"Yes, I'll be inside." Rich went inside to call June, inform her of what had happened, and tell her to go on to her apartment. He would be there as soon as he could.

Cassidy and Holly walked across Calhoun Street. The police photographers were finishing up. The forensic team moved in to begin collecting physical evidence. Cassidy could see that Carleton James, the Medical Examiner, had already arrived and was now inspecting the body of the late Jab Brown, which was still sprawled over the fallen microphone stands.

Cassidy knew that the M E would brief him when he was ready, so he turned his attention to the photographers. Protesting vehemently, they surrendered all of their film, both still and moving, to Randy Holly. Cassidy assured them that they could pick it up at headquarters as soon as copies had been made. Cassidy collected business cards from each of the journalists and requested that they remain in Charleston until he could question them. None had any plans to leave.

Ken Wall drove up in his official black Lincoln, lights flashing and sirens wailing. He spotted Cassidy. "What have we got?" he asked.

"We arrested a suspect on the roof of the Holiday Inn." Cassidy had the good sense not to remind Wall that he had expressed concern to Wall about the roofs of the nearby buildings only yesterday. "I'm going in to question him as soon as I talk with Dr. James."

"Okay," the Chief said. "I'll handle the reporters. Can I tell them we got the shooter?"

"Looks that way," Cassidy replied. "When they got up there, he was waiting with his rifle, dressed in a Klan robe."

"Okay. Keep me informed." The chief walked over to the reporters for his fifteen minutes of fame.

Cassidy walked over to the body, which the M E had moved off of the microphones. His assistants had enclosed the body in a bag and were lifting it onto a gurney. "Whatcha got?" Cassidy asked.

"One shot to the head," the M E said through a cloud of pipe smoke. "Looks like he was dead before he hit the ground. I'll know better this afternoon."

"Okay. I won't bug you, but you need to hop right on this one."

"No problem," Dr. James replied and went to accompany the corpse to the morgue.

"Let's go," Cassidy said to Holly. They headed for headquarters.

They brought Long, still in his Klan robe, into the interrogation room. Cassidy, Holly, and two other detectives were waiting along with a police stenographer, who would take down everything that was said in the room.

"I'm Detective Cassidy," he said to Long. "It's hot in here. Don't you want to take that robe off?"

"No, sir," Long replied calmly. "I'd like to keep it on, if you don't mind."

"Up to you," Cassidy said. "Do you want a Coke or something?"

"Yeah. I'm kinda thirsty."

Cassidy nodded to Holly, who left to get some Cokes. "You understand that this lady is a police stenographer and will take down everything that is said in this room," Cassidy began.

"Yeah. Sure." Long seemed unconcerned.

"What is your name?"

"Jimmy Long."

"Is that James Long?"

"No, it's Jimmy. Jimmy Long. No middle name, either."

"And where do you live, Mr. Long."

"Eighty four Westside Drive, near the marina."

"Do you mind if we search your house? We can get a search warrant, you know."

"No, I don't mind. Here's the key."

The two detectives took the key, wrote down the address, and left.

Cassidy decided to wait until Holly returned with the Cokes. He was getting thirsty, too.

"Some shot, huh," Long said.

"What?" Cassidy asked, not sure he heard Long correctly.

"That was some shot," Long repeated.

Okay, Cassidy said to himself. Let's play it that way for a while. "Yeah, it was, Jimmy. How far do you make it?"

"Oh, I don't know. A hundred yards, maybe one fifty."

"I make it more, maybe two hundred," Cassidy said. "Remember, you were six stories up, and he was at ground level."

"Shit, you're right. Damn. I dropped that mother fucker with one shot from two hundred yards. That'll show them."

"Show who?" Cassidy asked almost matter-of-factly, as if he was just keeping the conversation going to kill time. He looked over at the stenographer.

She wasn't missing a word and hadn't even flinched at Long's language. She heard it every day.

"Those pussies who call themselves Klan members. Burn a cross. Big deal, I told them. We have to hit the coloreds and hit them hard, so they know we mean business."

"So you did it yourself?"

"Damn straight," Long said proudly.

"Tell me about it," Cassidy said.

And Long did, starting with the previous night and the argument at the Klan meeting. Holly returned with Cokes and doughnuts, as Long was describing the actual killing. Holly paused to take a telephone call from the detectives searching Long's house. He hung up the phone, scribbled a note to Cassidy saying that the detectives had found a bullwhip, and sat back down across from Long.

"Now let's talk about Monday night," Cassidy said, playing a hunch.

"Oh, you know about that, too," Long said, surprised. "You're good."

"Thanks," Cassidy replied, "but I'm not that good. I know some of it, but I need your help."

"Sure. What do you need?"

"Well, I know that Monty Simmons was there and, oh, yes, the photographer from the News and Courier. What's his name? I've got it somewhere here in my notes?" Cassidy thumbed through some blank pages of his notebook.

"Gentry," Long offered. "Ray Gentry."

"Yeah, that's it," Cassidy said. "And I assume that you are the one who wielded the whip."

"Right, again," Long said proudly. "Twenty lashes from twenty feet. Really tore his black ass up."

"Why him?" Cassidy asked. "Why Shine Rivers?"

"You see, he works for me as a mechanic, and when I saw him marching along with those Communists, I knew that he was doing it to spite me. He knows how I feel about those marches going on in Birmingham and Atlanta."

Cassidy wanted to throw this slime ball out the window, saving the court's time and the State's money. Instead, after getting the names of all of the participants in the whipping of Shine Rivers, he had Long returned to the holding cell and drove himself to the morgue. Dr. James was conferring with an assistant when Cassidy arrived.

"Hello, Frank," he said. "Is this one going to be a political hot potato?"

"Probably," Cassidy answered, sitting down on a stool. "Quite frankly, I've been too busy to surface and sniff the air."

"Well, you can smell it all the way over here. I've already had two calls from Chief Wall and one from the Mayor."

"Well, they can relax. I got a full confession, plus a bonus. The shooter is the same guy who whipped the black preacher Monday night."

"Well, well. A regular Sherlock Holmes. Good work, Frank."

"Thanks, but we kinda got lucky. So, what do you have on this one?"

The coroner took out his notes. "A single bullet in the head. He died instantly. There was hardly any bleeding. Come over here and I'll show you." Frank followed the M E across the room to a full skeleton suspended from a hook. "The bullet entered here on this trajectory." James used a pencil to indicate the angle from which the bullet entered Jab Brown's head. The pencil was pointing to the right front of the skeleton's forehead, from an angle slightly right of center, say one o'clock, and angling downward. "Looking where he was probably standing, preparing for the press conference, I'd say the angle of entry was consistent with being fired from the roof of the Holiday Inn. The bullet passed through the brain and lodged here." He pointed at the base of the brain, where it meets the spinal column. "That's why death was instantaneous. The damage immediately shut down his entire nervous system, like turning out the lights. Here's the bullet."

The coroner handed the bullet to Cassidy. A white tag was attached to the bullet with a piece of white string. Cassidy added his initials to the coroner's on the tag, put the bullet in a small evidence envelope, sealed it, and put it in his pocket. "Anything else?" Cassidy asked.

"Not really. Pretty cut-and-dried."

Cassidy headed back to headquarters to brief the Chief and take the heat off. When he arrived, he called Rich at the Holiday Inn and made an appointment to interview him the next day. Rich hung up the phone and raced to June's apartment.

Chapter 30
Day 4—Thursday
10:00 PM

It was an eerie scene. The setting sun had not produced the breezes which normally come when the land cools down more than the water in the harbor. Tonight, a still dome of warm, humid air covered Charleston like a blanket. The people of Ansonborough were outside, as they usually were on nights like this, escaping the heat of their houses and apartments, sitting on the porch or the stoop and talking with their neighbors. Tonight, however, there was no talk. The black people of Ansonborough were just there, quiet, milling around or just standing still. The silence was ominous and foreboding.

The council had met for three hours after the shooting, trying to reach agreement on what to do next. They had decided to pray for guidance overnight and meet again the following morning. Shine Rivers had then stayed in town for a while to join Reverend Lyle in offering comfort to Jab Brown's family, whom Lyle had brought to the parsonage for their safety. Rivers left the parsonage, about to walk the three blocks back to the church, where his car was parked, and immediately sensed that something was wrong. In their grief and concern about Brown's family, they had forgotten that the community also needed comfort. As he was about to return to the parsonage to speak to Lyle, several black teenagers, walking in the middle of the deserted street about half a block away, picked up some pieces of brick and broke a store front window. They then began running up the street in Shine's direction, throwing rocks at other windows.

Shine knew that Ansonborough was moments away from full scale rioting and looting. He walked out to the middle of the street and stood in the path of the running teenagers. The lead teenager stopped in front of Shine.

"Get outa the way," he said to Shine. "We tried it your way, and look what they did. They shot Reverend Brown. Now, we'll do it our way."

Please help me, Lord, Shine prayed. "No," Shine said, staying his ground. "You will not do this. This is exactly what the white man wants us to do. He wants us to act like a bunch of ignorant savages. If we act like children, they will treat us like children. If we act like grown-ups, maybe one day they will treat us like grown-ups."

More black teenagers joined the small mob and surrounded Shine. The self appointed leader of the teens said nothing, continuing to stare at Shine. The tension grew.

Reverend Lyle, having heard the breaking glass, had walked onto the sidewalk. He started walking towards Shine to stand with him, as he saw two youths at the edge of the growing crowd stoop and pick up large chunks of brick. Lyle was about a block away. He picked up his pace, convinced that the youths were about to begin stoning Shine.

Suddenly, a loud clap of thunder startled Shine and the youths. For a brief moment, Shine thought it was a gunshot. Then, the heavens opened up, taking away the heat and humidity and driving the residents inside. The youths ran for cover, and Shine walked in the rain to his car, unaware that Lyle had been coming to join and support him. Thank you, Lord, he said.

Reverend Lyle stood for a moment in the downpour, turned, and walked slowly back to the parsonage. He had seen and heard the message from the Lord and now knew what he had to do.

A cop stopped by and alerted Rich to the potential trouble in Ansonborough, only three blocks away. After Charley agreed to close up, Rich drove to the High Hat and took June home. He stayed the night with her, just in case there was more trouble.

Chapter 31
Chapter 5—Friday, June 8, 1962
8:00 AM

The March Strategy Council gathered at the AME Church. Reverend Lyle suggested that they meet in the sanctuary instead of the classroom. The first marchers who arrived were asked to remain outside and inform other marchers to please wait in the parking lot until the Council meeting had concluded.

Reverend Lyle climbed the steps to the pulpit to address the Council. "A message was sent by the Lord last night," he began, using his preaching voice. It was vital that the Council agree to his proposal. "A riot was averted in Ansonborough when Brother Rivers, acting alone, stopped a mob of teenagers who were getting out of hand."

"Reverend Lyle," Shine interrupted, standing. "Pardon my interruptin' you, but I was not alone. God was with me. He sent the rain that stopped the riot. I didn't do it. He did." Shine sat down.

"Thank you, brother," Lyle went on. Shine had just made his task easier. "My point exactly. I checked this morning. It didn't rain anywhere else in Charleston County last night. Only in Ansonborough. At the precise moment when Shine stepped into the street and halted the vandalism, God sent rain. God acted through his instrument, Brother Rivers, to help his afflicted people avoid a terrible mistake, just like he acted through Moses, Job, Aaron, and Paul. I believe that he will continue to act on our behalf through Reverend Rivers. Dr. King called me early this morning to offer his condolences and concerns about the assassination of Reverend Brown. I assured him that we will press on with the marches, just as we all know Jab would want us to. I told him about Brother

Rivers. He was, of course, well aware of the sacrifice for the movement Reverend Rivers endured Monday night. He agreed that Reverend Rivers is the right choice to lead us in our struggle. I propose that Reverend Rivers be named as the new leader of the Civil Rights Movement in Charleston."

The aging minister walked slowly down the winding pulpit steps. Shine sat, stunned and speechless. He was so unworthy of such an honor and position that he didn't know where to begin.

One by one, the other members of the Council rose to voice their agreement with the proposal. "Reverend Rivers," Pastor Lyle said, standing before the group and addressing Shine. "Will you accept this charge of your brethren?"

"I cannot," Shine said, rising to his feet once more. "I am not worthy to lead you and them." He motioned towards the parking lot, where the marchers were now gathering. "I ain't got…I don't have a college education. I didn't even finish high school. All I know, I learned through studying and with the help of my wife, God bless her. I'm a simple auto mechanic and island preacher. I'm not a good speaker. I cain't do the things that Jab Brown did."

"Shine, no one's asking you to be Jab Brown. We are all telling you that we want you, Shine Brown, to lead us your way through your faith, your strength, and your actions. Jab Brown led us with words, and he was brilliant at it. We are asking you to lead us with your faith, strength, and actions. If you don't want to speak, then don't."

"Shine," a voice said softly from the rear of the church. It was Rebecca. Reverend Lyle had arranged for her to be brought into the city. Mrs. Lyle was minding the children. "Shine, it's time. This is the moment you have been preparing yourself for. You are a man of strong faith and convictions. The battle ahead will be tough. These people need your strength."

Shine, surprised by the unexpected sound of his wife's voice, turned to face her across the expanse of the empty church. He trusted Rebecca's wisdom and judgment beyond question. If she thought he should do it, then he must do it.

"I will need your help," he said to his wife. The Council was silently witnessing a deeply personal moment between a man and wife. "I'll be there, Shine," she answered, "just like always."

Shine walked forward and stood next to Reverend Lyle. "If this is the judgment of the Council, then I will accept your charge." The Council members stood and applauded, while Rebecca came forward to stand beside her man.

"Now, let's get the people in here. We've got a demonstration to put on," Shine shouted. The Council broke into laughter, as several went out the side door to beckon the marchers to come in.

"Shine, I'm going to march today beside you," Rebecca said.

"No, honey," he protested. "It's too dangerous. Look what they did to Jab."

"Shine, I said I'll be with you. Today, I'll be with you on the march. Tomorrow, I'll stay home with the kids, but today, since Mrs. Lyle was kind enough to watch the children, I will walk beside you. Besides, God is watching out for you, Shine Rivers. I'm not afraid."

When the marchers were told by Reverend Lyle that Shine Rivers had been named as their new leader, the spontaneous reaction of joy and approval could be heard for two blocks. The cops and reporters outside were perplexed. Why were these people, whose leader had been killed only yesterday, so happy? When the doors opened, they had their answer. Shine and Rebecca Rivers came out into the sunshine at the head of the line, leading the day's march.

Chapter 32
Day 5—Friday
8:15 AM

Charles Terrell emerged from the front entrance of the apartment building, looked carefully for anything unusual in the parking lot (more out of habit than from any sense of foreboding) and walked through the parking lot to his baby blue Cadillac Coupe Deville convertible. He had received enough liquor and gambling equipment to get back into business the night after the raid, but a larger shipment was due in this morning. He wanted to be sure that the club was ready for the weekend crowd.

He started the car, unlatched the top, and engaged the electric motor to retract the convertible top. It was a beautiful, sunny day, and he might as well enjoy the ride to the club. As the top settled into place behind the back seat, a shot rang out, and Terrell slumped forward, his falling arm shifting the car into drive. The car began to inch forward, climbed a low divider into the street, and finally stopped in the street, the front bumper against a fire hydrant. A passing Charleston Police squad car stopped to investigate.

Frank Cassidy was in his office, completing the paper work on the Brown shooting, when the phone rang. "Cassidy," he answered, erasing a typo and rolling the paper back through the typewriter in a vain attempt to position it in exactly the right place to make the correction.

"Got another shooting, Frank." It was the Chief's voice. "You want it?" Frank always had first call on homicides. "After what you've had on your plate, you can pass, if you want."

"No, thanks. I'll take it. Give me the details."

"On the street in front of the Harbor View apartments. A black and white is there. Forensics and Doc James are on the way."

Frank yelled for Holly to finish his doughnut, as he took his revolver from his desk drawer and donned his jacket. Holly caught up with him in the parking lot.

"You found the car just like this?" Cassidy asked the officer at the scene.

"Yes, sir. I turned the motor off. Other than that, I haven't touched a thing."

Cassidy walked behind the car and spotted the tire indentations on the grass divider between the parking lot of the apartment building and the street.

"I figure he got shot in the parking lot," the uniformed officer said, "somehow put the car in gear, and its idle was fast enough for it to end up here. It was still pushing against the fire plug when I turned it off."

"Know who he is?"

"The car is registered to a Charles Terrell. Address is that apartment building there. I don't know any more yet." The officer had not been able to get to Terrell's wallet, because the forensic team and the M E weren't finished yet.

"Okay," Cassidy said. "Get a tow truck. We'll have to clear the street as soon as we can."

"Lieutenant!" one of the forensic technicians called out. "See ya' a minute?"

Cassidy walked back over to the Cadillac.

"This guy doesn't have any fingerprints," he said.

"What?" Cassidy exclaimed. "What do you mean?"

"Here. Look." The technician took out a clean paper, rolled fresh ink onto the fingertips of Terrell's right hand, and touched the fingers to the pad. "See? Nothing."

"Yeah. I see. Are the photogs finished?"

"Yes, Lieutenant," one of the photographers called out.

"Stick around for a few minutes. Okay?"

"Sure, Frank," the senior photographer said.

Dr. James was examining the body.

"Can we push him back?" Frank asked.

"Yes," the M E answered. "Let's get a look at this guy."

Together they eased the body off the steering wheel and rested the head against the seat back. Frank looked the dead man straight in the face. Except for a single bullet wound in the chest and lots of blood down the front of his shirt, he looked like a man asleep. There was something about the man that was familiar to Frank. He didn't recognize him or know who he was, but Frank was familiar with the look, having seen types like this on the streets of Brooklyn every day when he was growing up. He would bet a week's pay that this guy was an Italian from New York. Put that suspicion together with the expensive suit and no fingerprints, and he might have some kind of bad guy here.

"Joe," he called the photographer over. "Get me a good shot of his face."

The photographer took a whole roll.

"I need it right away," Cassidy said.

'They'll be on your desk when you get back," Joe said, heading for his car.

"Okay, Doc," Cassidy said to the M E. "What do you see?"

"I see a bad trend, Frank. Two shootings in two days. This was a shot in the heart, single shot I expect. I'll tell you more as soon as I get him back. Is this a rush, too?"

"Nah, take your time on this one. This afternoon will be fine," Cassidy joked.

Cassidy took Terrell's wallet and found a business card showing him as owner of the Jaguar Club. He sent Holly to check out the man's apartment, giving him the key. Holly then was to go to the club and check it out. Cassidy wanted to run the photograph.

Sure enough, the pictures were on his desk. He selected the best one and picked up his phone.

"Manhattan South Detectives," the voice answered. "Sergeant Auteri speaking."

"Lieutenant Cassidy, please," Frank said.

"Yeah, can I tell the Lieutenant who's calling?"

"Yes, It's Lieutenant Cassidy," Frank answered.

"Just a minute, buddy," the Sergeant said. "Is this some kind of joke?"

"No, Sergeant. This is Lieutenant Frank Cassidy of the Charleston, South Carolina Police Department calling for Lieutenant Kevin Cassidy."

"Sorry, Lieutenant. I'll get him."

"Frankie, how's it going?" his brother's voice boomed through the phone. "You made the New York Times, today. Ain't that a bitch? I bust my ass up here for twenty years, solving all sorts of crimes, and it's my brother in some hick town down south who makes the Times. Go figure."

"Yeah, well, if you get the doughnuts out of your face and hit the street, you might make the papers, too."

"Hell, you're probably right," his brother laughed. "What's up?"

"Kevin, I'm faxing you a picture of a DB I've got with no finger prints. Has an English name, but he looks Italian—New York Italian—to me. See if someone can make him and give me a call back, will you?"

"Sure. In fact, hold on. It's coming through right now. Let me be sure it's a good transmission."

Frank heard his brother lay the phone down. While he was waiting, one of the forensic technicians walked into Frank's office, looking as if he were about to wet his pants. As Frank was about to ask him what he wanted, his brother came back on the line.

"Got it," Kevin said.

"Is it good enough?"

"Hell, yes. I know this guy. His name is Carmine Terenzi." Kevin spelled the name. "He is…I guess now was a capo in the Genovese family. Wondered what happened to him. What's he doing in Charleston?"

"Owns a club called the Jaguar."

"Uh oh," Kevin said. "If Terenzi's down there, then he is, or at least was, bringing in drugs and maybe gambling. Brother of mine, you've got trouble."

"Yeah, well, he's dead now."

"They've got others," Kevin responded. "This wasn't his action alone. Terenzi was a doer, not a thinker. I'll bet there is a new owner of the Jaguar by Monday. Good luck."

"Thanks," Frank said. "Give Pop my love. Tell him we'll call on Sunday." He hung up the phone.

"Lieutenant?" The forensic technician was beside himself.

"For God's sake, sit down, Artie," Frank said. "You're making me nervous."

The technician remained standing. "Lieutenant, the bullet that killed that Negro minister yesterday did not come from the rifle the perp had."

Frank stood straight up. "What?! Are you sure?"

"This is the bullet you gave me from the M E. After the first test came up negative, I fired two more from the rifle. These are those three bullets. The three from the rifle match each other exactly. None of them come anywheres close to this one. You've got the wrong man, Lieutenant."

"Holly!" Cassidy roared.

Tom Watson, one of the other detectives, stuck his head in the door. "You sent Randy out to the Jaguar," he reminded Frank.

"Yeah, right. Look, Tom, we've got a problem. Artie here says that the bullet that killed that Negro minister yesterday didn't come from Long's rifle."

"Jeez, Artie," Watson said. "You sure?"

"Yes, he's sure," Frank answered. "And if Artie says he's sure, that's good enough for me. Tom, do me a favor. Take a couple of uniforms and search the roof of the Holiday Inn. Maybe the bastard had another rifle up there."

"Sure thing, Frank," Watson said. "Jeez," he muttered, as he went off to find some uniformed cops.

Frank dialed the M E's number.

"James," the M E answered.

"Doc," Frank began, "I've got to ask you a crazy question, and don't get pissed. Is there any chance that you gave me the wrong bullet yesterday?" Frank knew it was a stupid question when he asked it, but he had to ask.

"No chance. Took it out myself. Tagged it myself. Kept it on my person until I gave it to you. What's the problem? Ballistics doesn't match?"

"Right."

"Then, it's simple," the M E said. "Your man didn't do it."

"Come on, Doc. The bastard confessed."

"Frank, he may truly believe that he killed that minister, but if the ballistics doesn't match, then somebody else fired the murder weapon. Dig deeper and you'll probably find other evidence pointing the same way."

"Thanks, Doc." He hung up.

"Artie, do you guys have the film that we confiscated from the photographers?"

"Yes, sir. I don't think anybody's looked at them yet."

"Then let's go do that right now."

The still shots weren't much help. No one had taken a picture at the moment of impact. However, the moving film camera had been on and rolling when the bullet was fired, and it told the story. As he was about to speak, something made Jab Brown look to his right and lean ever so slightly to the right. That's when the film clearly showed the bullet hitting him. When Carl James, the Medical Examiner, had showed Cassidy the angle of entry of the bullet, they had both assumed that Brown was looking straight ahead towards the cameras at the time of impact. Now, the film clearly showed that he was looking to his right, putting the shooter to the west of the Holiday Inn, probably across Meeting Street on the roof of a building along Calhoun Street between Meeting and

King. Furthermore, the sound track clearly has two gun shot sounds very close together, so close that the second could be mistaken for an echo of the first.

Frank had one more thing to check before he blew the lid off the case. He hustled Artie with his forensic kit out to his car and drove, lights and sirens on, to the AME Church. Sure enough, allowing for Brown's height and the angle from the roof of the Holiday Inn, they found a bullet embedded in the wood of the charred cross. Artie took the bullet back to the lab and had a match with Long's rifle in two minutes.

Frank went to see the Chief.

Chapter 33
Day 5—Friday
12 Noon

The POETS Club was assembled for its usual Friday meeting.

"Gedney," Mayor Jerry Anderson began, "we have new information about yesterday's shooting. It turns out that the man who was arrested and confessed is not guilty of shooting the Nigra minister. However, he is guilty of Monday night's bull whipping on Wadmalaw Island. We got the names of all the Klansmen who were there that night, including two cops—one city and one county—and" he nodded to Manigault "the News and Courier photographer who took the pictures. We rounded them all up last night except for the city cop, who we think has left town. We issued an APB for him."

"Go on about the shooting at the church," Gedney Middleton said.

"I'll let Chief Wall explain."

"The bullet taken from the body does not match the test bullets from the rifle that Klansman had. We have re-intensified the investigation," Ken Wall said.

Beano Martin leaned over and whispered something to Middleton, who nodded his agreement. "Chief," Beano said, "you should invite the FBI and the State Law Enforcement Division in to review and verify your evidence."

"But we don't need…," Wall began to protest.

"It's the right move," Gedney interrupted. "The Feds and the Northern press will be skeptical about any claim that a white man, especially a Klan member who confessed, is in fact not the killer. We have to be sure that we have outside confirmation. It's no reflection on the professionalism of your department, Ken. It's a political matter. Okay?"

"Okay," the Chief said, not convinced, but also not willing to go against

Middleton. "Also, there was another shooting this morning. The victim was a Charles Terrell, the owner of the Jaguar Club."

"Jesus! What's going on?" Jim Tucker complained. "Two shootings in two days?"

"Who's got that case?" Middleton asked.

"Cassidy," the Chief responded. "He took it before we knew about the ballistics report."

Beano whispered something to Middleton.

"I recommend," Middleton said, nodding to Beano Martin, "that you give the…what's the name…Terrence shooting to someone else. Cassidy still has his hands full."

"The name is Terrell," Chief Wall corrected Gedney. "I'll take care of it this afternoon."

"Good," Middleton said, leaning back in his chair. "Considering all that's happened this week, things aren't so bad. We arrested the bastards who whipped that other nigra minister on Monday night in three days. Very good. That, along with this turn of events in the Brown shooting, will take the wind out of the Kennedys' sails. They'll waste time trying to prove that the Klansman did it. Anything that buys us time helps us. The nigras can't march forever."

"Now, all we need is for Cassidy to prove that a nigra shot Brown," Jim Tucker chuckled.

The group laughed long and hard at that one. Actually, all but one laughed. He made a mental note to make a phone call immediately after the meeting.

Chapter 34
Day 5—Friday
4:00 PM

After spending most of the afternoon talking with the reporters and marchers who witnessed the shooting at the church, Frank Cassidy had an appointment to meet Rich Newton at the Holiday Inn to interview him about the events surrounding the shooting. As he took the report out of the typewriter and placed it on the growing pile in the manila folder, his phone rang. "Cassidy," he answered.

"Frank, Ken Wall. Come in here for a minute."

Frank walked down the hall to the Chief's office. Detective Tom Watson was with the Chief.

"Frank, we have a tip from a reliable snitch that the cook at the Holiday Inn, name of Marvin Watkins, killed Brown. He works the evening shift. Here's an arrest warrant and a search warrant. Take Holly, pick him up, and search his house. The snitch says the rifle is there. I'll have a couple of uniforms and a forensic team meet you there. If you find the rifle, execute the arrest warrant and bring him in. Look, I want your full attention on this case. You know how important it is, so Tom will take over the Terrell shooting. Give him the file before you leave. Okay?"

"Sure. Watkins? Let's see. I know that name." He thumbed through his book. "Here it is. He was late for work right after the shooting. Chief, this guy is a Negro. Do you think a Negro did this?"

"How the hell would I know? If the rifle's not there, apologize and take him back to work. If it's there, book him."

Cassidy gave the file on the Terrell shooting to Watson, found Holly, and hurried to the Holiday Inn in Holly's black and white.

Rich was waiting for Cassidy at the front desk.

"Are you the restaurant manager?" Cassidy asked.

"No, I'm the assistant manager. Charley Innis is the manager," Rich answered.

"Is he here?"

"Yes, probably in his office."

"Show me." The three men went to Innis's office.

Cassidy introduced himself and Holly. "We have a warrant for the arrest of one of your employees, Marvin Watson," Cassidy said. "We need to take him with us."

"Can't you pick him up after his shift?" Innis asked. "What's he done?"

"I'm not at liberty to discuss the charges. We are only starting the investigation. I want to emphasize that he has not yet been charged with anything. I'm afraid, though, that we must take him now. If there's nothing to it, he'll be back in an hour."

"Okay," Innis said. "Rich, you go with them. I have to get another cook in here quickly. Lieutenant, can you take him out the back door?"

"Sure," Cassidy said.

Rich took the two men to the kitchen, while Charley Innis began making telephone calls.

"Marvin, this is Lieutenant Cassidy of the police," Rich said. "He needs to speak with you."

"What'd I do?" Marvin became very excited. "I didn't do nothin'!"

"We need to ask you some questions, that's all," Cassidy answered. He wanted to get him away from the knives on the table in front of him and, hopefully, out of the kitchen without a ruckus. Watkins's fright was very apparent.

"Questions about what?" Watkins persisted.

"We're interviewing everyone who was in the area when the shooting occurred. We just want to ask you a few questions."

"I doan know nothin'! It was all over when I got here. I gots to work now. I doan know nothin'."

Cassidy walked around the table and stood close to Watkins. "Look, Marvin," he said, softly and calmly, his hand on the cook's shoulder, so he could sense if Watkins was about to make a sudden move. "We can do this one of two ways. You can come with us willingly, and we can probably clear this up in about an hour. If you're in the clear, we'll bring you back to work. If you force us to, we'll arrest you right here and take you out of here in handcuffs. Which way is it going to be?"

Holly reached to his hip and thumbed the safety strap off of his revolver.

"Okay," Watkins said. "I'll come, but I didn't do nothin'." He took off his apron and followed Cassidy out the back door, Holly taking up the rear.

They drove to the apartment. A black and white was parked outside next to the forensic team's station wagon. They walked up the three flights to the apartment and found Artie and the two cops standing in the living room. Marvin's grandmother was sitting in a chair, crying.

"We found it, Lieutenant," one of the cops said, holding up a rifle inside a long, transparent plastic bag. "In the back of his closet."

Idiots, Cassidy thought. He had the search warrant in his pocket.

"Artie?" Cassidy said.

"No prints, Lieutenant. Wiped clean."

That doesn't make sense, Cassidy thought. Why wipe the prints off a rifle and then leave it in your own closet.

"What's that?!!" Watkins shouted, becoming excited again. "What's that!!? That ain't mine! What's goin' on?!!"

Holly removed his handcuffs from his belt and silently stepped behind Watkins.

"What about the bullets?" Cassidy asked.

"I'd rather take them out in the lab," Artie answered, "so I don't smear anything."

"Right," Cassidy said. He turned to Watkins. "Marvin Watkins, you are under arrest for the murder of Jeremiah Brown."

Marvin's grandmother screamed and fainted. Holly cuffed Watkins, who was yelling that he hadn't killed anyone.

"Oh, lord. Oh, lord," Watkins repeated, as they took him down the stairs. "Help me, lord. I didn't do nothin', Mr. Policeman. Please let me go. I didn't do nothin'. Oh, lord, help me."

They put the struggling black man in the back seat of the squad car, drove to headquarters, and took him immediately to an interrogation room. They would print and photograph him later. Cassidy wanted to interrogate him as soon as possible.

Word spread through the building. By the time Holly could round up a stenographer, the Chief and two other detectives were in the room.

"Good work, Frank," the Chief said. "Must have found the weapon."

"We found a rifle," Cassidy answered. "Artie's got it. We'll know soon."

"Oh, go ahead and get started," the Chief said. "My gut says it's the murder weapon."

Watkins, still cuffed and sitting uncomfortably in a metal chair, watched silently, his eyes wide as saucers. Halfway to headquarters, Holly had finally told Watkins to stop with the 'oh, lords', or he would smack him one. Watkins had not uttered a sound since.

"Marvin," Cassidy began, "we're going to take your handcuffs off. I want you to behave. If you cause any trouble, these men are going to hurt you. Do you understand me?"

Watkins nodded that he understood.

"Do you promise to behave?"

Watkins nodded again. Holly removed the cuffs, and Watkins rubbed his wrists.

"Marvin, we found the rifle in your closet. We know you did it. Why did you kill Reverend Brown?"

"Mister, I didn't kill nobody. Like I tole you, I never seen that gun before. I doan own no gun. Never did."

Artie came in.

"Rifle checks out," Artie said.

"Thanks," Cassidy said. Artie left.

"Hear that, Marvin?" Cassidy said, turning back to face the suspect. "He said the rifle checks out. That means that a bullet he fired from that rifle matches the bullet that we took from Reverend Brown's head. That means that the rifle we just found in your closet is the same rifle that fired the bullet that killed the Reverend. Do you understand that?"

"No, sir," Marvin whined, "cause I never seen that rifle before. I didn't put it in my closet, and I never killed that Reverend or nobody else."

"Come on, Marvin. If we have to go on like this all night, these men will just get mad. Tell us now and make it easy on yourself. The rifle is the one used to kill the Reverend, and we found it in your closet. We know you did it. We just don't know why. Why did you do it, Marvin?"

"I never killed nobody, and that's the truth. Oh, lord, why won't they believe me?"

"Marvin," Cassidy said, trying a different tack. "You were late to work yesterday. Why were you late? Where were you? If you didn't do it, then tell us where you were. We'll check it out. If you were somewhere else and somebody can testify to that, then we'll believe you. Where were you? Why were you late?"

Watkins would not tell anyone that he was late because he was looking for his mother who was back on drugs. He was too ashamed. And besides, the police would arrest his mother if he told them she was a drug user. So, he said nothing.

"This is not going anywhere," the Chief said. "We've got enough. Lock him up and let him sleep on it. Maybe tomorrow, he'll tell us the truth."

"Book him, Randy," Cassidy said to Holly, who took Watkins downstairs for mug shots, finger prints, and processing into the City jail.

Cassidy found Artie in the forensic lab. "What else did you find?" Cassidy asked.

"I got a partial thumb and forefinger from two of the four bullets," Artie responded.

"Let me know," Cassidy said over his shoulder. He still wasn't sure.

Chapter 35
Saturday, June 9, 1962
9:00 AM

Cassidy was sitting at his desk, sipping a cup of black coffee, having spent the last hour grilling Watkins with all of the skill and tricks he possessed. Watkins would not break and continued to insist that he didn't commit the murder.

Artie burst into the office, startling Cassidy who spilled his coffee.

"Damn, Artie," he said, wiping up the mess.

"Sorry, but…"

"Did you match Watkins' prints with the bullets?" Cassidy interrupted. This case was getting to him. He wanted to close the file and go home to his family.

"Inconclusive," Artie said.

"What do you mean, inconclusive?"

"Lieutenant, the prints are only partials. I can't get enough points to confirm a match. Maybe the FBI can."

"Okay," Cassidy said, wearily. "I'll ask the Chief."

"Uh, Lieutenant?"

Artie again looked like he was about to wet his pants. Cassidy had a bad feeling. "Yes, Artie?"

"The bullet from Terrell and the bullet from Brown both match to the same rifle."

"What?!" Cassidy bellowed. "Are you trying to tell me that poor, ignorant cook killed a black civil rights leader AND a mafia hood from New York? Is that what you're trying to tell me?"

"All I'm saying, Lieutenant, is that the same rifle was used in both killings. That's all."

"Sorry, Artie,' Cassidy said apologetically. "It's been a rough week. Sit down."

This time, Artie accepted the invitation and took a seat in front of the desk. "How sure are you?"

"Lieutenant, I've never seen matches any closer. I need eleven points to confirm. I've got fourteen from the Brown bullet and fifteen from the other. I'd stake my life on it. Also, the FBI would confirm it, hands down."

Cassidy got up and took his cup to the coffee pot on the book case. "Coffee?" He asked Artie.

"Yes, thanks. Two sugars."

Cassidy put a cup of coffee, two sugar packets, and a stirrer on the desk in front of Artie, filled his own cup, and sat back down behind the desk. "Who else knows about this?" Cassidy asked, nonchalantly.

"Nobody," Artie answered. "I just made the match. Couldn't believe it myself."

"Artie, keep this to yourself for a while, will you? I need some time to think."

"Sure thing, Lieutenant. Thanks for the coffee."

Artie went back to the lab to tag and store the evidence. Cassidy sat at his desk, sipping his coffee. Deep in thought, he nearly spilled his coffee again when the phone rang. "Cassidy."

"Hello, Frank."

"Pop, how are you? We were going to call you tomorrow. Didn't Kevin tell you?"

"Yes, he did. He also told me about Terenzi. Frank, I'm worried about you. Terenzi was bad news. Busted him myself, twice. If this was a mob hit, you might be in danger."

"Well, this whole thing is getting weirder by the minute. I assume that you know about the murder of the Negro minister."

"Yes. It made the front page of the Times. Some Klansman did it. Your name was in the article. You're famous, son!"

"Well, maybe not. First, the Klansman didn't do it. Ballistics didn't match. Second, an anonymous tip fingered a black cook who works at the Holiday Inn across the street from the church where the black minister was shot. We found the rifle in his closet. He denies it, by the way. This time, the ballistics matched. Then, this morning, right before you called, forensics matched the bullet from the Terenzi shooting to the same rifle."

"Frank," his father asked, "are you saying that the same rifle was used in both killings?"

"Yes. I can't figure it out. What's the connection?"

"Hell if I know," his father said, laughing. "What do you think I am? A cop? Seriously, though, I'm glad to hear it."

"Glad? Why?" Cassidy asked.

"If the same weapon was used in both shootings, it means that it wasn't a professional hit, Frank. A pro would never do that. The same weapon links the two crimes. Find the link, and you narrow your search."

"But what possible link could there be between a Negro civil rights leader and a hood from New York?" Frank wondered.

"I don't know," his father said, "but there is one. You have to find it. Give my love to Rita and the kids."

"I will, Pop, and thanks. You just gave me a direction to head in. Love ya."

Cassidy pressed the button on his phone, dialed the turnkey, and asked that Watkins be returned to the interrogation room.

"Marvin," he said, sitting next to the black man. "I need your help in another investigation. Will you help me?"

"What investigation?" Watkins asked, suspicious.

"Do you know a man named Charles Terrell?"

"Doan know him," Watkins said. "Know bout him, though."

That surprised Cassidy. Why on earth would this black cook from Ansonborough know about a gangster who both lived and worked miles from Ansonborough and Watkins' world?

"What do you know about him?"

"He owns a club, called the Jaguar, I think. He's bad. He sold...he tried to sell drugs to my mother."

"You mean this Terrell personally offered to sell drugs to your mother."

"No, not him," Marvin said, becoming upset. "His people did it. I fixed it, though."

"How did you fix it? What do you mean?"

"Doan mean nothing. Just fixed it. That's all. A friend of mine...I just fixed it. That's all."

Cassidy thought for a minute.

"Do you know where the Jaguar Club is?"

"No. Somewhere uptown, I think."

"Do you know where he lives?"

"Who?" Marvin asked, confused.

"Terrell. Do you know where Terrell lives?"

"No, I don't. Where does he live?"

Cassidy checked the sheet showing Watkins's effects when he was booked. There was no driver's license.

"Marvin, do you own a car?"

"No, suh."

"Do you know how to drive?"

"No, suh. No need. Doan own no car."

"Marvin, where were you yesterday morning?"

"Why? What's this all about?" Marvin was getting very nervous.

"Marvin, this Terrell was shot yesterday morning with the same rifle we found in your apartment last night. You killed him because he sold...tried to sell drugs to your mother, didn't you?"

"No!"

"You got mad. You had to protect your mother."

"No!"

"You killed this bad man, just like you killed the minister!"

"No," Marvin screamed. "Like I tole you before. I never killed nobody. Not Terrell. Not Reverend Brown. Nobody!"

Cassidy continued the pressure, but Watkins had now shut up and would not utter another sound. After another half an hour, Cassidy had him returned to the lock-up.

Before Cassidy called the Chief at home, he had one more thing to check. He drove alone to the Holiday Inn. Cassidy sat in the dining room, sipping coffee and waiting for Rich, who arrived for work fifteen minutes later. Rich spotted the detective, walked over, and sat down at the table.

"Hello, Lieutenant. How's Marvin?"

"Hello, Mr. Newton. He's been arrested for the murder of the Negro minister."

Rich was shocked. "I can't believe that," he said. "Why would he do that?"

"I was hoping you could tell me," Cassidy responded, watching Rich.

"Me? What could I tell you?"

"Well, for instance, did he say or do anything that might lead you to believe that he was upset with the minister or the marches?"

Rich thought for a minute. "As a matter of fact," Rich began, "he did. The other night, when we seated the Negro couple, he at first refused to cook their dinner. I thought at the time that it was ironic. Here I had white waitresses who had no problem with the new decision to serve Negroes, but the Negro kitchen staff balked at serving them. On one level, I understood it, but on another level, I thought it was strange."

"Why did Watkins refuse to cook?" Cassidy asked. "What do you mean that you understood?"

"Marvin told me that he was afraid that the marchers would run off the tourists, and the hotel, or at least the restaurant, would close, which would cost him his job."

"So, that was it? He thought these marchers would cause him to lose his job?"

"Basically, yes," Rich answered, knowing that the answer was more complicated but that Cassidy was not wrong.

Cassidy was satisfied. He had motives in both killings, means because the rifle was found in Watkins's possession, and opportunity in that Watkins refused to give an alibi for his whereabouts in both instances. More than enough for a Grand Jury.

He left and returned to the station. One more thing to do and maybe he could spend the rest of the day with his family. Sammy Boutry's funeral had been yesterday. As he had promised, he had not bothered the mother or sister until the funeral was over. Now, it was time to revisit them. He rounded up Holly and headed for Ansonborough.

"Mrs. Boutry," Cassidy began, after the daughter had let them into the house, "you and your daughter remember us from last Monday, don't you?"

"Yes, Lieutenant Cassidy," the mother said. "And we promised to talk to you after the funeral. We'll keep that promise. Please sit down."

The two men sat at the dining room table, while the elderly woman poured them coffee in her best Sunday china.

"What do you want to know?" the mother asked, sitting down opposite Cassidy.

"Do you know who did this to your son?"

"Sir, we doan know for sure, and it wouldn't be Christian to falsely accuse…"

"Mother," the daughter interrupted, "the undertaker tole us how Sammy was killed. If'n you doan tell, I will!"

"Okay, Lucia," the mother said with a sigh, "I suppose you're right. Just please remember, Lieutenant, that while we might suspect—strongly suspect, we doan know for sure."

"Yes, ma'am," Cassidy said. "We would need other proof in any case. We just need to know where to begin."

"Very well," the mother said and looked off in the distance while she told her story, ashamed to look Cassidy in the eye. "Sammy was a good boy up until about two years ago. Then, he started selling drugs on the street, working for Junior Hutto."

"Who's that?" Cassidy asked.

"You mean you don't know who Junior Hutto is?" the daughter asked, truly amazed. "He only controls all of the drug traffic in all the Negro communities in Charleston. Everybody knows who he is."

"Well, ma'am," Cassidy said, turning to the daughter, "I don't work on drug cases. I handle homicide—murders, so I wouldn't know. Thanks for telling me."

Cassidy, too, wondered why he had never heard the name, if what the daughter was saying was true. "Please go on," he urged the mother.

"Well, bout three weeks ago, Sammy came home all excited. He said he was movin' up in the world, that he was now workin' for a new man—a white man name of Terrell—and that he would soon be as powerful and rich as Junior. We both warned him not to fool with Junior. Everybody know how mean Junior Hutto can be."

"Lieutenant," she continued, turning to look directly at Cassidy, "we think that Junior Hutto probably found out what Sammy was doin' and killed him for it."

"Where can I find this Junior Hutto?" Cassidy asked.

"Oh, he doan hide," the daughter sneered. "He struts all over town like his you-know-what doan stink. Has breakfast every morning over to Dave's Coffee Shop, rain or shine. It's like it was his headquarters or somethin'."

Cassidy and Holly thanked the pair and returned to police headquarters. Cassidy went to Records and requested the file on Junior Hutto. There wasn't one. He then went to talk to the vice cops. They said they had never heard of him. Cassidy and Holly then planned the arrest of Junior Hutto.

Chapter 36
Sunday, June 10, 1962
6:30 AM

Cassidy scanned the Sunday morning newspaper headlines, as he waited for the policemen to take their seats.

NEGRO COOK ARRESTED IN ASSASSINATION OF NEGRO CIVIL RIGHTS LEADER

NINE KLANSMEN ARRESTED IN WADMALAW WHIPPING—ONE STILL AT LARGE

He could imagine the discussions around Charleston's breakfast tables that morning.

"All here, Lieutenant," Holly said, taking a seat at the other end of the conference table.

"Okay," Cassidy said, standing up. "Here's what we have. Junior Hutto is a Negro about five foot eight, close cut hair, medium dark complexion, mid thirties. He will probably be accompanied by a large Negro, built like a weight lifter. Hutto is apparently a snappy dresser and wears a big, gold ring on the middle finger of his right hand. We don't expect him to be at the coffee shop when we arrive. However, Lucia Boutry, the victim's sister, has agreed to meet us there. She will go in to buy some coffee and sweet rolls. When she leaves, she will let us know if Hutto is inside or not. If he is not there, she will simply walk home. If he is there, she will "accidently" spill one cup of coffee on the sidewalk and then walk away. No one is to acknowledge her in any way. Everybody got that so far?"

The seven uniformed officers sipping the coffee and eating the doughnuts supplied by Holly nodded or grunted yes.

"If he is inside, you two will cover the back door. The rest of us will charge through the front door, guns drawn. Holly and I will take Hutto. You two take the weight lifter. You two cover everyone else in the shop. Everybody got that?" They did.

"Okay. If he isn't inside, Holly and I will go in through the rear and hide in the storeroom in the back of the restaurant. You two will still cover the rear door from the outside. You will be parked in your squad car down the block. When Hutto arrives, you will hit your siren and drive away, making sure that the sound of the siren appears to be moving away. Dispatch knows not to have any cars squealing in the area during this period. Drive around the block. When you get back, you four move to the front door. When you're ready to come in, fire one shot in the air and hit the door. Same assignments. Everybody got that?" Again, they indicated that they had it.

"Remember, these guys are extremely dangerous. However, if at all possible, I want to take Hutto alive. Okay. Let's move out."

Cassidy sat in the squad car at the end of the block with Holly and one other cop. The other cops were two blocks away in two cars. Right on time, Lucia Boutry came walking past them and entered the coffee shop. Brave girl, Cassidy thought. After a lifetime, she came out, turned to her right, and walked away. She had not spilled any coffee. Cassidy prayed that she had the signals right.

Cassidy picked up the microphone. "Hutto is not, I repeat, not inside. Holly and I are moving in. Rear entrance back-up take your positions. Everybody else stay put until you hear the signal."

Cassidy and Holly got out of the squad car and walked to the rear of the coffee shop. The door was locked. Holly picked the lock in thirty five seconds. As the back up officers moved into place, Cassidy opened the door and stepped into the dimly lit storeroom, Holly right behind him. The room was long and narrow, shelves on both sides full of canned, bottled and dry goods. A cat meowed, complaining about the intrusion. Cassidy walked as quietly as he could to the front of the storeroom, stopping at the door which led into the dining room of the coffee shop. As he was about to gently push the door ajar to get a peek at the layout, he heard the siren outside howl and then gradually fade as the squad car sped by, turned the corner, and raced off. Cassidy and Holly drew their guns and waited. It was now too risky to crack the door. They would have to go in blind, not knowing the layout of the dining room.

Cassidy waited. Where the hell were…CRACK!!

Cassidy hit the door running, gun out in front. His eyes swept the room as he ran in. He spotted the huge weight lifter first. The smaller black man next to him must be Hutto, he decided. Cassidy ran up to the two men, who were still trying to comprehend what was going on with cops coming in from two directions. He crouched in front of Hutto and leveled his gun at him.

"Freeze!! Cassidy shouted.

The huge weight lifter lunged at Cassidy. Holly intercepted him and altered his path. The two men crashed into a table, knocking it and two chairs across the room. Cassidy remained still, his gun pointed at Hutto, who was standing frozen about three feet away.

Two cops ran to help Holly. One of them hit the huge man as hard as he could over the head with his night stick. The blow didn't appear to faze the weight lifter, who grabbed Holly around the neck and lifted him off the floor, choking him. The cop hit the huge man again, harder, breaking the night stick. The blow only made the large man madder.

Holly, gasping for air, drew his weapon, put the barrel against his assailant, and shot the huge man five times in the stomach. Ever so slowly, the grip loosened, and Holly finally fell free, almost blacking out. The large man fell over backwards, completely demolishing a table and landed on the floor, bleeding to death.

When Holly fired his weapon, a black man sitting at one of the tables drew a gun and shot one of the cops, whose attention was momentarily diverted to Holly. The cop's partner shot the black man with the gun and in his anger, also shot the other black man sitting beside him. He then finished off both men.

Cassidy never took his eyes or gun off of Hutto. Slowly, Cassidy walked forward.

"On your knees," he said to Hutto. He could tell that Hutto was weighing the odds. "ON YOUR KNEES!! NOW!!" Cassidy shouted.

Holly, rubbing his throat with one hand, walked towards Hutto from a different angle, his gun also pointing at Hutto's head.

Hutto slowly sank to his knees. As Cassidy and Holly kept their guns on Hutto, a third cop came up behind him. He took Hutto by the left wrist and pulled his left arm down behind him. He handcuffed Hutto's left wrist to his right ankle. Then, he took his right arm down and, using a second pair of handcuffs, cuffed his right wrist to his left ankle. Hutto was immobilized.

Cassidy and Holly holstered their weapons, as one of the cops went out to a squad car to call an ambulance for the wounded cop. He then called the M E. James would have to haul three bodies away.

Holly and another cop picked Hutto up by his armpits, carried him outside, and tossed him into the back seat of one of the squad cars. A cop got in the back seat with Hutto and pointed a shotgun at his head, as they transported him to headquarters.

Hutto was strip searched, photographed, finger printed, and booked. Dressed in prison grey with handcuffs and leg irons, he was brought to a small interrogation room, where Cassidy, Holly, a stenographer, and two other policemen were waiting for him. Hutto, hands still cuffed behind his back, sat stiffly in a metal chair.

"What's your name?" Cassidy asked. Hutto sat silent. Cassidy lit a cigarette, sat down across the table from Hutto, and crossed his legs. "I can stay here all day," Cassidy said, sipping a cup of hot coffee. "If you want to get out of those cuffs and leg irons, you had better start talking. Otherwise, you are going to get very uncomfortable, not to mention hungry and thirsty. Now, what's your name?"

"Hutto," he spat. "Junior Hutto."

"Where do you live?" Hutto gave his address.

"Where were you last Sunday night, about midnight?"

"I don't remember," the prisoner sneered.

"Well, let me help you out. You and your large friend were near Hampton Park, murdering Sammy Boutry. What I want to know is why."

"You find a rat in your house, what do you do?" Hutto answered. "I was exterminating. He was a drug dealer. Why do you give a shit?"

"I didn't ask you what you did," Cassidy said, softly. "I asked you why you did it."

"I tole you. He was a rat. He broke the rules. What's this town gonna turn into if'n we let everybody walk around breakin' the rules?"

"Okay," Cassidy said. "Let me tell you why you did it. You discovered that Sammy Boutry was selling drugs from another source. You tortured him to find out who it was. He told you it was Charles Terrell. Then, you finished the job. Actually, you had your friend do it. I don't think you have the guts to do it yourself."

"Wrong, Cop!" Hutto shouted. "Take off these cuffs, and I'll do you like I did Sammy with my bare hands!"

Suddenly, alarm bells went off in Cassidy's head. He had a terrible hunch. "Junior, do you know Marvin Watkins?"

"Yeah, I know him."

Cassidy motioned to Holly, who walked over to Cassidy. Cassidy whispered something in Holly's ear. Holly left the room.

"Tell me about him," Cassidy said, turning back to face Hutto.

"Who?" Hutto asked.

"Watkins."

"What's he got to do with this?"

"Humor me," Cassidy said. "Tell me about Marvin."

"Good guy," Hutto answered. "Helped my brother out once."

"So, you paid him back by selling drugs to his mother."

"Never!" Hutto insisted. "My people never did that. It was Terrell's people, probably Sammy, who sold drugs to Marvin's mother. Not me. Not anybody who worked for me."

"What makes you think Terrell's people sold drugs to Marvin's mother?"

"Marvin tole me. Came looking for me. He was crazy mad. Then, he went looking for his mama."

"Did he find her?"

"Doan think so," Hutto answered. "He was still looking for her Friday morning. Saw him myself."

"I'll be right back," Cassidy said. "Cuff his left wrist to the table leg and give him a smoke."

"Thanks." Cassidy heard Hutto say, as he went into the next room down the hall. Marvin Watkins was sitting there next to Holly.

"Marvin," Cassidy began. "Junior Hutto is in the next room. He told me about your mother. He says you've been looking everywhere for her. Why didn't you tell me about that?"

"He's lying!" Watkins shouted, tears streaming down his cheeks.

"No, Marvin," Cassidy said calmly, "you're the one whose been lying—lying to protect your mother, I suspect. Marvin, these charges against you are very serious. You could spend the rest of your life in prison. Unless you start telling me the truth, you WILL spend the rest of your life in jail. Do you want to go to jail?"

"No, suh," Watkins said, looking down at his feet.

"You have been lying to me, haven't you?"

"Yes, suh."

"Okay. Let's tell the truth now. Why were you late to work on Thursday?"

"I was lookin' for my mama. I had to run three blocks."

"And where were you Friday morning?"

"Looking for mama. I finally found her. She was bad. I had to take her to Roper Hospital."

Cassidy glanced at Holly, who left the room to call the hospital.

"Who told you about Terrell?"

"Junior."

"Did you tell Junior that you were upset about the marches?"

"No, I doan think…No, that ain't right. Yes, suh. I did."

"When?"

"Lemme see. Wednesday, I think. Yeah, it was Wednesday. That's the first day I went looking for Mama. That's when Junior tole me 'bout Terrell."

"What time did you drive your Mama to the hospital?"

"Didn't drive her. I don't know how to drive. Had to take a cab. It was early. I found her about six thirty or seven."

Holly returned to the room. "Hospital says he brought his mother into emergency on Friday at six forty eight AM. She was in a bad way. Real strung out. She stayed in emergency until about eleven and was then admitted. The nurse says that Watkins stayed with her the entire time she was in emergency and left only when she was taken to a room."

"Marvin, you would have saved us a lot of time, if you had told me about this Friday night. Randy, take him back to his cell."

Cassidy went back into the other interrogation room. "Junior," he said, again sitting down opposite Hutto, "I think you killed Charles Terrell and framed Watkins for the murder."

Hutto became very nervous. One black man killing another black man was one thing, but a black man accused of killing a white man was a different matter. He would never make it to jail alive. "No, suh," he insisted. "I ain't never killed no white man. Sure, I killed Sammy. Good riddance. But I didn't kill Terrell."

"If you didn't, who did? You're the one with the motive. You control the drugs in the Negro community, and he was moving in on your territory. He was going to put you out of business."

"No, suh." Hutto was becoming agitated. "I don't control nothin'. I work for the man. He's the one with the control. Maybe he killed Terrell. He asked me about Terrell. I tole him. That's all."

"Who is the man?" Cassidy asked softly.

"Danny Costellano."

"What else do you know about Costellano?"

"Owns the High Hat. Asked me about Terrell. Man, he was mad as hell. Said he'd take care of it. Said somethin' about how this wasn't supposed to happen."

"What wasn't supposed to happen?"

"Somebody else selling drugs in Charleston."

"What did that mean?"

"I doan know. He just said it. That's all."

"What else do you know?"

"Nothin'. Nothin' else."

"Book him for the murder of Sammy Boutry," he said to one of the cops.

Cassidy went back to his office, poured himself a cup of coffee, and reviewed what he knew. He now believed that Watkins had been framed. If he didn't kill Terenzi, then he didn't kill Brown, since the same weapon and presumably the same shooter committed both crimes. It made sense that Costellano, if he did in fact control the drugs in Charleston, killed Terenzi, or at least had him killed. But now, the other problem re-emerged. Why would Costellano, a drug lord, kill a civil rights leader? It made no sense.

Chapter 37
Day 7—Sunday
2:00 PM

June came running up from the surf, her wet hair streaming down her back, and plopped down on the blanket. Rich almost hurt every time he looked at her. She wasn't strikingly beautiful, just very pretty with a body that was perfectly proportioned and skin that seemed perpetually lightly tanned. And she was lighthearted with a perpetually positive attitude.

But not today. Today, she was quiet, almost withdrawn. Rich was scared that maybe she was tiring of him and their relationship, 'falling out of love' if there was such a thing. When am I going to learn? He thought to himself. When his father had died, he had promised himself not to become vulnerable again, and here he had gone and let June into his heart in less than a year.

"Rich," she said, turning over on her back and staring up at the sky, "there's something I want to talk to you about."

His heart went into his throat. "What is it?" he asked lightly, trying to hide his fear that she was about to dump him.

"I don't know how to start," she said, still studying the clouds.

"Just say it," he said.

"Well, it's about something Peaches told me last night."

"What? Peaches? What do you mean?" He had hardly heard her.

"Last night she told me something that she asked me to keep secret, but now I want to tell you about it. I feel I have to tell you."

"Well," he began, trying to be serious and not signal his considerable relief. "You have to use your judgment. I get the idea this is serious."

"Yes, it's serious. Okay. Here goes. Sometimes, between lunch and dinner,

Peaches and Mr. Howe get together in his office and…well, I guess they do the same thing that you and I do in my apartment." She giggled.

"Well, I know that what you and I do is make love," Rich responded. "I think that what they are doing is something else."

June flipped over and kissed Rich very hard and long. "I do love you, Rich Newton. You're right. What we do is different."

She lay back down on her back. "Anyway, that's not what I have to tell you. Last night, at the High Hat, she told me that they got together on Friday. After they had sex, Howe started drinking and smoking marijuana. After he got high, he started bragging to Peaches that he had killed two men in two days. When Peaches laughed and accused him of kidding, he suddenly got mad, as if…how did she put it…like she was questioning his manhood. He insisted that it was true. Peaches got very scared. She still is."

Two men in two days, Rich thought. Jesus, he might be talking about the Negro Reverend and that other shooting that he had heard about from the cops who drank coffee in the restaurant while waiting for the marches to start.

"June," he said, sitting up. "I think we better tell this to Lieutenant Cassidy. What do you think?"

"You really think so? I don't want to get Peaches in trouble."

"I think she may be in danger," Rich answered. "Also, if this is what I think it might be, I know a Negro cook who is sitting in jail for something he didn't do."

"If you think we should tell him, then let's go." June stood.

Rich gathered the beach blanket, and they walked to the car. Rich found a pay phone, took Cassidy's card from his wallet, looked on the back where Cassidy had written his home number, and dialed. "Hello," Rita Cassidy answered.

"This is Rich Newton, Mrs. Cassidy," Rich said. "Is the Lieutenant home?"

"Yes, just a second."

"Cassidy."

"Lieutenant, this is Rich Newton. I might have some important information about the shootings."

"What is…Did you say shootings—plural?"

"Yes, I did. It's a little crazy, but I think you better hear it."

"I think we'd better talk about this in person," Cassidy said, suddenly not sure that his phone was safe. He knew that Mafia money could open doors, even at the phone company. "Where are you?"

"Folly Beach," Rich answered.

"You know Bootle's?" Bootle's was a popular drive-in restaurant near Cassidy's house.

"Yes."

"Meet me there. I'll be waiting."

Fifteen minutes later, Rich and June drove up to Bootle's. Rich ordered two barbecue hot dogs and Cokes, as Cassidy walked over and got in the back seat. After Rich introduced June, she told Cassidy the story.

Cassidy sat and thought, while Rich and June ate their sandwiches.

"Do you think you can convince Peaches to talk to me?" Cassidy asked June.

"Rich thinks that she might be in danger. Do you think that, too?" she asked.

"I agree with Rich. There have been three killings in the last week that I think are all connected. If what Howe told Peaches is true, then he is in this up to his…neck. But, before I can do anything, I have to hear the story from her."

"Okay," June said. "I'll try."

"Good girl," Cassidy said. "Let's do this. Rich, can you pick June and Peaches up at the Colonial Steakhouse tomorrow after the lunch shift?"

"Yes," Rich said. "I usually pick June up anyway, so that wouldn't look odd."

"Good. You pick them up and take them to…let's see…"

"How about my apartment?" June offered.

"Good," Cassidy said. "Your apartment will do fine."

June gave Cassidy her address, and he went back to his car.

Cassidy was so engrossed in his attempt to assimilate this new information, information which was only deepening his confusion about this case, that he nearly hit the strange car that was parked in his driveway. He became alarmed when he noticed the New York plates.

"Frank!" Rita said. "Look who's here!"

Cassidy took his hand off his gun handle under his jacket and hugged his father and brother, who were standing in his kitchen drinking a beer.

"What are you guys…"

"Frank," his father interrupted. "Good to see you. Why don't you get a beer and let's go out back and light off the barbecue. We brought some steaks down from New York. Figured you couldn't get good meat down here in the sticks."

"You damn Yankee," Frank laughed, as he went to get a beer. Obviously, whatever this was about, his father wanted to discuss it in private. The three men, beers in hand, went into the backyard.

"We got worried," Kevin said, as Frank poured charcoal onto the grill. "After Pop told me about your conversation yesterday, I made a few calls. Apparently, the Gambino family has controlled the drug traffic in Charleston for fifteen years. Now, the Genovese family is trying to move in."

"Gambino? Genovese?" Frank didn't believe what he was hearing. "This is Charleston, not Canarsie. We don't have that kind of stuff down here."

"See, Pop," Kevin said, kidding his brother. "A crack detective. He's got the mob crawling all over his town, and he doesn't even know it."

"Pop," Frank said. "Is he serious?"

"Dead serious, Frankie. That's why we came down. Knowing how these wise guys operate, some of your city officials may also be involved. We thought you might need some help."

"Now, that I don't believe," Frank insisted. "Sure, with our crazy liquor laws, there's probably a little bit of graft going on, but it doesn't amount to a hill of beans. But drugs? I don't believe it!"

"Okay, Frank," his father said, soothingly. "Maybe you're right. Anyway, here we are and Kevin already put in for a few days vacation, so...do you want some help from a couple of damn good detectives?"

"Yeah," Frank said, "I sure do. I could really use some help on this one."

"Good," his father said. "Get me another beer, and let's get started." Frank fetched three beers and briefed his father and brother on the events of the past week, concluding with the story he had just heard from June.

"It just doesn't make sense," Frank concluded. "If Costellano fingered Terenzi, why did Howe do the shooting? Second, who wanted Brown dead? Costellano or Howe? And why? What was the motive?"

"Let's take it one step at a time," Kevin began. "It makes sense that Costellano wanted to hit Terenzi. If Howe did the deed, then Costellano has something on Howe or Howe is connected to the drug operation somehow. From what you told us about Howe, my money says Costellano's got something on him. But why Brown?"

"Why did they shoot him on Thursday?" The father mused.

"What?" Frank asked.

"Why did they shoot the Negro minister on Thursday?" his father repeated. "Why not Wednesday or Friday? Why Thursday?"

"I don't know," Frank answered. "Probably no particular reason."

"But you don't know," his father persisted. "Maybe you have some more questions to ask. What was he going to say in that press conference?"

"Okay," Frank relented. "I'll ask—first thing tomorrow morning."

"Good," his father said. "Perfect timing," he shouted as Rita and the kids came out of the house, carrying the steaks. "I'm starved."

Chapter 38
Monday, June 11, 1962
8:00 AM

Cassidy was sitting in the front pew of the AME Church when Shine Rivers came in through a side door from the parking lot.

"Good mornin', Lieutenant," Shine said.

"Good morning, Reverend. How's your back?"

"Oh, it sometimes stings a little. Otherwise, it's okay. What can we do for you?"

"Can we get the others together? That Council?"

"Sure. C'mon. They're probably all waitin' in the back."

Cassidy followed Rivers into the classroom in the rear of the church. "Good morning, gentlemen," Cassidy said. Some of them looked at each other in wonderment. It was the first time in their lives that a white man had referred to them as 'gentlemen'. "I know you have a busy morning, so I'll try to be brief. I need your help."

"What can we do, Lieutenant?" Reverend Lyle asked.

"I'm trying to determine if there is any significance to the timing of Reverend Brown's murder," Cassidy explained.

"Well," Lyle said, "he always came out the same time everyday to have his press conference, so I imagine that's what determined the timing." Lyle thought it was a strange question.

"That's not what I mean, Reverend," Cassidy said patiently. "We know why it happened in the early afternoon after the march. I am wondering whether or not there was any reason why it happened on Thursday rather than, say, Wednesday or Friday. Was there anything different about Thursday?"

"I cain't think of anything," Lyle began.

"I can," Rivers interrupted. "That's the day Jab was gonna talk about the drugs and numbers. Remember? You see, Lieutenant, before Thursday, he would talk about the same subject in the press conference that he had talked about during the march. That day, though, he changed and talked about the burning of the cross at the church during the march, but he still planned to talk about drugs and numbers in the press conference. Said it probably worked out for the best. He thought it would get a bigger impact. So, he put out the word that the press conference topic would be different and very important."

"What was he going to say?" Cassidy asked.

"Reverend Lyle can probably explain it better'n me," Rivers said.

He looked over a Lyle who was frowning and motioning for Rivers to explain.

"As Reverend Lyle explained to Jab, there are drugs and numbers all over the Negro neighborhoods here in the city. The drugs sap our people of their drive and hope and both the drugs and the numbers suck the money out of the Negro areas—money that could be spent at the Negro businesses. Yet, the police doan seem to do anything to stop it. They just turn their heads, so long as the drugs stay out of the white community. That's what he was goin' to say, I think. Isn't that right, Reverend Lyle?"

Lyle nodded in the affirmative, a solemn look on his face.

Cassidy had part of his connection. If such a story had been printed in the northern papers, it would have brought tremendous pressure to bear on the local authorities to focus on a problem they had been ignoring. That was Costellano's motive. Now, he had to link Howe to Costellano. He thanked the assembled ministers and drove home to confer with his father and brother.

"Let me be sure I have this right," Frank's father said after Frank's briefing on his meeting at the church. "You arrested this Junior Hutto who you now believe heads up an organization of young Negroes who sell and control the distribution of all kinds of illegal drugs as well as numbers in the Negro community. Yet you, a detective in the police force, have never heard of him. Moreover, there is no jacket on him at the station, and the vice cops say they don't know his name. Now, the Negro community leaders say that the drug traffic is widespread in their communities but is withheld from the white community. Then, they tell you that the minister who was shot was about to blow this story open with the northern press. That's when he was shot. Is that about right?"

"Yes, that's right," Frank said, sipping his coffee.

"Tell me what you know about this Howe," his father asked, continuing to pace in Frank's kitchen, while Kevin sat next to Frank at the breakfast table, taking notes.

"Let's see. He owns the Colonial Steakhouse Restaurant, one of the better, upscale restaurants in town. His wife is society. Her sister is married to Gedney Middleton, a prominent lawyer from an old Charleston family and the President of the Ashley Cooper Society, which is THE men's society in town. All the power brokers are members. Howe's daughter made her debut last month."

"So, you can't just go and investigate this guy without clearing it with your Chief. Right?"

"Right," Frank agreed.

"Good," his father said, taking a seat opposite Frank. "The more I hear, the more I think that this isn't a case of apathy by the authorities. I think something smells. Frankie, I suggest that you go see your Chief, now, and lay the whole case as you now know it on the table. If he supports your theories and turns you loose to discretely investigate Howe and Costellano, he's in the clear. But if he calls you off, my money says you've got a problem here with at least high level protection if not high level involvement and corruption."

"Okay," Frank agreed. "I hope you're wrong, but I see your point."

"I hope I'm wrong, too, Frank, because I know what you'll do, and I don't want that pain and agony for you."

Frank Cassidy drove to police headquarters and briefed the Chief, using the elaborate and detailed flow chart that he, his father, and his brother had drawn up to explain what they believed had actually happened the previous week.

"Frank, here's what your story and this chart tell me," the Chief began. "First, we have a suspect in custody for the shootings of Brown and Terrell. The confirmed murder weapon for both shootings was found in his home, wiped free of prints. He refused to give an alibi until you suggested one."

Frank began to protest, but the Chief held up his hand to stop him.

"Let me finish. Then, you arrest this Junior Hutto, evidently a notorious drug dealer, for the murder of Boutry. He doesn't deny killing another black man. But when you suggest that you might charge him with the Terrell murder, the murder of a white man, he panics and tries to cut a deal by implicating Costellano. We have no other evidence to implicate Costellano in these murders than the statement of a self-admitted, drug dealing nigra murderer. Who do you think a white jury will believe? As for the theory that Costellano had Brown killed because he was about to talk about drugs, that was a threat to Hutto more than anyone else, assuming that he or anybody else, except those nigra ministers, knew in advance what Brown was going to say. You have no indication that anyone else, much less Hutto, knew that. But assuming he did, I would sooner accept the theory that Hutto encouraged Watkins, who they both admit were friends, to make the hit. Finally, based on hearsay evidence about what a known hooker said, you are ready to accuse one of Charleston's most prominent citizens of murdering two people in the last five days, and you have no motive or link to anyone. That's what I heard."

The Chief walked around his desk and sat down. "Frank, you are my best detective, but I can't support you on this one. The ink is hardly dry on the headline that says Watkins killed Brown. We have everything we need to indict and probably convict him. The rest of your theory wouldn't make it past the DA. You've done very good work. Book Hutto for Boutry's murder and spend some time with your family. You've solved three murders and one whipping in one week. Take some time off. You deserve it."

Cassidy was feeling a mixture of emotions, anger, disappointment, and resignation that his father was right. Deep down, he had probably felt, ever since his father had first mentioned it, that he might be right. But he had tried to write it off to the fact that his father's police experience had been in New York, where such high level corruption, fueled by Mafia money, was commonplace. He had hoped—no, prayed—that Charleston was different. Now, he knew it wasn't. He felt betrayed, but most of all, he was angry.

He revealed none of these emotions to the Chief sitting across the desk from him, whom he now regarded as a bad guy—one of them. He thanked the Chief for his time and left. He drove home to plan his next moves, which would begin with the afternoon meeting with Peaches.

Chapter 39
Day 8—Monday
3:00 PM

Peaches was nervous and uncertain about telling the police what she knew. June finally convinced her to come with her and Rich and listen to the detective. If she didn't want to talk after hearing what he had to say, she didn't have to. Peaches reluctantly agreed. All three were quiet as Rich drove the two young women to June's apartment. Neither he nor June wanted to say anything which might spook Peaches. Cassidy was waiting outside in his car as they drove up. Rich introduced Peaches to the detective, and they all went into June's apartment.

As June went to the kitchen for some Cokes, Cassidy invited Peaches to sit down on the couch. He took a seat in a chair next to her. Rich sat at the opposite end of the couch.

"Peaches," Cassidy began in as gentle a voice as he could muster, "you now know that June and Rich told me what you told June about Howe. Please don't be mad at them. They told me because they were worried about you—worried that you might be in danger because of what you know. I believe they are right to be worried. If what I understand Howe told you was true, he has killed two people. He won't hesitate to kill again, if he thinks you might be a danger to him. And it won't matter whether or not you tell me anything. He might feel in danger because you might tell. Do you understand?"

"Yes," Peaches said so softly that Cassidy, sitting less than two feet from her, could barely hear her.

"We can protect you," Cassidy went on, "but I have to hear what happened and what you heard directly from you. Hearing it from June and Rich is hearsay evidence, and that's not enough for me to go after a man as powerful as Howe. I need to hear it from you—everything you know. Will you tell me?"

"Maybe I should," she said, a little louder this time. "I'm not mad at June or Preacher, I mean Rich. It's just that I don't like snitches, and I don't want to be one. But…, Mr. Howe got really mad when I didn't believe him at first. I never saw him so mad. Maybe he would hurt me."

June handed Peaches a Coke. "Thanks," Peaches said to June. She looked back towards Cassidy. "Like I told June, it was last Friday. After I finished cleaning up the dishes from the POETS Club meeting, I came into his office, like I usually do. He was really horny, so we had sex. Man, was he ready. After we finished, he refilled his drink—that's when I knew he had been drinking before I came in—and lit a joint. He offered me one, but I said no. I don't do drugs. I did have a drink, though. The marijuana hit him almost immediately. Maybe it was because of the booze. Anyway, he started bragging about how good our sex had been, taking the credit for his manhood. He said he felt more like a man than he had since the Marines. Then, he said it—that maybe it was because he had killed two men, one that morning and one the day before. He said his adrenalin hadn't stopped running yet. I laughed and told him to stop joking. That's when he got mad and told me—no, he shouted—that it wasn't a joke. He even showed me the rifle he said he used. It was right there in the office. That's when I got scared. I calmed him down. Then, I got out of there."

"He showed you the rifle?" Cassidy asked, taking notes.

"Yes. He asked me if I wanted to hold it—the rifle, I mean. I said no."

"Can you describe the rifle?"

"No. I don't think so. It was just a rifle with one of those telescope things on it. He said it was his sniper rifle from the Marines—that he had been the best shot in his company and it looked like he still was."

"Would you recognize the rifle if you saw it again?"

"Maybe."

"Peaches, thanks," Cassidy said. "I know that wasn't easy. Now, I need to ask you some questions. Okay?"

"Sure," Peaches said, taking a cigarette from her handbag. Cassidy produced a lighter.

"Do you know if Howe has any connection to Danny Costellano?"

"Sure. Last winter, Mr. Howe had some financial problems. They were really bothering him. That was the first time we had sex. Anyway, I introduced him to Danny. Danny loaned him enough money to solve his problem. Danny did it because I asked him to. Danny's a good guy."

"Yeah, a good guy," Cassidy mumbled under his breath. "Do you know how much money Danny loaned to Howe?"

"Not exactly. I think it was around forty or fifty thousand."

"Do you know if Howe paid the money back?"

"I don't think so. I think he had a year to pay Danny back, vig and all."

Cassidy knew that 'vig' meant vigorish, a New York term for the interest paid to a loan shark. "Why didn't he borrow the money from his brother-in-law?" Cassidy asked.

"I'm not sure. Maybe he was worried that his wife would find out. I don't think he told his wife very much. It's funny that you should mention it. Mr. Middleton was there that day."

"What day?"

"Friday. Last Friday. In fact, the POETS Club met everyday last week. They usually meet on only Friday."

"Gedney Middleton is a member of this POETS Club?"

"Yes. I think he's the President—that is, if they have a leader. At least, he pays the bill."

"What is the POETS Club?"

"I don't know. I just know that they come in the back door, in small groups of one or two. They leave the same way—the back door one or two at a time."

"Do you know who all the members are?"

"Yes, sir." She gave the names, including the two police chiefs.

"What do they discuss?"

"They usually don't talk about anything important when I'm in the room, taking their orders or serving the food. They pour their own drinks, so they are mostly alone in there. But I have to stand outside by the door after they first come in so I can hear when they are ready to order. Sometimes, when they raise their voices, I can hear what they are saying. Last week, they raised their voices a lot. Mostly, it was about the marches and what they could do about it. Mr. Middleton got really mad the day after the Klan beat that poor nigra man."

Cassidy sat back and thought for quite a while. Peaches sat quietly and sipped her Coke. "Do you know where Howe is right now?" he asked.

"No, I don't. He left about one and said he wouldn't be back today or tonight. I've never known him to do that before. Ever since I've been there, he's been there every night...Except of course Sundays."

"Okay," Cassidy said. "Thanks again. You've been very helpful. I suggest that you go back to the restaurant tonight for your normal shift. Otherwise, if he's there and you don't show, he might get worried. Did he act differently towards you at any time since Friday?"

"No. I don't think so."

"Okay. We'll try to find him and pick him up. In the meantime, you should keep your normal routine."

Cassidy left and drove to Howe's home on the Battery. Mrs. Howe told him that Howe had driven to Columbia on business earlier that afternoon and would not be back until very late that night. Cassidy told her it was nothing important, that he had to ask Howe some routine questions about a former employee. He would stop by in the morning. He then drove home for another strategy session with his father and brother. Except for them, Frank Cassidy was now on his own.

Chapter 40
Tuesday, June 12, 1962
8:00 AM

While his father was taking a shower, Frank went out to retrieve the morning paper from the front yard. He knew that his father could not drink his morning coffee without a newspaper to read. Besides, Cassidy wanted to see if there was any more coverage of the past week's events. Walking back up the steps, he noticed another newspaper, folded over, on his front porch. When he picked it up, a dead flounder fell out onto the porch.

Cassidy froze and then turned and looked up and down the street. Seeing nothing unusual or out of place, he picked up the fish, put it back inside the second paper, and went into the house. He put the paper on the table in front of his brother and flipped the fold back.

"On the porch," he said softly.

"Shit," Kevin said, looking at what was clearly a Mafia warning to back off. "What are you going to do?"

"What is that?" Rita asked, bringing the coffee pot to pour Frank a cup.

"It's a Mafia warning," Frank said. He had always been honest with Rita. He knew no other way to have a relationship.

She sat down in a chair and poured two cups of coffee, one for Frank and the other for herself. "What are we going to do now?" she asked.

"I want you to pack some things for yourself and the kids," Frank answered. "You can fly to New York and stay with Mom until this thing blows over."

Frank's father walked into the kitchen. "What's up?" he asked.

"This," Kevin said, pointing to the fish. "On the front porch."

"I think that Rita and the kids should fly to New York and stay with Mom," Frank said to his father.

"I agree," his father said. "She'll be thrilled."

"There's another option," Rita said. "Why not give it up, Frank. It's not your fight. Anyway, maybe the warning was for you, not us."

"I can't, Rita. You know that. Unless I do something, they'll crucify Watkins, and these scum bags will walk. I can't let that happen."

"I know," she sighed. "It was worth a try, though. I don't want to go to New York. No offense, Pop. Under different circumstances, of course we would love to see Mom. But I don't want to be that far away from Frank. I do agree we should leave town, though, so Frank won't have to look over his shoulder, concerned about us. Besides, if the Mafia wants to find us, they might figure out to look at Pop's house. And they have a lot of people in New York to look. Frank, we can go to my sister's in Orangeburg. It's close, and I doubt if they know or can find out about her."

"She's got a point," Frank said to his father, amazed at his wife's calm, clear thinking in such a situation.

"Okay," his father said, "but they should get going as soon as possible."

Frank tried to assure his wife that he would be alright. It was safe to assume that nobody knew his father and brother were with him, so he had more help and back-up than the opposition (whoever they were) knew about.

Within an hour, Rita and the kids were driving towards the Interstate Highway which would take them to Orangeburg about an hour away. Kevin followed them until they were clear of Charleston and well on their way.

Frank drove alone to Howe's house, only to learn that he had called home the previous night and changed his plans. He had stayed in Columbia and would return to Charleston sometime that day.

Frank drove to headquarters to put in an appearance. He called his father, and they planned their next move. Frank thanked the Chief for the offer of taking a few days off, telling him he had decided that it was a good idea. He would be back on Thursday or Friday. Chief Wall was glad he was taking the time and told him to take a week, if he wished. Frank dropped by Forensics and got copies of the prints Artie had lifted from the bullets found in the rifle used to kill Brown and Terrell. He also got a photograph of the rifle. There wasn't a rap sheet on either Howe or Costellano.

He was on his way out when the phone rang. "Frank!" Watson called out. "It's for you—a Rich Newton." Frank Cassidy retraced his steps and walked into his office to take the call. He glanced at the clock on his desk, as he walked around it. Almost noon.

Chapter 41
Day 9—Tuesday
11:15 AM

June couldn't remember when Peaches had been any later than eleven. She had already called Peaches' number three times in the last fifteen minutes. No answer.

June made up her mind. She walked out the front door of the Colonial Steakhouse, hailed the cab that was dropping off the day cashier, and went to Peaches' apartment. When Peaches didn't answer her knock, June let herself in with the key she still had in her purse from the time when she roomed with Peaches.

The apartment was messy; not dirty, but not straightened up. June knew that Peaches was a stickler for leaving the apartment neat. At first, June thought that she was just a very neat person. Later, after she learned what Peaches was, she figured that Peaches never knew when she might be bringing someone back, so she wanted to be sure that the place was neat. Whatever the reason, today, the apartment did not look right.

"Peaches!" June called out. No answer. Then, June noticed that no lights were on. Peaches always left the lamp on the table near the front window lit when she left.

June made the gruesome discovery in the bathroom. Peaches was nude, lying in a half-filled bath tub, a needle protruding from her left arm. June leaned over and put her right ear against Peaches' chest between and slightly above her breasts. Nothing.

June was pretty sure she was dead. Yet her skin was warm. June realized that Peaches couldn't have been dead very long. Suddenly, she wondered if the killer was still in the apartment, and she became frightened. As quietly as she could, she walked back into the bedroom, sat on the edge of the bed, picked up the phone, and dialed the Holiday Inn restaurant.

"Holiday Inn," she heard. Thank God, she thought. It was Rich. No need for stupid explanations.

"Rich," she whispered. "I'm at Peaches' apartment. She's dead. I'm worried that the killer might still be here. What should I do?"

"June? Is that you?" Rich asked. "I can hardly hear you. Speak up."

"Rich, I can't," June whispered only slightly louder. "Can you hear me now?"

"Yes, I can," he said. "Did you say you were at Peaches?"

"Yes. She's dead, and I'm not sure if maybe the killer is still here."

Rich heard her that time. He thought furiously, not knowing the layout of Peaches apartment. "Is there a back door?" Rich asked.

"No."

"Can you get out of a window where you are?"

"Yes, I think so."

"Okay," Rich said. "If you can, go ahead. I'll wait here for ten minutes. If I don't hear from you, I'll assume you made it out okay. I'll meet you at the corner of Coming and Smith Streets in front of the Alpha fraternity house."

"Okay," June whispered and hung up. She tiptoed around the bed to the window, which was slightly ajar. She was able to raise the window all the way without making a racket. She climbed through the window, dropped to the ground, and ran as fast as she could to the place Rich had said he would meet her.

Rich had glanced at his watch when June hung up. He pulled Cassidy's card from the drawer of the menu stand and called. After telling Cassidy what June had said and where he planned to meet her, he hung up. The second the ten minutes were up, Rich took off running for the parking lot.

After his short conversation with Rich, Cassidy called Artie and Carleton James, asking both to meet him at Peaches' apartment. He picked up the copies of the fingerprints and the photo of the rifle and walked calmly and casually out of the headquarters.

Cassidy, the Forensics van, and the Coroner all converged on the apartment at the same time, lights flashing and sirens wailing. If the perpetrator had not already left, he should be doing so now, if he had any sense.

When Cassidy saw Peaches' body, he wasn't sure if it was an unintentional overdose, suicide, or murder. Her face was all made up, like she was going out to dinner or something, not like she was going to work. Artie took some photographs and was carefully removing the needle from her arm when June and Rich came in.

"Do you think she committed suicide?" Cassidy asked them, primarily asking June.

"Absolutely not," June insisted. "I've known her for nearly a year. I even lived here for a while. I never saw her so much as smoke a joint, much less snort or shoot up. You heard what she said yesterday. She doesn't do drugs. I believe that."

Dr. James was examining Peaches' body very closely.

"Pure, uncut horse," Artie said after analyzing a minute amount of the contents of the syringe. "If she took what's missing in the syringe, she took enough to kill a horse three times. Whadda ya think, Doc?"

"I think, Artie, that she was murdered, that she was hit over the head—here—hard enough to knock her out and then her killer injected what you are saying is pure, uncut heroin into her arm. Frank, I'd say she has been dead about a couple of hours—maybe less, surely no more. I can be more specific when I get her on the table. I'll look again, but I can't find any evidence of injections other than the one that killed her, not in her arms, her legs, beneath her nails, or any of the places that some people hope will not be detected. If she did take drugs, she didn't inject them. This will be a popular autopsy. Standing room only in the amphitheater," he said, as his assistants lifted the body from the tub and placed it on the gurney.

"Was Howe at the restaurant when you left?" Cassidy asked.

"Yes, he was," June answered. "He had just arrived, maybe a few minutes after eleven. Do you think he did this?"

"What do you think?" Cassidy asked, not expecting an answer. "I would at least like to know where he was between ten and eleven this morning."

Cassidy, after determining that the phone had already been dusted, called his home and spoke to his father and brother. The plan was in place. Cassidy waited about ten minutes and then drove to the Colonial Steakhouse. Cassidy showed his badge and ID to the man standing behind the counter next to the cash register.

"I'd like to speak with Mr. Howe," Cassidy asked.

"I'm Bob Howe, Lieutenant," Howe said, walking around the counter and extending his hand. "Come on into the office. My wife said you'd been around. Something about some questions about Marvin Watkins?"

Cassidy walked into the office after Howe and closed the door. "Actually, I'm here about another matter," Cassidy said. "One of your employees, a Peaches Parker, was found dead in her apartment a few minutes ago. I'll need to see your personnel file on her. We need to notify her relatives."

"Peaches dead?" Howe acted surprised. "That's terrible. She was one of my best waitresses. What was it? An overdose or something?"

Howe pulled open a drawer in his desk, thumbed through some files and removed one, which he handed to Cassidy. "Hope it's some help."

"Why did you ask that?" Cassidy inquired, as he scanned the contents of the file.

'Ask what?" Howe responded.

"You asked me if it was an overdose. All I said was that she was found dead"

"I don't know," Howe said. "I guess—Peaches being so young and healthy—I guess I just assumed that she didn't die of natural causes or anything. And she was a hooker. Maybe you don't know that. It was common knowledge here. She always did a good job here, but after she got off at night, she was a prostitute. You know how they are—into all kinds of things, including drugs. At least, that's what I'm told."

Cassidy was fighting to keep his cool. So far, he was winning. "Well, since you asked, at first we thought it was an overdose, maybe a suicide. Now however, we believe it was murder, and we don't have a suspect yet. Which means I have to ask you—where were you this morning between, say, ten AM and when you arrived here shortly after eleven?"

"What the hell are you asking me a question like that for?!" Howe exploded. "Do you know who I am?"

"Just routine, Mr. Howe," Cassidy said calmly. "Just tell me where you were between ten and eleven, and I'll be on my way."

"I was on my way back from Columbia," Howe responded angrily.

"Who can verify when you left Columbia?"

"I actually left Columbia at seven thirty, but I stopped along the way."

"You stopped for an hour and a half? Where?"

"At a restaurant near Monck's Corner for breakfast."

"Give me the name," Cassidy persisted. "I'll check it out."

"Am I a suspect?" Howe asked.

"Not yet," Cassidy answered. "If I can verify that you were at that restaurant for as long as you say and left no earlier than, say, ten, you're probably off the hook."

"Well, I don't remember the name right now. When I do, I'll give you a call."

"Okay," Cassidy said, handing Howe one of his cards with his telephone number. "While you're remembering, also try to remember where you were last Thursday afternoon and Friday morning. I need to check out those times, too."

Cassidy left a dumbstruck Howe, standing in his office with his mouth open. Howe quickly recovered his cool and dialed a telephone number.

"Yeah?"

"It's Howe. We have to meet. Now."

"Jesus. Calm down," Costellano said. "What the hell's wrong?"

"A cop was just here, asking me where I was on Thursday and Friday."

"Jesus, man. Calm down," Danny repeated. "Keep your cool. Why do we have to meet?"

"I want my IOU back now. Without that, they've got no link between us and no motive. I did your dirty work. You're paid back in full."

"I totally agree," Costellano said. "Okay. If that'll calm you down, come on over here and I'll give it to you. On second thought, maybe we'd better meet some place. How about the Market Street market?"

"Fine," Howe said. That was just a couple of blocks away. "I'll meet you right across from Henry's."

"Bob," Danny added, "drive around until you're sure that you're not being followed."

"Sure," Howe agreed. "I'm leaving now."

Howe left by the rear door and drove out the back way. Kevin Cassidy picked him up as he turned onto Meeting Street, heading south. As he followed Howe, Kevin Cassidy talked with his father, who was paralleling him two blocks away, using a couple of old Navy walkie talkies that Frank had bought at the Army Navy surplus store. As soon as it became apparent that Howe was doubling back on himself to uncover anyone who might be tailing him, Kevin and his father went into a standard New York City police "loose" tail arrangement, where they constantly traded off who was following and who was paralleling. After five minutes, Howe parked the car and went the rest of the way on foot, Kevin and the elder Cassidy following.

Costellano came walking up about ten minutes later. The Cassidy's recognized him from Frank's description. They would have spotted him any way. He looked exactly like a New York hood.

As the two men met and began talking, Frank's father walked up next to them, examining some corn spilled out on a table. Normally a dapper dresser, he was wearing a striped, short sleeved blue and white shirt, red and green plaid Bermuda shorts, a white belt, white socks, and black dress shoes. When Frank had complimented him earlier on his "tourist" disguise, his father had responded, "What disguise?" It had taken Frank a full minute to realize that his father had been kidding. Although he was talking to the black island woman sitting behind the table about the freshness of her corn, he was listening to the conversation between Howe and Costellano.

"You should have kept your mouth shut," Costellano said, as he handed an envelope to Howe. "Telling Peaches was stupid."

"Don't I know it," Howe responded, taking the envelope and putting it in his inside coat pocket. "I could have shit when you told me she had told the cops. How did you find that out?"

"Don't ask. Maybe you should get out of town for a while," Costellano said.

"No need, now that I have this," Howe responded, patting his coat. "No need to worry now."

"Why do you say that? It seems to me…"

"Don't ask," Howe said, mocking Costellano.

As the two men left, Kevin walked to telephone Frank, who was waiting at a pay phone a couple of miles uptown. He then hurried to his car.

Frank's father bumped into Howe, spilling his bag full of fresh, Charleston corn. He apologized and bent to pick up his corn. Howe walked quickly away, leaving the envelope which Frank's father had lifted from his coat. The envelope containing the IOU was now safe in the brown paper sack under the fresh, Charleston corn.

Chapter 42
Day 9—Tuesday
2:10 PM

Costellano parked in the rear of the High Hat and let himself in through the rear door, which opened into his office.

"What the…," he began, and then he recognized the man sitting in front of his desk. That detective named Cassidy. "Hello, Lieutenant. I'll have to have a word with my staff. This is supposed to be a private office. Well, you're here now," Costellano continued, sitting down behind his desk. "What can I do for you?"

"Are you Danny Costellano?" Cassidy asked.

"You know I am. What's this all about?" Danny was concerned that he hadn't been tipped off about this visit.

"Mr. Costellano, I have reason to believe that you are involved in three…no, four murders in the last week."

"That's ridiculous. I'm simply a businessman providing entertainment to some of Charleston's tourists. Clubs like this are one of the reasons why Charleston gets so many conventions, like the Shriners. I don't kill people. Why would I do that?"

"I'll run them down, one at a time," Cassidy said calmly, standing up and pacing slowly back and forth in front of the desk, his coat unbuttoned and his eyes always on Costellano. "Eight days ago, a young Negro man was killed, rather brutally by the way, and his body was set on fire in Marion Square. That murder was committed by Junior Hutto. Junior Hutto works for you and runs all the drugs and numbers in the Negro parts of town. Murder number two. You know about the killing of the Negro minister at the AME Church on Thursday. He was fixing to speak to reporters about the drugs and numbers in the Negro communities. Bob Howe killed him. Bob Howe owed you a large sum of money. Stop me when I stray from the facts."

Costellano merely sat, looking at Cassidy and saying nothing.

"Murder number three. The next morning, that's Friday morning, Howe shot and killed Charles Terrell, who was actually Carmine Terenzi, a Mafia hood from New York, a capo in the Genovese family. Genovese was trying to move into your action. Finally, murder number four. This morning, you killed Peaches Parker, one of your employees, because she had learned that Howe was the shooter. It's been a busy week. Now, you're going down hard and long."

There was a knock at the back door. Cassidy continued talking as he walked over to let his brother in.

"Let's go downtown," Frank said to Costellano.

"Wait. Now wait just a minute. Maybe you don't know, but I'm protected. Just pick up that phone and call your boss, Chief Wall. He'll tell you."

"This man is a detective from New York," Frank said, referring to his brother. Kevin flashed his gold detective's badge. Costellano had seen enough New York detectives' badges to know that it was real. Suddenly, he was unsure of what was going on or his ability to control the situation.

"What the hell's going on? New York? Why's he here?"

"We have a problem. We want you, and New York wants you. Something about a murder years ago. I don't know what you mean—protected—but I don't think anybody will want to help you with this one. You're going down. Maybe here. Maybe New York. Maybe both."

"Can we make a deal? How about a drink? Let's talk."

"Okay. Get some coffee in here, and we'll listen until we finish the coffee. That's how long you have to convince us," Frank said, sitting back down. Kevin remained standing.

Costellano picked up the phone and ordered some coffee, which came immediately.

"First," Costellano began, "I had nothing to do with the nigra kid or Peaches. Hutto did the kid, and Howe probably killed the girl. The other two—yes. I won't deny involvement in those. You'll find out anyway. I want a deal. There's a lot involved here—a lot going on that you don't know about."

"So you're paying off the police," Frank said matter-of-factly. "Don't you think we know that?"

"It goes higher than that. Yeah, I deliver cash every month to the city and county police chiefs. But I also pay money every week into a bank account. Lots of money. It goes higher—all the way to the top. Let me tell you a story."

Costellano told them his story.

"Who is this Mr. X?" Cassidy asked.

"No more," Costellano said, sitting back. "Get me my deal, and I'll tell you how to blow this whole thing wide open. Trust me. This is very big. It goes all the way up."

"What do you want?"

"Deportation to Sicily," Costellano answered. "I'm in this country illegally anyway. Just send me home. Trust me. I won't come back. Give me deportation, and I'll give you this city on a silver platter. Now, I guess I'll find out if you're honest cops."

"Okay," Cassidy said. "Let me use your phone."

He took two business cards out of his wallet. Chief Wall had called in both SLED (the State Law Enforcement Division) and the FBI to review the evidence that indicated that Jimmy Long had, in fact, not been the killer of Jab Brown. Both had found the opportunity to indicate to Cassidy that if he needed their assistance in his investigations, he should contact them. He was about to take them up on their offer.

First, he called Jordan Mack of the FBI. He agreed to meet Cassidy in the FBI office. At Cassidy's request, the FBI agent called Wayne Stowe of the local SLED office and conferenced him in on the conversation. Stowe agreed to meet Cassidy at the FBI office also. Ironically, the FBI's offices were in the Federal Building and the SLED offices were one floor above the State Court, both at the corner of Meeting and Broad Streets, the destination of each of the Civil Rights marches.

Cassidy then called the Holiday Inn. Rich was not there, so he made his arrangements with Mackey, the Innkeeper.

"Here's what we'll do," Cassidy said to Costellano. "As you heard, I'm going to meet with the state and federal authorities. In the meantime, I want you to go with this detective here. Based on what you've told us, we can't take you to headquarters."

This was actually somewhat of a bluff. Since Cassidy was operating on his own, he could not take Costellano to headquarters. If he did, they would probably cut Costellano free and put Frank and Kevin behind bars. Since

Costellano didn't know this, he was visibly relieved when Frank said what he said about not taking him to police headquarters.

"This detective will take you to a suite at the Holiday Inn. Kevin, park in the underground parking lot and take the elevator directly to the sixth floor, room 614. You will be met there by the Innkeeper, Mr. Mackey. Stay there. I'll call you. Is that agreeable with you, Mr. Costellano?"

"Yeah, sure," Costellano answered. "Just get me that deal. They won't be disappointed."

Costellano went to collect the records and ledgers he would need. Kevin would stay with him and take him to the Holiday Inn, keeping Costellano in his custody until Frank called.

Frank drove to the Federal Building. The SLED agent had already arrived.

"What's up, Frank?" Jordan Mack asked, as the men shook hands.

"I'm not sure," Cassidy said, taking a seat at the conference table. "Here's what I've got." Slowly, step-by-step, Cassidy walked the two men through the events of the past nine days, concluding with his recent conversation with Danny Costellano.

"I don't know exactly what he can or will reveal," Cassidy said. "However, I can speculate, based on what I know. Costellano runs drugs and numbers in the Negro sections of town. He apparently has a deal with Charleston authorities that if he pays them a cut—a sizeable cut, I might add—and keeps the drugs out of the white sections, he has exclusivity. A monopoly. He makes weekly deposits into a local bank account. He also pays off the chiefs of the city and county police. He has indicated that the corruption goes all the way to the top. He may not know who he is dealing with. It seems to me, though, that the FBI can probably gain access to the bank's records, hopefully without tipping the bank off…"

"We can do that," Mack interjected.

"…and we can trace the money. That may tell us something. What do you think?" he said to the two men.

"Since murder is a state crime," Mack said, "SLED must first agree. I'm pretty sure I can get my people to go along."

"Let me make a phone call," Stowe said. The SLED agent pulled the phone on the conference room table towards himself and dialed a number in Columbia. He spoke briefly with the head of SLED and hung up.

"He'll get right back to me," he told the two men. "Has to talk to the Governor. He thinks it might fly."

The three men sat, drinking coffee and talking shop. Sooner than they expected, the phone rang. "Mack," the FBI agent answered. He handed the phone to the SLED agent.

"Stowe here." He listened for a long time. "I understand." He hung up the phone.

"Here's what I've got," he told the other two men. "One, we'll agree to a conditional deal, conditioned on Costellano's information leading to the arrest and conviction of high level Charleston city officials or leaders. Second, the next steps have to be taken very discretely. They have to know who the target is before they will authorize us to proceed."

"Who is 'they'?" Cassidy asked.

"The Governor," the FBI agent offered. The SLED agent merely nodded in the affirmative.

"Okay," Agent Mack said, pulling the phone across the table. "This will probably be brief." He had permission to proceed within three minutes.

"It's a go," the FBI agent said. "Where's Costellano?"

"He's with my brother in a suite at the Holiday Inn."

"Your brother?!" both men exclaimed in unison.

"Calm down," Cassidy laughed. "He's a Lieutenant with the New York City police—a detective. My father, who by the way is also down here, was also in the NYPD. It runs in the family. They identified Terenzi for me. Then, they got worried about the mob being in Charleston and came down to help me. Damn good thing they did. Otherwise, I would have been on my own. Anyway, they're at the Holiday Inn."

"Can you get them over here?" The FBI agent asked.

"Sure." Cassidy dialed the Holiday Inn. "Meanwhile, can you run these prints?" He handed the envelope containing the fingerprints to the FBI agent. "They were lifted from the cartridges in the rifle used in both the Brown and Terenzi shootings. Tell them to check Bob Howe's prints. He was in the Marine Corps, I believe." The FBI agent took the envelope down the hall and returned.

Kevin Cassidy and Danny Costellano drove into the private garage in the Federal Building and came up the private elevator. They were immediately ushered into the conference room. After delivering Costellano, Kevin Cassidy left and drove across the Ashley River to Frank's house, where his father was waiting.

"Danny, this is Special Agent Jordan Mack of the FBI and Agent Wayne Stowe of SLED. You've admitted complicity in two murders. Murder is a state crime, so I'll let Agent Stowe talk to you about your request."

"Mr. Costellano," Stowe began, "my understanding is that you claim you have been making payoffs from money earned through the numbers racket and the sale of illegal drugs to what you believe are high level Charleston city officials, and you have offered to tell us what you know and testify for the prosecution in exchange for deportation to Sicily instead of prosecution for the crimes you have acknowledged you committed. Is that right?"

"Just so there's no misunderstanding," Costellano said, "I didn't commit the murders and I didn't say I did. I said I was involved. That's all. The rest of what you said is essentially correct."

"Okay. On the condition that the information you provide us leads to the arrest and conviction of high level city officials or leaders, you can have your deal."

"By high level officials or leaders, do you mean only elected officials?" Costellano asked.

"No, not necessarily," the SLED agent answered. "We are aware that certain business leaders exercise a very high level of influence over the affairs of this city. Your information must uncover and expose the leaders at the top, regardless of who they are."

"Okay," Costellano agreed. "Can I have that in writing?"

"Sure," Stowe said. "Here it is and here are my credentials." He slid a sheet of paper and his ID across the table. Costellano read the paper and examined the credentials. Satisfied, he returned the ID and put the sheet of paper in his pocket.

"What's the FBI's involvement?" he asked Mack.

"Mr. Costellano, unless other information is forthcoming and right now I don't expect any, we have no interest in you. We are merely offering our assistance to these two gentlemen in their investigation."

"Okay," Costellano said. "Might as well get started."

A stenographer was summoned, and they began. Cassidy asked the questions, again slowly and painstakingly leading Costellano through the events of the past week. Then, he asked about Costellano's arrangement with Mr. X.

"The deal was arranged by people in New York. Someone high up in the organization."

"What organization?" Cassidy asked.

"Some people call it the Gambino family. The deal was and still is as follows. I run the numbers and drugs in Charleston. Nobody else is allowed in. I can sell numbers and drugs only to the coloreds. No sales to whites. I also have to keep them—the drugs, that is—cheap. I never understood that. We are charging about twenty to thirty per cent less than they get in New York. I raised prices once. The bastards raided me. Took all the drugs. I had to pay for a new shipment out of my end."

"Let's go back for a second," Cassidy interjected. "Who from the Gambino family set the deal up?"

"That's not part of the deal," Costellano complained. "I'll give up these Charleston goombahs, but not New York. My life wouldn't be worth a plug nickel, even in Sicily. Hell, especially in Sicily."

Mack nodded to Cassidy that it was okay.

"Go on," Cassidy said.

"Well, right away, the Charleston police—both city and county—began continuous raids on all numbers and drug operations in the county. Within two weeks, I was the only game in town. The deal went like this. I paid all expenses out of the weekly take, including covering the numbers winnings, paying for the drugs which came each week from New York, paying off the two police chiefs, and taking care of overhead. Then, one third went to New York, one third was deposited into Mr. X's bank account, and I kept a third."

"How did they know you weren't skimming?"

"Well, you don't skim New York. I mean, you just don't. It ain't worth the risk. When I shorted the bank account one week—honest to God it was an honest error—I got a call. I guess that New York and Mr. X compared numbers. Anyway, I never did again."

"How much are we talking about?"

"Well, the drug take has been growing. Lately, the deposits to Mr. X have been around sixty thousand."

"A week?!" Cassidy asked.

"Yes. Sixty thousand a week. Drugs and numbers are very profitable."

"What is the bank account number?"

Costellano opened his briefcase, took out a blank deposit slip, and handed it to Cassidy, who passed it to the FBI agent. The FBI agent left the room to make arrangements.

"Who do you think Mr. X is?"

"I honestly don't know. Don't you think I've asked myself that same question over the years? I didn't like having to deal with a mystery person who had power over my operation. But there was nothing I could do about it."

"But I take it you don't think Mr. X was the Chief of Police?"

"No, I don't think he is either Wall or Leech. First, I pay them both in cash every month. Chump change, but to them it's a good stash. Most of all, though, I have talked to both of them several times. Mr. X is educated. He uses good English and big words. They don't. I think you can fake that down, but not up, if you know what I mean."

"Yes, I get your drift. Is there anything else at this point?"

"I think you know everything I know now," Costellano said.

Special Agent Mack came back into the conference room.

"Just in time," Cassidy said. "I think we're through for this session."

"Okay," Mack said. "We're prepared to baby sit Mr. Costellano at a safe house outside of the state."

"Mr. Costellano," Mack said, "we'll abide by our agreement. However, I want you to consider another proposition. We believe that you are wanted for other crimes, perhaps a killing in New York. Also, the IRS may come calling about your take from the illegal operations. We can arrange to have the murder charge lifted and the IRS look the other way, if you will tell us, in total confidence, what you know about the operations of the Gambino family. In this situation, you won't have to testify. Your cooperation will be kept totally confidential. Will you think about that?"

"Yeah, I'll think about it. Sure." Not in a million years, Costellano thought to himself, as he rose to begin the next leg of his trip. Another FBI agent took Costellano immediately to a waiting car. He was driven to a safe house in Georgia.

"The prints are Howe's," Mack said, after Costellano had left. Mack quickly briefed the other two on the next steps, which would be carried out by the FBI.

Stowe and Cassidy drove to the Colonial Steakhouse. Howe was not there, and the staff didn't know where he was. They went to Howe's house. He wasn't home, and his wife claimed not to know his whereabouts. Stowe agreed to have SLED officers stake out the restaurant and the house, promising to call Frank immediately if Howe showed up. A tired Cassidy drove home to brief his father and brother.

Chapter 43
Wednesday, June 13, 1962
9:00 AM

When the doors of the Old South National Bank's main branch on Broad Street opened for business, among the customers impatiently waiting on the sidewalk were two men in blue, pinstriped suits carrying briefcases. Since Broad Street was Charleston's financial district, the two men didn't look out of place in the least. However, instead of walking up to tellers' windows, they walked through the bank's main teller area to the rear of the bank and entered through a door marked 'Executive Offices'.

"Good morning," one of the men said to the secretary seated at her desk outside the closed door marked 'President'. "We're bank examiners from the Federal Reserve." Both men handed business cards to the secretary. "We would like to see the bank's president, please."

The secretary picked up her phone, dialed two digits and informed John Mason of the unexpected visit. Mason immediately came from his office, greeted the bank examiners, and invited them into his sunlit, spacious office.

"This is your unscheduled annual inspection," the first examiner said. "I'll be checking on checking and savings accounts. My colleague here will examine your loan portfolio. We'll need an office or a conference room. If you'll have someone bring us a list of your checking and savings accounts—just a listing showing the numbers will be fine—I'll select accounts at random."

"Certainly," Mason replied. "How long do you expect this to take?"

"Unless we find something which warrants further study, we should be out of your way by lunch time."

Mason showed the men to a small conference room, usually used for closings. A clerk brought in a listing of checking and savings account numbers. The examiner selected five checking and five savings accounts 'at random'. Among the checking accounts he selected was the account into which Costellano had made the monthly deposits.

Chapter 44
Day 10—Wednesday
9:17 AM

As Frank filled his father's empty coffee mug, the kitchen phone rang. "Hello," Frank answered.

"Cassidy? Stowe. Howe's at the restaurant. Just showed up. I'm on the way."

"Try to wait for me," Cassidy answered, swallowing his coffee. "I'll be there in less than fifteen minutes."

"Howe," Frank said to his father. "Wanna come along?"

"No, thanks. I've got to see that Times reporter."

The elder Cassidy had learned that he knew one of the reporters covering the Charleston marches for the New York Times. They had decided to see if they could enlist his help for part of their plan. They had planned to go together to see him. Now, the father would go alone, while Frank went to arrest Howe.

Frank sped to town, a portable light flashing on the hood and his siren wailing. Three blocks before the turn onto Vendue Range, he turned off the light and siren and slowed down to the speed limit. As he turned onto the short street, he could see Stowe sitting in his car in front of the restaurant. Good, he thought. He had gotten there in time.

As Cassidy drove up and stopped, Stowe got out of his car. The two men trotted up the steps. The front door was unlocked. Frank led the way to Howe's office, opened the door, and stepped into the office, followed by Stowe. Howe was squatting in front of an open floor safe, removing packets of cash and putting them into a briefcase. He looked over his shoulder when Cassidy and Stowe entered the office.

"Good morning, Lieutenant," Howe said, continuing to squat in front of the safe. "What can I do for you?"

"This is Agent Stowe of SLED," Cassidy said. "Mr. Howe, we are placing you under arrest for the murders of Jeremiah Brown and Charles Terrell. Please stand up."

"This is crazy," Howe answered, ignoring the request to stand. "Why would I kill…"

While he was protesting, Howe reached into the safe. He then stood up with a revolver in his hand. As Cassidy and Stowe drew their weapons, Howe stuck the barrel of the revolver in his mouth and pulled the trigger.

The back of Howe's head exploded, sending scalp, brains, blood and other tissue flying against the wall behind him. His body collapsed in a heap on the carpet, blood staining the light blue fabric.

"Shit," Cassidy said, returning his gun to its holster.

"Just as well," Stowe remarked. "He saved the State a lot of time and money. If you'll call the M E, I'll stay and take care of this."

"Thanks," Cassidy said. They both knew that until Wall and Leech were out of the picture, it was better to let SLED take the heat for the investigation. Cassidy had no power to protect himself.

Cassidy called Carleton James, who agreed to retrieve the body and perform an autopsy on behalf of SLED, and then left the restaurant. He headed for the Federal Building.

Chapter 45
Day 10—Wednesday
10:30 AM

Frank's father, Tim Cassidy, spotted the reporter from the New York Times waiting for him in the lobby of the Francis Marion Hotel, just as they had agreed over the phone.

"Hi, Captain," the reporter hailed, as Tim Cassidy strode across the lobby. "What are you doing in Charleston?" The two men shook hands.

"My son is a detective on the force here," Cassidy said.

"So, that's your son," the reporter said. "I wrote about him a few days ago. He must be one good cop. Chip off the old block, huh."

"Yes, he's good," the father agreed. "But right now, he has a tough one. That's why I called you. I'm helping him, and we need your help."

"You know I'll help you if I can," the reporter said. "God knows you helped me over the years, especially when I was getting started. I can remember even today at least three times when you saved my ass by stopping me from going off in the wrong direction in a story. What can I do?"

"It's nice outside," Tim Cassidy said. "Let's take a walk, and I'll tell you a story." The two men walked outside, crossed King Street, and walked into Marion Square towards the statue where Boutry's burned body had been discovered nine days earlier.

"The lid's about to blow off this town," Tim Cassidy began. "Apparently, the people who run this city have been protecting an operation for years that has been running drugs and numbers in the Negro areas of town. There's a guy named Danny Costellano. He used to be a member of the Gambino family, may still be for all I know. He runs the operation out of the High Hat Club. He has had a protected monopoly for ten or twelve years. If anybody else tries to move in, the cops run them out of town. That black minister who was shot was about to talk to you guys about the drugs and numbers. That's why they killed him."

"Hold on a minute," the reporter said, as they walked up to the statue. "You've lost me. I thought that Negro cook killed the minister. Are you telling me he was part of this drug operation?"

"No. He didn't do it. He was framed by those who did it. The day after the killing at the church, they killed Carmine Terenzi…"

"You mean the Terenzi from New York?" The reporter interrupted. "The one in the Genovese mob?"

"Yeah. He was trying to move in on the drug operation. Anyway, my son, along with the State boys and the FBI, are moving closer to breaking the whole thing wide open. Costellano is in custody and is apparently willing to cooperate. My son is arresting the actual shooter in both killings right now."

"Who is that?"

"A guy named Howe. Owner of the Colonial Steakhouse restaurant."

"I've heard of him," the reporter said. "Why would he make the hits? Was he in on the drug deal?"

"We don't think so. He owed Costellano money. Quite a bit of money."

"Did Costellano finger those at the top?"

"Not really. He knows the Chiefs of the City and County police are dirty. He pays them off in cash personally each month. But he says it goes higher than that. He also deposits cash in a bank account each week. But his communication is only over the phone with some man he knows only as Mister X."

"How much money are we talking about?"

"Two to two and a half million a year."

The reporter whistled.

"That's a lot of money. What do they use it for, and who are 'they'?" he asked.

"We don't know yet where the money goes. And we don't yet know exactly who they are. We think we've narrowed it down to a small group of men, members of the Ashley Cooper Society who meet once a week in a group they call the POETS Club. This group consists of the Mayor, head of the County Council, a judge, the owner of the newspaper, two bankers, a real estate developer, a minister, a lawyer, and a college professor. We don't know if the whole group, some of the group, or only one man, is involved in the drugs and numbers. That is, we don't know yet. That's where you come in. We are willing to give you an exclusive on this. As this thing unravels, we want to be able to isolate the person or persons who are really behind this drug thing from the rest. We have to strip him or them of their power. Then, we can bring them down. We want to tell those who are not in on the drug operation that how you treat them in your story will depend to some extent on whether or not they turn away from those involved. If they help them or tip them off to our investigation, then your story will include them as part of a conspiracy. However, if they cooperate with us and are truly not involved in this thing, you will not mention them in your story or will at least treat them favorably as unwitting dupes in the drug thing. What do you say?"

"Sounds to me like all you're asking is that I report what actually happens. Is that right?"

"Yeah. That's the way it looks to me. We're just asking that you take your normal care with the details and not inadvertently paint the wrong picture."

"No problem," the reporter said. "In fact, I'll run my story past you and your son before I file it, just to be sure I've got it right."

"Thanks," Tim Cassidy said, extending his hand and sealing the agreement with a handshake.

"No," the reporter said. "Thank YOU. This is a huge story. Any reporter would give his right arm for an exclusive on this. Why me?"

"Because you're a rare breed," Cassidy said. "An honest reporter who gets his facts right. Not many of you around." The street hardened reporter actually blushed. Tim Cassidy pretended not to notice.

Chapter 46
Day 10—Wednesday
12:30 PM

The two Federal bank examiners, who were actually FBI agents from the Atlanta field office, walked into the FBI conference room. SLED Agent Wayne Stowe, FBI Special Agent Jordan Mack, and Frank Cassidy were waiting. One of the fake bank examiners sat down and pulled out his notes. The other walked to the blackboard at one end of the room and began writing as he began his briefing.

"The checking account is in the name of the Lowcountry Political Fund. Current balance is five point seven million dollars. The only person authorized to draw against the account is Gedney Middleton. Deposits come from two sources. Once a week, a sum of cash is deposited. The amount varies, but recently has been between fifty and sixty thousand dollars. The other source of deposits comes from checks, deposited irregularly but usually once a month, from Merrill Lynch. We examined checks drawn against the account over the past two years. Again, there are occasional checks to Merrill Lynch. Our guess is that some of the money in the account is invested in the stock market. All of the rest of the checks drawn appear to be campaign contributions. We have a list of the names. You guys will probably know who they are. We don't."

The Atlanta agent seated at the table distributed copies of the names of those who had received money from the bank account. It read like a political Who's Who of the State of South Carolina.

"Holy Crow," the SLED agent said. He quickly scanned the list and was relieved to find that the Governor's name was not on the list. Cassidy and Mack had already made the same discovery. The Atlanta agents went to an office to complete their paper work.

Cassidy waited impatiently while Stowe and Mack called their superiors to brief them on the findings from the bank. Each received clearance to proceed.

"Here's my suggested plan," Cassidy began, as the three men reassembled in the conference room. "First, we should take Wall and Leech out of the game."

"I can arrest them on Federal charges," Mack said. "There's a Federal law against police officers, regardless of their jurisdiction, taking bribes when the money comes from the sale of drugs. We can also arrest them for violation of Federal gambling laws."

"How about for just being scum bags in general?" Stowe quipped.

"No," Mack laughed. "If that was against the law, we'd have to clean out Washington."

"Can you do that today?" Mack asked.

"One of my guys is downstairs right now getting a Federal warrant signed by a Federal judge. As soon as he gets it, we'll move."

"Good," Cassidy went on. "Next, I think we have to visit the rest of the members of the POETS Club. We need to isolate Middleton. We also need to freeze the bank account and the Merrill Lynch account."

"I can lock the accounts," Stowe said. "We can seize them as proceeds from the sale of illegal drugs."

"What can we say to the others to insure that they don't tip Middleton off?" Mack asked. "We can't really threaten them if they didn't do anything, and we have no evidence that there was a conspiracy? We won't know that until we take Middleton. Maybe we should go for him first."

"Gedney Middleton is a very powerful man," Cassidy said. "We need to isolate him, financially and otherwise, before we take him. Otherwise, he might be able to marshal his forces and blow a lot of smoke over the whole situation." He explained the plan he and his father had developed about using potential exposure in the New York Times as the inducement for the members of the POETS Club to cooperate.

"Okay," Mack agreed. "This is going to take some time. When should we plan to take Middleton?"

"If we take Leech and Wall today," Stowe said, "we should be able to interview the others tomorrow and take Middleton on Friday. That warrant may be harder to get, anyway. What charges will we use?"

"It would be better to take him on a State charge," Mack said. "Hell, he's tied to drugs, illegal gambling, and three, maybe four, murders."

"He might have every judge in the State in his pocket," Stowe said.

"I'll bet there's one judge that will issue the warrant," Cassidy said.

"Which one?" Stowe asked.

"This one," Cassidy answered, poking his finger at the list of POETS Club members. "If he doesn't, the New York Times will crucify him."

"Yeah, that'll probably work," Stowe agreed. "Okay, who does what?"

"I want to be in on the arrest of Wall," Cassidy said. "It's personal. I'd also like to go with you, Stowe, to see Judge Whittington. Other than that, we can divide them up any way you want. One thing, though. Peaches said that Middleton usually comes to the POETS Club meetings with that professor from the College of Charleston—what's his name—oh yeah, Martin. We might want to take Middleton at the restaurant Friday when he comes for the usual meeting. Might be easier than taking him at his office surrounded by lawyers or at home. In that case, maybe we shouldn't interview this Martin in advance. Anyway, he probably doesn't have the power these other guys have to hinder us and help Middleton. He's probably only some kind of advisor."

They agreed.

Two hours later, the FBI arrested the Chiefs of the City and County Police Departments. During interrogation, each man separately confirmed the identities of the members of the POETS Club and the fact that the Club, unquestionably headed by Gedney Middleton, controlled all important decisions about the City and the County. Piecing together the stories told by each man, Cassidy, Stowe, and Mack now had a pretty clear picture of Gedney Middleton's concerns about the blacks becoming a political majority in the City and his plan to forestall that eventuality through the forced gentrification of Ansonborough and the annexation of white areas west of the Ashley River. It was a picture of a powerful man obsessed with Charleston; a man who would stop at nothing to "save" his City.

Chapter 47
Day 11—Thursday, June 14, 1962
9:00 AM

Cassidy, Mack, and Stowe crossed the busy intersection from the Federal Building to City Hall to keep the scheduled nine o'clock appointment with the Mayor. The remainder of the meetings with POETS Club members would be held in the SLED offices. One of Stowe's agents was already contacting the other six POETS members who would be interviewed that day, scheduling them at one hour intervals beginning at ten o'clock.

The three men were escorted into the Mayor's spacious office overlooking the historic corner of Broad and Meeting Streets with a view of Charleston Harbor and the prominent white steeple of St. Michael's Episcopal Church. They sat on couches and easy chairs placed around an ornate coffee table, which had been a gift of the French Government to Charleston some sixty years ago. The Mayor's secretary poured coffee into delicate china cups, a gift from Queen Elizabeth.

"Mr. Mayor," Mack began. It had been agreed that the FBI would lead off this meeting, since the police chiefs had been arrested on Federal charges. "I believe that you were informed that we arrested Chief Wall yesterday afternoon on bribery and corruption charges. You may also know that we arrested County Police Chief Leech on similar charges."

Jerry Anderson merely nodded. Trying to appear calm, he was in fact scared to death. It had been difficult to comply with the demand of the FBI agent who had called him to schedule the meeting that he inform no one of the meeting. He had no idea what this was about, but he feared that the FBI might believe that he was involved in some way with whatever Wall and Leech had been doing. He knew that he was clean, but the mere allegation would be enough to ruin the career of any politician. He prayed that he wouldn't start sweating before they got to the point.

"Actually," the FBI agent continued, "the information that led to yesterday's arrests was uncovered in an investigation into other matters. It's those matters that prompted us to request this meeting. Mr. Mayor, have you ever received campaign contributions from Gedney Middleton?"

"Yes, I have, as has virtually every office holder from here to Columbia. What's this all about?"

"Sir, the funds that Mr. Middleton used for his political war chest came from payoffs from criminals who control the numbers racket and the sale of illegal drugs in the Negro sections of Charleston."

"What?!" Anderson blurted. "Are you sure? You can't be right! Gedney Middleton is one of the finest…Oh, my God. You are sure, aren't you?"

"Yes, sir," the FBI agent replied, "we're sure."

SLED agent Stowe took over the dialogue. "We also believe that within the past two weeks, four murders have been committed in Charleston in an effort to protect and cover-up those drug and gambling operations."

The Mayor stood and began pacing, as the SLED agent recounted what the law enforcement officers had pieced together of the events of the past eleven days, beginning with the murder of Sammy Boutry in Marion Square.

Now, it was Cassidy's turn. "Mr. Mayor," he began, "we also know about the POETS Club, that the POETS Club effectively runs this city, that Gedney Middleton is the leader of the Club, and that you are a member. What we don't know is how much did the other Club members know about the sources of the money in the campaign fund and the murders that Agent Stowe mentioned. Can you help us with that?"

The Mayor sat back down on the sofa. "We knew nothing. Nothing at all," he answered, attempting to remain calm and mayoral. "I'm flabbergasted. I simply can't believe what you're telling me. Drugs? Gambling? Murders? The people who meet at the Colonial Steakhouse for lunch are the top business and public leaders of the City and the County. Surely you don't believe that we are gangsters!"

"What was the purpose of the Club?" Cassidy asked.

"Before the marches began, we met every Friday simply to maintain a dialogue between the political leaders and the business leaders of the City.

When the marches began, the focus changed. We knew that changes were coming. But we were concerned that any change in the political make-up of the City might hurt tourism, and without robust, growing tourism, Charleston will begin to fade economically."

"You were worried that the Negroes would set the political agenda for the City and elect its leaders, so the numbers and drugs were one way to keep them down and drain money out of their communities," Cassidy challenged.

"We didn't know about that," Mayor Anderson insisted. "If we had, we would have put a stop to it. I still find it incredible. Our plan involved the rebuilding of Ansonborough to entice whites to move back into the City and the annexation of certain white areas west of the Ashley River. The objective was to ensure a continued white voting majority in the city."

It was now Stowe's turn to get to the real point of the meeting. "Mr. Mayor," Stowe began, "we are inclined to believe that you didn't know about the numbers, the drugs, or the murders. If that's true, then you'll want to cooperate with our investigation. Right?"

"Of course. What can I do to help?"

"Several things. First, you are to appoint Lieutenant Cassidy as the new Chief of Police."

"Whoa," Frank said, startled at this request. "Excuse us for a minute," he said to Anderson and Mack. He led Stowe out of the office into the corridor. "What in hell is this?"

"First of all," Stowe said, "you deserve to make the arrests. You are the one who broke this case. Second, the Governor wants to make sure that things get cleaned up here without throwing out the baby with the bath water. In other words, there are certain aspects about Charleston, like its bars. Even though they are technically illegal, they play an important role in attracting tourists and conventions. An insider understands these things. The Governor wants an honest insider to take charge and clean things up. That's you."

"Okay," Frank relented. "I'll do it on a temporary basis. I'm not sure I'm the right person for the long run."

"Fair enough," Stowe said. "We'll start there and see where it goes."

The two men returned to the Mayor's office. "Mr. Mayor," Stowe began again, "Frank has agreed to the appointment on a temporary basis. However, the temporary nature of the appointment will be just between you and Frank. You will announce the appointment as permanent. You can begin a discrete search for a new Chief, but you can replace Frank only with the agreement of the Governor and Frank. Is that agreed?"

"Yes," Anderson agreed. "I'll put the announcement out this morning."

"Good. Second, you are not to inform anyone else of what we have told you this morning, especially Gedney Middleton or anyone else who might alert him to our investigation. You are also not to avoid him or act in any unusual manner that might tip him off that something is wrong. If he calls with concerns about the arrests of Wall and Leech, you are to inform him that's where the investigation stopped. Agreed?"

"It'll be tough, but yes, I agree."

No, the next condition is the tough one, Stowe thought. It was purely political, but what the hell, everything about this case was going to be political.

"Finally, the Governor has asked for a letter from you to him stating that you will not seek another term as Mayor."

"Why? Why does he want that?"

"The Governor feels that these events happened on your watch and that a change will be good for Charleston's image."

"That's bullshit!" Anderson exploded. "He wants to put his own man in here. I won't do it."

"Mr. Mayor," Cassidy said. "There's a reporter from the New York Times here covering the marches. We have agreed to give him an exclusive on this story, which will be printed in the Times this coming Sunday, I understand on the front page. In return for the exclusive, he has agreed to paint some of the participants in these events either sympathetically or unsympathetically, based on our direction. How do you want to be painted?"

"Blackmail is not appropriate for the new Chief of Police," Anderson sneered.

"The way we see it," Stowe interjected, "if you are truly clean, you will cooperate with us in all requests for the good of the City. Otherwise, maybe you aren't as clean as you claim."

"Okay. Okay. I'll dictate the letter this morning. Anything else?"

"No, sir," Stowe said, standing up. "That just about covers everything. We're going across the street to SLED's offices to meet with the other members of the POETS Club. Please send over both letters—Frank's appointment and the letter to the Governor—as soon as you can."

The three men left the Mayor, staring sullenly at the view of the harbor, and returned to SLED's offices. Arthur Manigault, the publisher and owner of Charleston's daily newspaper, was waiting on them. They went through the story pretty much in the same order as they had with Jerry Anderson. Besides admonishing him to tell no one, they also extracted a reluctant agreement from the patrician publisher that for the first time in history, a story written by a reporter from the New York Times would be printed on the front page of the News and Courier in the Sunday edition.

The reactions of the POETS Club members to the revelations of the investigation varied. The politicians worried about re-election. The bankers worried about their reputations. The developer worried about his business deals, especially the Ansonborough project. Only one, Judge Whittington, felt any responsibility for what had happened. After leaving his appointment at SLED's offices, he returned to his chambers, issued a warrant for the arrest of Gedney Middleton, and dictated a letter of resignation.

After the interviews were completed, Cassidy, Stowe, and Mack were convinced that the POETS Club members they had interviewed that day had not known of the criminal activities that had taken place. They then began preparations for the next day, drawing up the papers necessary to support the arrest warrant for Gedney Middleton and court orders freezing the bank account and the Merrill Lynch brokerage account. A tired Frank Cassidy went home for a well deserved dinner with his father and brother. After the arrests tomorrow, he would call Rita at her sister's house in Orangeburg and have her come home. He missed his family.

Chapter 48
Day 12—Friday, June 15, 1962
Noon

Cassidy, Stowe, and two other men, a SLED agent and Randy Holly dressed in an ill-fitting suit, waited in the private dining room of the Colonial Steakhouse. Another SLED agent was in the restaurant's executive office, insuring that Bob Howe's wife, who was attempting to manage the restaurant until she could sell it, didn't call her sister Jane or her brother-in-law, Gedney Middleton, to alert them. It was a needless precaution. Her stability, already fragile with the suicide of her husband and the disclosure that he had murdered three people, fell totally apart upon learning that her brother-in-law was about to be arrested for drugs, gambling, and complicity in murder. At first, she had fainted. When the agent revived her, she sat on the couch in the office sobbing, her head in her hands. The agent had already decided that after the arrest, he would call an ambulance to take her to the hospital.

Cassidy was pouring himself a cup of coffee, when the back door opened and Middleton entered, followed by Beano Martin. Middleton immediately stopped in his tracks.

"What's going on," he asked. "Where is everyone? Who are you?"

"Mr. Middleton," Cassidy said, stepping forward, "I'm Lieutenant…Chief Cassidy. This is Agent Stowe of the State Law Enforcement Division."

"I've heard of you," Middleton said to Cassidy, stepping forward and extending his hand. "Congratulations on your appointment. Too bad about Ken Wall. My office will be defending him, you know, so I can't comment on that case. Where are all my friends?"

"They won't be here. Mr. Middleton, I have a warrant for your arrest for conspiracy to distribute illegal drugs. Other charges may be added later."

"You have a what?!" Middleton protested. "Drugs? What in the name of God are you talking about?!"

"Sir, we have traced payments made by criminals who control the drugs and numbers rackets in Charleston to a bank account under your control which we believe you use to make political contributions. Under the law, anyone who knowingly profits from the sale of illegal drugs is equally guilty of the sale of those drugs as are the people who actually participate in their sale and distribution."

While enduring a sudden coughing spasm that turned his face beet red, Beano Martin placed a hand on Gedney's arm, as if to restrain him from saying anything further. After a few moments, the spasm ended.

"You've got the wrong man," Beano Martin whispered, the lingering effects of the coughing spasm still affecting his throat.

"What did you say?" Cassidy asked.

"I said you've got the wrong man," Martin said in a louder voice. "Gedney knew nothing about it. He thought the money came from corporate contributions to a political fund. I'm the one you are after."

"What are you talking about, Beano?" Middleton asked. "Don't say anything more until we can talk privately. Chief Cassidy, I am Beano's attorney. He has the right to confer with me before answering any questions."

Cassidy was confused. They had been so sure.

"I think you two gentlemen had better accompany us to headquarters voluntarily," Cassidy said, "so we can sort all this out. That way, I can put off executing this warrant until we have a better handle on what Mr. Martin is saying."

Beano Martin whispered something in Middleton's ear. "Okay," Middleton said to Cassidy. "Let's go now. The sooner we straighten this out, the better."

Middleton and Martin rode in the back of Cassidy's unmarked car with Cassidy and Stowe in the front. After Cassidy gave instructions over the radio for the court orders freezing the bank and brokerage accounts to be served, the four men drove uptown to Police Headquarters in silence, Holly and the SLED agent following in another unmarked car.

At Middleton's request, he and Martin were escorted to an interrogation room and left alone, so they could confer. "What are you doing?" Middleton asked Martin. "You know very well that…"

"Hush," Martin said in a low voice. "This room might be bugged."

"That would be unconstitutional," Middleton said.

"These cretins aren't constitutional lawyers," Martin replied softly. "They're cops, for Christ's sake. Give me a pad."

Middleton reached into his briefcase and placed a legal sized yellow pad of paper on the table.

I HAVE CANCER. GOT ABOUT SIX MONTHS TOPS. Martin wrote.

Middleton read the message several times. He sat and thought.

I PROMISE YOU YOU'LL NEVER SEE THE INSIDE OF A JAIL CELL. Middleton wrote.

THANKS, FRIEND, Martin wrote.

NO! THANK YOU, FRIEND, Middleton scribbled.

Gedney Middleton tore up the piece of paper and put the scraps in his briefcase. He then summoned Cassidy and Stowe.

Beano Martin was, if anything, smart. During the interrogation, which was constantly interrupted by Middleton, he forced the two policemen to gradually lay out their case, confirming their details rather than giving any details of his own. After the interrogation, Beano Martin was able to dictate a fairly complete confession to a police stenographer.

Chapter 49
Day 13—Saturday, June 16, 1962
8:00 AM

At Reverend Lyle's request, the Marchers Strategy Council convened prior to the day's march. Again, the Council met in the sanctuary with aides posted at the doors to keep the marchers outside until the meeting was concluded.

Reverend Lyle slowly and painfully climbed the circular staircase to the pulpit. "Brothers," he began, "I stand before you today, heavy in heart, to confess a grievous sin—a sin that has been plaguing me ever since our meeting Monday with that police lieutenant. The day before Reverend Brown was assassinated, you will remember that he decided to speak the next day about the drugs and the numbers. As usual, he admonished us not to reveal the subject of his talk to anyone. God knows, and now you will know, that I am weak. That evening, I got in a heated argument with my nephew. He maintained that the white man would never clean the drugs and the gambling out of the Negro areas and because of that, our marches and protests would do no good. In my anger at his attitude and lack of faith, I told him that he should remain strong and have hope, because Brother Brown was going to blow the cover off the dark secret the next day. Yes, brother, I told. My nephew was encouraged. Now, he said, maybe the protests and the marches could accomplish something. I now know that he later told some of his friends in an effort to bolster their confidence and hope, as his had been bolstered. I can only assume that as the word spread, and spread we can be sure it did, it finally fell on the wrong ears. Brothers, I am the one responsible for the killing of Reverend Brown, as guilty as if I had pulled the trigger myself."

"Brother Lyle," one of the assembled ministers called out.

"Please," Lyle interrupted. "Let me finish. I do not ask for your forgiveness for this terrible sin I have committed. I don't know if God will forgive me. I do know that I cannot forgive myself. I also know that I am old, weak, and tired. I am no longer able to lead this Church. Last night, I met with the Elders, confessed my sin, and offered my resignation as Pastor of the Calhoun Street African Methodist Episcopal Church, a church I have headed for thirty five years. I pray that I will be remembered for some of the good things I tried to accomplish rather than this vile act I have committed."

The elderly minister held up his hand, commanding continued silence on the part of his audience.

"I recommended my replacement to the Elders. After conferring, they agreed. Reverend Rivers, the Elders of this Church have issued a call to you to become the Pastor of this Church. Will you accept this call from God and from this Church?"

Shine Rivers was stunned. He stood. "Reverend Lyle, this is the largest and most important Negro church in the County, maybe the State. I am an ignorant, uneducated automobile mechanic and island preacher. I am not worthy or qualified for such a position. I am honored and humbled by the call, but I cannot accept. It would not be fair to the people of this Church or to the Negro people of this City."

"Shine," Reverend Lyle said tenderly with a smile on his face. "Do you want me to call Rebecca in again?" All the men, including Shine, laughed. "She's right outside. She knows what I have asked you to do, and I can tell you she is in favor of you accepting."

Shine closed his eyes and prayed. Suddenly, he felt warmth and a sense of new strength engulf his body. God had answered him. This was the path he was to take.

"In light of that information," Shine said with a chuckle shared by the others, "I guess I'd better accept. God have mercy on me and give me strength."

The marchers filed in, also applauding. Shine shook the hand of each Elder, as Reverend Lyle climbed down from the pulpit. He walked over to Shine and embraced him.

"This is a wonderful church," Reverend Lyle said, his hands on Shine's shoulders. "I'm sure you'll make it even better. Now, I recommend that you skip today's march. You will be installed tomorrow as Pastor of this Church. You have a sermon to prepare."

As the realization of what was happening sank in, Shine almost panicked. "I think you're right," he said. "Please excuse me, gentlemen."

He quickly left the Church sanctuary, found Rebecca, and told her of his acceptance. Together, they drove home to prepare the most important sermon of his life.

Chapter 50
Day 14—Sunday, June 17, 1962
9:00 AM

Gedney Middleton was sitting at the breakfast table in his townhouse, sipping coffee and looking out of the window at his Azalea garden, lost in his thoughts. The Sunday paper was sitting on the table in front of him. He didn't notice his wife, Jane, as she came into the kitchen and sat down next to him.

"Are we going to be alright, Gedney?" she asked, bringing him back to the moment.

He reached over and patted the back of her hand. "Yes, I think we'll be okay," he said in a quiet voice. "This is a mess, though." He gestured toward the paper and the lead article on the front page by the New York Times writer. "People are scared. I have some rebuilding to do. It will come, but it'll take time."

"Do we have the time?" She got up to pour herself a cup of coffee and refilled Gedney's cup.

"I hope so," he responded "and I think so. Talk happens fast. Action takes longer. My concern is the political power base. Without the campaign money, my grip on that will weaken. I just might have to go into the fund raising business."

"Poor Beano," Jane said, sitting back down next to him. "What was he thinking?"

"Beano loves Charleston. Apparently, he was willing to do whatever he felt was necessary to preserve our way of life."

"But drugs and gambling. That's pretty bad. Are you clear of all that?"

"Yes. Beano was very clear with the police. We should be just fine."

"Do you want to go to church this morning?" she asked.

"No. I think I'll lay low today. Maybe work in the garden. I have some planning to do. I might walk over to the office later."

"Okay. I'm going to spend some time with Frances. I'm really worried about her. She took Bob's suicide really hard. I might be there for a while." Gedney gestured absently, already lost again in his thoughts. Jane finished her coffee and stood for a few moments watching Gedney. Still worried about Gedney and the family's standing in society, she went to get her purse and visit her sister.

Chapter 51
Day 14—Sunday, June 17, 1962
10:00 AM

The restaurant at the Holiday Inn, already a hubbub of activity, buzzed with a higher level of excitement and curiosity as Frank Cassidy arrived with his wife and children to have breakfast prior to attending the eleven o'clock service at the AME Church, having been personally invited by Rebecca Rivers. Just as Rich greeted them and was about to escort them to a table, June arrived to have breakfast with Rich. They all decided to eat together at a table for six near the front window. Charley Innis took over for Rich and escorted the six to their table.

Copies of the Sunday paper were everywhere, the huge black banner headline trumpeting Friday's arrest and exposing Charleston's "secret"—drugs and numbers in the black community. People came over to the table to congratulate Frank on his promotion, only to leave in mild disappointment when he politely declined to reveal any juicy tidbits about the investigation. A waitress walked up, handed Rich a note, and took their orders.

"Is the restaurant usually this busy on Sunday morning?" Frank asked, looking around. He was surprised to see that about one third of the patrons were black.

"No," Rich answered, "it isn't. We had to call Marvin in to help. If you have the time, he would like you to step into the kitchen, so he can thank you for what you did for him."

"I didn't do anything special," Frank protested. "He was innocent."

"Well, anyway, he would like to thank you. Please go. It's important to him."

Frank rose and walked into the kitchen, returning after a few moments. As he sat down, Russ Mackey, the Innkeeper, entered the restaurant and walked to their table.

"Congratulations, Chief," he said to Frank, extending his hand, which Frank shook. "Glad you came in. I want to thank you for helping Marvin."

"You're welcome," Frank responded, deciding not to protest again. "Pretty busy, I see."

"Yes," Mackey said, looking around. "Most seem to be here for the service across the street. I hear that the minister who was whipped is going to be installed as the Pastor today."

"That's right," Frank said. "That's why we're here. We've been invited to attend."

"Good for you," Mackey said. "Looks like it's the hottest ticket in town. By the way, did Rich tell you?"

"Haven't had the chance, yet," Rich said, taking June's hand. "Go ahead."

"Mr. Wilson himself—he's the Chairman of Holiday Inn—well, he's appointed Rich as Innkeeper of a small Holiday Inn in Florence. Rich agreed, as long as we also appointed June here as Restaurant and Bar Manager. They both leave this afternoon for Memphis for training."

"Congratulations to y'all," Frank said to Rich and June.

"Thanks," Rich said, blushing slightly. "How does it feel to be Chief of Police?"

"I'm not sure," Frank said. "I took the job on a trial basis. If it turns out to be as political as I'm afraid it might be, I'll step down. We'll just have to see."

Their food arrived, and they ate and talked about the events of the past two weeks.

"So, what happened with Costellano and Hutto?" Rich asked.

"Costellano is on his way back to Sicily as we speak," Cassidy answered, buttering another slice of toast. "Hutto will stand trial for the murder of Boutry."

"What about Beano Martin?" June asked.

"The judge released him on half a million in bail. Gedney Middleton pledged the bail. Apparently, Martin is pretty sick. We'll have to see how that plays out. At least the drugs are off the street. We're gonna see if we can keep it that way."

"What about Middleton?" Rich asked.

"We'll have to wait and see about him, too. As far as the law is concerned, right now he's in the clear. Unless something else comes to light, he should stay that way. His power and standing in the community and in the Ashley Cooper Society may be a different matter."

When they had finished, Rich and June said their goodbyes, telling the Cassidy's that they were on their way to Lake City to visit June's family before heading on to Memphis.

"What a beautiful girl," Rita said, after Rich and June had left.

"Smart and tough, too," Frank said. "She probably has as much to do with cracking this case as anybody else."

"She's obviously in love with him, too. Did you see her glow?" Frank, while agreeing that June appeared to be in love with Rich, didn't notice a 'glow'.

"Men!" Rita said, chuckling. "You men never notice that sort of thing." A light bulb went off in Rita's head. "Frank," she whispered, "I remember when my sister had that glow. I think that June is pregnant."

"Women!" Frank retorted. "The things you get in your head. You can't tell something like that just by looking at someone." Rita said nothing, but she knew better. And Rita was right. June would begin to suspect in about a week.

Frank protested again, when the waitress told him that there was no check and that Rich had paid it when he left. Frank left a few dollars on the table for the waitress, and the Cassidy family went across the street to the Church for the installation of Pastor Rivers.

It was a beautiful Sunday morning in Charleston, not overly hot, especially for the middle of June. The humidity was thankfully low, and there was a nice sea breeze blowing. As a result, with the windows opened, the packed church was not that uncomfortable. Nevertheless, the hand fans were in use.

Fourteen days earlier, on that first morning when Jab Brown had addressed the marchers, he had set four empty chairs in front of the choir section facing the congregation, pointing out that Charleston's white religious leaders were not there to lend their support to the cause. Today, those same chairs were again there, but this time they were occupied by Monsignor O'Brien of the Blessed Sacrament Catholic Church, Bishop Carroll of the Episcopal Diocese, Pastor Boyd of the Ashley River Baptist Church, and Rabbi Cohen of the Charleston Hebrew Temple.

As the congregation sang Amazing Grace, the church Elders, the ministers of the Marchers Strategy Council, and Reverend (soon-to-be Pastor) Shine Rivers processed from the rear of the church, Shine resplendent in a new, dark blue robe with light blue piping, a gift from the Episcopal Bishop. Shine knelt. One of the Elders read the words of the installation service as the Strategy Council ministers stood in a semi-circle around Shine, each placing a hand on Shine's head. After the installation, Shine rose and ascended the circular steps to the pulpit to deliver his first sermon as Pastor of the Calhoun Street AME Church.

"Brothers and sisters," he began, "we have seen more things happen and change in the last two weeks than many of us have seen in our lifetime. The Negroes in this City and in other cities of the South have finally stood up and demanded, peacefully, thanks to the wisdom and leadership of Dr. King, but demanded in any case, their rights as human beings and Americans. There is still a long road ahead, but we have now started the journey, a journey to create a better life and a better world for our children and our children's children."

A scattering of "Amens" was heard.

"Today, though, on this day of rest, we need to pause and think about this journey we have begun. What does it mean? Where will this journey take us? What are we seeking? I say that if we want to be treated like adult Americans, we must act like adult Americans. We must stand on our own two feet and make a life for ourselves and our families. But that isn't enough, because we claim to be children of God and of Jesus. Therefore, we in this church must behave like adult, Christian Americans. What does it mean to be an adult, Christian American, Brother Rivers, you ask. Well, I'll tell you what I think it means. First, if we want things to change, we must exercise our rights within the system to bring about that change. And that means to vote. How many of y'all are registered to vote?"

All of the whites and a smattering of the blacks raised their hands.

"See there? How can we expect anybody to take us seriously and care at all about what we want when we don't exercise that most fundamental right that an American has—the right to vote? By the way, don't think I'm up here pointing a finger at you. I hope you noticed that I didn't raise my hand, either. My wife did, but up until two weeks ago, I didn't think it was worth the trouble to register. Well, I was wrong. And it is not easy for a Negro to register to vote. I know that. I believe it's fixin' to get easier, but that doesn't matter. It doesn't matter how hard or easy it is. We have to do it anyway. Starting tomorrow after the march, Brother Reynolds—stand up, Brother Reynolds—Brother Reynolds will begin holding classes to show you how to get registered to vote. How many of y'all who aren't registered promise to attend those classes and get registered?"

Virtually every black arm in the church was raised.

"Looks like you better get some help, Brother Reynolds."

The congregation laughed.

"Voting is an important step in us becoming full fledged Americans. But there's something else more important. What do we want, and what do we expect? I tell you that what we want is a place at the table—OPPORTUNITY. We don't want or need hand outs. We don't want or need special treatment. We don't want or need to take somebody else's job. All we want is the opportunity to do better, to get an education, to have an equal chance at a job, to not be denied anything merely because of the color of our skin. If we can get better jobs, we will have more money to spend. And if we have more money to spend, we will spend it, won't we, ladies?"

The women laughed louder than the men.

"If we spend more money, the economy will grow and everybody, Negro and white, will prosper. The incoming tide raises all boats. So, mister and missus white person, don't be scared of us and what we are seeking. We don't want anything you have. We just want the opportunity to do better, to be better, to live better, to earn better, and to learn better. Just make room at the table, give us that opportunity, and watch us as we do better!"

"Adults take care of themselves. Adult Americans work for change peacefully within the system and that means they vote. But what about adult, Christian Americans? Here my friends is where it gets tough. Our Lord Jesus said, 'Thou shalt love the Lord thy God with all thy heart and all thy soul and all thy mind. This is the first and great Commandment. And the second is like unto it. Thou shalt love thy neighbor as thyself. On these two Commandments hang all the Law and the Prophets.' How many of y'all call yourselves Christians?"

All but a few in the congregation raised their hands.

Pastor Rivers turned his to his left. "Of course, Rabbi Cohen and a few members of his Temple who he brought with him here today to show the support of the Jewish community didn't raise their hands. Rabbi, we welcome you and your people here, and thank you for your support. And I'll bet that even though you don't follow Jesus as the Messiah, you have words in your Bible similar to those I just read that place the same obligations on you."

Rabbi Cohen nodded his head in the affirmative.

"The rest of us, though, call ourselves Christians. As such, we say that we follow Jesus' teachings and obey God's commandments. Well, it seems that the New Testament was written in the Greek language, and in the Greek language, there are different words that we translate into the word 'love'. In the passage we just heard, the word for the love of God is 'agape'. It is like the love a son or daughter has for their father or the love we have for God. It means respect and obedience, not because we have to, but because we want to. As Christians, we believe that it is our duty to respect and obey God and his laws. The Greek word for love of our neighbor is 'filio'. It is like the love that a brother or sister has for another brother or sister, a love where we trust and protect our brothers and sisters from harm and stand with them against those who would harm or threaten them. Now, what does this passage tell us? It tells us that God commands us to love our fellow man. 'Thou SHALT love thy neighbor as thyself'. Brothers and sisters, our neighbors include white folks. God says that we SHALT love them—filio them—as we love ourselves. He doesn't ask us to love the white man. He doesn't say that we should love them if we get around to it, maybe by next Tuesday. He commands us to love them every hour of every day of every week. But Brother Rivers, you say, you ask us to love the white man when he has kept us down, sold us drugs, led us into gambling, kept us out of his movies and bathrooms and hotels and restaurants and beaches and jobs and schools? How can we do that? I tell you that it is not Brother Rivers that tells you to love the white man. It is the Lord your God who commands you to love the white man. He might not promise that it'll be easy, but he says that we must do it."

"So, in our journey, we must take care of ourselves, work within the system by voting and participating in our communities and the government, ask only for the opportunity to better ourselves and our children, and say to the white man, don't be afraid of us. Don't be afraid of change. Don't be afraid of giving us opportunity. We are not your enemy. We love you, even if you don't love us. We forgive you for the way you have treated us. Giving us our opportunity will not in any way lessen or diminish your opportunity. We can all better ourselves and our children together. Let us live together among one another in peace with mutual respect and trust. The burden, brothers and sisters, is on us to love first. This, brother and sisters, is our journey and direction. This is our commandment from God. Let us pray for strength, and let us continue this journey we have begun. Amen.

The End